Novels by Kathleen O'Neal Gear
available from DAW Books:

Cries from the Lost Island

THE REWILDING REPORTS

The Ice Lion
The Ice Ghost
The Ice Orphan

THE
ICE
ORPHAN

THE REWILDING REPORTS #3

KATHLEEN O'NEAL GEAR

DAW BOOKS
New York

DAW Books
An imprint of Astra Publishing House
www.dawbooks.com
DAW Books and its logo are registered trademarks of Astra Publishing House.

ISBN 978-0-7564-1588-4 (hardcover) | ISBN 978-0-7564-1589-1 (ebook)

First Printing, November 2022

1st Printing

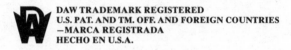

ACKNOWLEDGMENTS

Writing is not a solitary profession. It takes many people to bring you a book. I owe special debts of gratitude to the following: W. Michael Gear, the finest writer I know; Sheila Gilbert, the finest editor and publisher any author could hope for; and the amazing and dedicated staff at DAW Books.

Thank you all for helping me to write a better book.

DEDICATION

To Pia
When the time comes, I hope she leads me across the wasteland.

1

925 SUMMERS AFTER THE ZYME

*T*he beginning of the Book of Sticks the Virtuous, the Blessed Dog Soldier who witnessed what came to pass in those days. Forasmuch as many have taken in hand to set forth those things which are most surely believed among us about the Blessed Jemen, these are the events delivered unto us who were from the beginning eyewitnesses and sacred keepers of the story . . ."*

2

JAWBONE

Shh . . .

Do you hear him?

The other boy who tiptoes.

Sometimes I see him. He peeks around the dark wooly bison hide that hangs over the cave inside my head. I've tried to build a monstrous wall behind the hide to seal him up in there, but it keeps falling down. Stone by sacred stone, letting all the horrors that pant in the darkness slip out.

Shhhh.

Far away inside me . . . soft leather boots on stone.

Who are you, other boy who looks like me? Have you seen thirteen summers, as I have?

My voice bounces around my head, sing-song, almost loud enough to blot out the sound of your steps. Steps like a dying heartbeat. Slowing down, down, fading, melting away into a silent pool where the bison hide sways, and then turns to bright hot splinters. So bright my heart hurts.

NoNoNo.

Steps coming toward me. Thump, thumpthump.

Go back!

I shake myself and frown out across the glowing green blanket of zyme that covers the face of Mother Ocean. It stretches for as far as I can see to the west.

Quiet.

Is he still there? Waiting.

His footsteps are dead.

Exhaling hard, I hug myself and rock back and forth where I sit upon the ledge of the sea cave. Breathe the twilight. Breathe the storm pushing in from the west. Distant lightning flashes. In the brilliant green light cast by the zyme, the zigzags are purple. High overhead one of the Sky Jemen sails his ship of light through the few campfires of the dead that have begun to emerge with nightfall.

He must be gone, probably hiding behind the buffalo hide again.

Thank the Blessed Jemen.

My three little sisters laugh as they chase each other around the seven hide lodges in the rear of the sea cave. Little Fawn has seen eleven summers, Loon has seen seven, and my youngest sister Chickadee has seen six summers pass. They are not really my sisters. We were born Rust People, but three summers ago our village was destroyed and our families killed by giant lions. Two Sealion People found us and adopted us. Quiller and RabbitEar are our new parents.

My gaze drifts over Sky Ice Village. Made of mammoth rib-bone frames and covered with mammoth hides, the lodges resemble rounded domes. Firelight and smoke escape through the holes in the roofs and creep across the cave ceiling as though alive and seeking a way out into the open sky. Ten paces away, the central village fire blazes, lighting the faces of Elder Hoodwink, and Mother and Father. The rest of the villagers have retreated into their warm lodges. Mother and Father keep glancing at me. Worried. I'm sure they're talking about me.

Did I whimper when the boy came? I might have. I don't always realize it.

Blond hair blows over my blue eyes. Through the strands, I

focus on the towering thunderheads in the distance, studying the streaks of dusky blue rain that waver beneath them. The elders say that by midnight the rain will turn to snow, and I'll wake to a vast sparkling white sea. Such mornings fill my heart with longing, for they never last long. The blanket of snow that sheaths the zyme melts quickly. If we are lucky, for a few hands of time, the entire ocean appears to be rolling, snow-covered hills that rise and fall all the way to the horizon.

Our legends speak of the blue oceans that existed one thousand summers ago, before the Jemen planted zyme in Mother Ocean. There were blue oceans and dark night skies where the campfires of the dead glittered like millions of frost crystals, but no one among the Sealion People has ever seen such wonders. Nights along the shore are always filled with the luminous green shine of the zyme, and the campfires of the dead are faint. It's only when our bravest hunters climb high into the Ice Giant Mountains that they escape the glow.

Oh. No. Hear him?

Very soft. Almost not there. He whispers, *Come with me. Let me show you the way.*

"Stop talking to me!" I shout. "Go away!"

Elder Hoodwink, Mother, and Father turn in unison to gape at me. Elder Hoodwink leans sideways to speak softly with Mother. All I hear him say is her name: "Quiller."

She nods, rises, and walks toward me.

Tears clutch at my throat. I keep my eyes on the coming storm.

Who are you, other boy?

You live back there with my old mother and father in a long-ago darkness where huge lions roar and screams are bone knives. *But I don't know you!*

The elders of the Sealion People say I hear voices because I am a special child and will grow up to be a great shaman who

will lead our people to a warm world where the Ice Giants—
the glaciers that cover our world—do not exist.

I pray that's true. I have seen thirteen summers pass. In a
few days, I will go on my first spirit quest. I hope spirit helpers
find me worthy, but I'm not sure they will.

For I know I am a broken boy.

Like a shattered mica mirror, one dazzling splinter glitters
here, another dazzling splinter over there. They all reflect me
until nothing makes sense. Nothing connects.

Except on the most terrifying nights when my soul walks
backward to my old village, Great Horned Owl Village, and
then blazing threads spiral outward from the splinters and coil
up in the other boy's fractured blue eyes, making them whole
and clear, and I hear familiar voices shish and shush. Order me
to run. Drag me by the arm and fling me into the cold, where
the darkness pants and growls.

Don'tRememberDon'tRememberDon'tRemember!

My hands fly up to cover my ears. Please, spirits, don't make
me hear, don't make me remember.

Just let me sprout wings and soar to the far, far country
where I only have to hover in silent darkness for eternity.

I know another place. A better place.

"Stop it! Stop it! Stop talking to me!"

I loudly chant nonsense sounds, trying to drown out the
other boy's voice.

Mother sits down beside me and her buffalo-hide cape
spreads over the cave floor. Red hair frames her freckled face
and bulging green eyes. She's very tall, the tallest person in our
village. Some say that means she has Dog Soldier blood, for
they are very tall, as well. Sealion People believe the Dog Soldiers are half-human beasts, but I know they are not. They can
read. Among the Rust People, that means they are sacred. I
grew up with Dog Soldiers telling me wonderful stories about

ancient wars and strange beings who flew among the campfires of the dead.

Gently, Mother strokes my blond hair. "You're safe, Jawbone. Everything's all right. I promise you."

"But, Mother, he watches. He listens."

She gives me a worried smile. "Who? The spirit you were shouting at?"

I pick up a pebble from the lip of the cave and hurl it down where it vanishes into the luminous zyme. "He won't leave me alone. He scares me."

She slips an arm around my shoulders and hugs me. "In a few days, you will be a man and you will be initiated into the warrior society. Once you've learned all the secret ways of warriors, you will never have to be afraid again."

"But I'll have to fight if our village is attacked. I've heard warriors say they were scared during battles."

"Yes, that's true, but they are not scared the same way you are today, because they know how to fight. Training makes a big difference."

My mother is a respected warrior. I nod, but I can't imagine how being trained will allow me to fight the other boy.

"Can you fight spirits with spears or clubs?"

Mother's eyebrows pinch together. "Great shamans, like Elder Hoodwink, have special magical weapons they use to fight evil spirits. Are you saying that the spirit that's coming to you is evil?"

I have to think about that. "Mother . . . why won't Father let me become a shaman instead of a warrior? I don't want to be a warrior. Elder Hoodwink is an excellent teacher, isn't he?"

"Oh, yes, definitely. He taught the Blessed Teacher Lynx, you know."

"Of course," I reply, a little exasperated. I am almost a man and she still treats me like I've only seen eight summers.

Mother pulls her arm from around my shoulders and squints out at the ocean. "Would you like me to speak with Elder Hoodwink about training you after you've become a man?"

"Father won't allow it."

"You are of my clan. *I* will allow it. Let me speak—"

"No, Mother. I can speak for myself."

Lunging to my feet, I race away from her and straight to the fire to speak with Elder Hoodwink.

When I glance back at her, she looks hurt, but she must start treating me like the man that I will be in just a few days.

3

LYNX

Sitting upon a flat rock high above my cave, I let my gaze drift. Wind Mother has stripped the Ice Giants of their frosting of snow. For as far as I can see to the north and east, jagged ice mountains shimmer in the light of the rising full moon. The summer evening smells earthy and wet.

I draw up one knee and prop my elbow atop it to listen to mammoths trumpeting. The Ice Giants add their own rumbling voices to the music of nightfall. For a short while, I grant myself the right to just listen and look.

The air is aglow, turning the world faintly emerald. It's called *oxyluciferin 27*—the enzyme produced by Bioluminescent Algae Omega. The project was designed to feed the world, provide fuel, and cool the planet. My people, the Sealion People, named it zyme. It's been nine hundred twenty-five summers since Year Zero, the moment the zyme reached tipping point in the Pacific Ocean. There were many Jemen scientists involved in the algae project. My beloved teacher, Dr. John Arakie, blamed himself for the catastrophic consequences, but I don't think he was the only scientist responsible.

Locks of black hair blow around my face as I massage my heavy brow ridge. I have seen nineteen summers, hard summers of war, death, and starvation. Though two babies were born last winter, my people are almost gone. There are only twenty-two

Sealion People left in the world. We all know what that means. The hoofbeats of extinction beat in our hearts. It's inevitable now. Soon, we must plead with the Rust People elders to allow us to marry into their clans, but I doubt they will agree. Our peoples have warred since just after Year Zero. There is currently a peace agreement, but they continue to think Sealion People are ignorant sub-humans, beneath their dignity.

That's why I sit upon this black boulder, to consider the errors made by the ancient gods that we call the Jemen. From here, I can see my village, Sky Ice Village, nestled in a huge sea cave just above the algae line to the west. The seven mammoth-hide lodges glow like seashell lanterns. I miss my people. Almost no one comes to see me now, not even my best friend, Quiller. Over the past three summers, I have occasionally gone down to visit my family. But never for long. They're afraid of me. So long as I am there, women hide their children inside lodges, and warriors keep one hand on belted weapons.

Why wouldn't they? I live in a cave with a strange crystal being, a quantum computer named Quancee. That makes me exotic and alien. Not only that, the stories about me, spun by my former student, Sticks the Dog Soldier, are fantastic and terrifying, and untrue. At least, largely untrue, though I admit strands of the tales are accurate. That's what makes them powerful. No one really knows what is true and what is not. At first, I tried to counter them by constantly correcting people, but over the past two summers it has brought me nothing but heartache. People seem to want to believe I am a magical being. The more bizarre the story, the more they cling to it. In the eyes of both the Sealion People and the Rust People, I have grown strange beyond anyone's ability to understand.

So I am alone. My only company now is the wordless voice of an ancient quantum computer and the half-intelligible voices of the massive glaciers quaking through the earth around me.

This fact makes me neither happy nor sad. Each day I float suspended like a wing-seed in a haze of glittering information. I talk to myself a good deal, and to Quancee. No matter what anyone says, I know she's alive. Every moment I am with her, I feel her concern for me, her love for me. The solace of such love is this: only there, in the echoing silences that stretch between the qubits, can my life be molded into something that has meaning. But Quancee is dying. I've known it for three summers. She says I have almost learned as much as I can, and soon I must let her go and become the great teacher I am meant to be.

But I'm not ready to let her go.

Quancee's lessons are like unripe fruit rolling around inside me. They bang around my head and occasionally a sweet scent flies up, but for the most part my understanding is a thin veneer, so weightless it can blow away at any instant and leave me in despair and confusion. *Recite the solution to the Riemann hypothesis . . . the Yang-Mills existence and mass gap . . . Navier-Stokes existence and smoothness . . .* Quancee tells me there are patterns that tie everything together, and I await the joyous moment when all that has wounded or defeated me will fall away and I will finally *see*. But I don't. Not yet.

Until then, I can't bear to let her go.

I must continue to study and think. When I grow too exhausted to concentrate, I stride the glaciers looking for the bodies of ancient gods and the evidence of the great Jemen war that ravaged this land once called Merica.

With the arrival of summer, streams of meltwater constantly flow down from the Ice Giant Mountains and flood every low spot, every crater. To the south, vast lakes fill the craters and shimmer across the thin strip of tundra that lines the coast. The craters are the most obvious evidence of the ancient war, though I have found far more grisly evidence.

I will not climb into the Ice Giant Mountains without veering wide around the ice cave where a desiccated Jemen man sits silently in the rear with his hands folded in his lap, or quickly passing the woman lying on her belly near the glacial summit with her fingers embedded in the ice—as though still struggling to crawl away from her enemy after a thousand summers. Then there are the slaughter pens. Piles of bodies in various stages of undress that shame me to look upon. I refuse to go near those places again. The lolling thighs and shrunken genitals are agonizing . . . things that were never supposed to be exposed to casual strangers. But worst of all to me are the severed parts of giant creatures that should not exist. A monstrous scaled wing lying on the ice. Gigantic skulls three times the size of ours. Here and there, claw-like feet with tightly curled toes. Many of the skulls are shattered, as though they were dropped from some great height. Or perhaps they fell dead from the sky, killed by a Jemen weapon that I cannot even imagine.

Movement catches my eye.

Down the mountain slope, a pride of giant lions trots the trail through the pines. They are massive predators, taller than I am, with powerful front legs for grabbing and holding prey. I've sat here reminiscing for too long. The animals are out on their nightly hunts. Soon dire wolves and short-faced bears will silently creep through the darkness.

Rising, I pick up my spear and trot away along the icy bison trail that winds down the slope through the trees. The last windstorm tore many pine cones loose and tumbled them down the trail. I leap over them, afraid they will crunch beneath my hide boots and draw the lions' attention. The only time I've ever felt safe around the prides was when Arakie was with me, for the prides always left us alone—as though he was a member of the pride. Though I never saw my dear friend change into an animal, Sticks says he saw Arakie change into a giant lion the night he died. I don't disbelieve him. Our most ancient stories say that Jemen had to learn to change into animals to survive the crushing cold that descended upon the world after the zyme started to spread. I suspect, however, that Quancee projected those animal shapes to protect the last of the Jemen who'd been condemned to remain on earth while the rest flew to the stars. I've never asked, because it doesn't matter now. She's failing and too weak to shield me in that way, and I know it.

As I curve around the trail, I see the square entry filled with blue light—the entry to the last Jemen stronghold. Deep inside, Quancee stands hidden in a small chamber.

It's another three heartbeats before I realize a man leans back against the left side of the entry. The hood of his lion-hide cape is pulled up, but inside it, brown hair frames his small oval face with its long nose and pointed chin. The Rust People consider him to be the last god to walk the earth.

When he sees me, Vice Admiral Jorgensen calls, "Did you show them the cavern of the blue faces? What did they say?"

He seems unnaturally eager to know, as though it matters a great deal to his plans for the future. I don't answer right away. It's hard for me to fathom the way he thinks. Like a deadly spider, he builds an intricate web of words to trap his prey.

I finish climbing up the hill and sit down cross-legged opposite the entry, four paces away. I don't like being too close to him. Laying my spear across my lap, I hold tight to the shaft. The mammoth-bone spearpoint shines green in the growing zyme light.

For a few moments, my gaze locks with his. *Homo sapiens'* faces are so unlike those of my people, Denisovan reecur. Denisovans are closely related to Rust People, whom he calls Neandertals. Denisovans and Neandertals have similar heavy faces with broad noses and receding chins. And we are very different from the half-human Dog Soldiers who guide the Rust People. They have flat skulls and large feral ears.

Finally, I answer, "I'll walk down and find Quiller tomorrow. We'll go there together."

Jorgensen angrily slaps dust from his cape. "Which means you did not show them. That displeases me greatly, Lynx."

"I'll do it tomorrow."

"Why is it so hard for you to perform the simple tasks I give you?"

"I needed to think about it for a time. That's all."

Jorgensen heaves a breath, and it frosts the air before him. "Your archaic human brain is not very good at thinking things through. You should let me do that. All you have to do is follow my orders."

Over the past two summers, our relationship has grown increasingly strained. He gets frustrated with my apparent stupidity. The truth is that I must ponder the possible ramifications of his orders before I act upon them. He exhibits a perverse joy in showing me the horrors committed by his long-vanished people, and I don't understand why. It's as though he hates his own species.

Leaning forward, he waves a hand through the cold air. "Explain why you want to just take Quiller there. Why not take the entire village to see the caverns?"

"She is the matron of the Blue Dolphin clan now. It's her decision, not mine, and certainly not yours."

"Lynx . . ." he says through gritted teeth. "I don't show you these things for my own amusement. It's vitally important that they know the truth—"

"Why?"

"Why? That's the kind of ridiculous question that annoys me." He shoves back his hood, and his shoulder-length brown hair blows around his face. "Don't you think they ought to know the truth about their 'gods'?"

"Your truth. Not their truth."

"Truth is truth. Period." He glares, then turns away to gander southward at the line of volcanoes rising from the tundra. Smoke cloaks their cones, blotting out the campfires of the dead that sprinkle the glossy green sky.

"Quancee committed crimes against humanity. Your people should know that, Lynx. My family is in the first cavern. So is Arakie's. If your people are ever to get beyond their superstitions about the device and—"

"But we are not human—not *Homo sapiens*. So she committed no crimes against our people. She is innocent to us."

"Innocent?" He laughs the word. "Quancee is a weapon. The most powerful weapon the world has ever seen. Protecting it is a crime against life itself."

My heart starts to pound. "Arakie left me as her caretaker. I plan to carry out that obligation."

"Leaving you as her caretaker was another epic mistake on his part. God knows he made a lot of them."

Sighing, I reply, "Vice Admiral, I'm tired. I don't wish to argue with you tonight."

"Promise me you will—"

"I just told you I will show Quiller tomorrow. After that, it's up to her to decide if the rest of the Sealion People should be shown."

For a time Jorgensen peers out at the verdant glowing ocean. "After all that John Arakie taught you, you continue to think that the primitive ways of your people matter. Clan matrons and silly myths—"

Offended, I say, "My people are not primitive."

Jorgensen gets to his feet and props his hands on his hips.

"John agreed with you. He thought you were his greatest creation, did he ever tell you that?"

"Not exactly, no. He said—"

"He gave your species the genetic structure that would allow you to create a sort of mystical symbiotic relationship with Quancee after he was gone. Over the generations, most of you lost the genes. You, Lynx, are the rare exception. You may be the only one left who has the ability to bond with the computer—and that's why you are dangerous. Quancee can blind you and mislead you—"

"She is not blinding me to anything."

His smile is condescending. "The computer is not a *she*, Lynx. It's a mechanical device. You have to stop thinking it's alive."

I've never trusted Jorgensen. The Vice Admiral did not appear to me until after John Arakie was dead, and I suspect the timing was no coincidence. Arakie's death freed Jorgensen from ancient military obligations. Did he also think he would automatically become Quancee's caretaker?

"Can't you also be her caretaker?" I ask.

"Don't be ridiculous. I don't want to be its caretaker."

Solemnly, I reply, "Then I will take the best care of Quancee that I can. That's what Arakie wanted."

With a barely disguised glee, he says, "But you are a bad caretaker, Lynx. Quancee is almost useless now. It's falling apart. The only way to take care of it is to repair it. Can you do that?"

"No, I can't. Can you?"

He nods, but it's a faint gesture. "Within limits, yes, and it must be repaired. That computer has the ability to do things you cannot possibly comprehend. It can spin dreams from nothingness and leap through the coordinates of time. Not only that, if it was working properly, Quancee could extend your life for centuries and give you the ability—"

"I don't want to live forever."

"Of course you don't." He laughs again. "That's why Arakie chose you. He knew you'd never ask Quancee to do anything, because you're not smart enough to conceive the questions."

I wonder about that. It's possible. He does have a much larger brain than I do, and he seems to understand complex arguments that baffle me.

"Arakie said no one could repair her. He told me that when the supply ships stopped coming—"

"John was a geneticist." As icy wind gusts up the mountain slope, his cape whips and snaps around him. "He was my best friend, and my commanding officer after the treaty, but he should never have altered his genome so that he could become its caretaker. He developed an unnatural obsession with Quancee. I swear he looked upon that computer as his beloved child. He never understood the little details of how it works. Keep in mind, before I was forced into the military, I was a computer engineer, and I barely understand Quancee. She was created by the greatest minds on earth, but soon after her creation, she transcended all of our understandings."

Hope fills me when I look up at him. "What did you mean when you said you could repair Quancee 'within limits'?"

As though contemplating whether or not to answer, he tilts his head back and frowns up at the Road of Light that paints a swath across the pale green sky. Sealion People believe that at death souls follow that sacred road to get to the campfires of the dead where our ancestors wait to greet us. After a time, Jorgensen bows his head. "Even if I could find the necessary components, at this stage of its decay, I'll never be able to completely repair it, but I might be able to configure something useful from its last working parts."

"You mean the components to repair Quancee exist?"

"Of course they exist." He walks a short distance away to grimace out at the glowing ocean. "In the last days of the war—" he gestures to the cavern behind me—"we packed the Stronghold with supplies of every kind, including every possible component we might need for Quancee. But during the bombardment, many of the tunnels and caves collapsed. The tunnel where we stored Quancee's supplies is buried a mile deep beneath tons of debris. I'll never get to them, and even if I could, they've been lying unused for centuries. I doubt they're functional."

Bursting with hope, I ask, "But if we could find them and they were functional, couldn't Quancee tell us how to repair her?"

He pauses. "Well, yes, Lynx, but it doesn't want to be repaired. Didn't it tell you?"

The words hang in the air.

"Of course she wants to—"

"Don't you think both Arakie and I wanted to repair it? I crawled on my belly through every tunnel I could, despite the fact that Quancee told us to stop looking."

"But . . ." I spread my hands. "Why would she do that?"

"It wants to die." His preternaturally blue eyes shine even in the darkness, like a wolf's eyes. Another unholy creation of the Jemen.

"Why would she want to die?"

Jorgensen waves a hand through the moonlight. "The Stronghold switched hands several times. That computer was the key to winning the war. We all wanted it. Then, for no apparent reason, Quancee started shutting down systems of its own volition."

"Yes, Arakie told me about that. He said Quancee was heartsick over being used to kill thousands, and she—"

"Thousands?" Jorgensen stares at me like I'm an idiot. "Billions died, Lynx. But I'll bet you can't even conceive that number, can you?"

I stare at him with my mouth open. "I will speak with Quancee about it. She will explain."

He rolls his eyes. "You should be asking Quancee how to save Sealion People. That would be a productive use of your last moments with her. Don't you know extinction is right around the corner?"

I examine him through half-lidded eyes. "Do you care if my people go extinct?"

Another laugh as he shakes his head. "No. In fact, I think it's for the best. There's no doubt in my mind but that the earth is better off without hominins." He obsessively dusts off his cape again and starts walking away down the bison trail.

"Why is the earth better off without us?" I call after him.

He flips up his hood and continues walking. Over his shoulder he answers, "Ask Quancee about the original arguments."

"What arguments?"

Jorgensen halts in the trail with his back to me. At last, he turns. "Quancee calculated the probable consequences of *Homo recr.* Many scientists, including me, agreed with Quancee that re-creating archaic species would be a tragic mistake."

"Why?"

"For God's sake, Lynx." He stabs a finger at me. "The seeds of everything evil that we became are in you! And look at your history. It proves Quancee was right. You warred with the Rust People for centuries. You know why?"

I swallow hard. "Why?"

He pronounces each word separately: "The. Will. To. Survive. At. Any. Cost. That's the essence of what hominins are."

Jorgensen turns away so that I can't see his face, just the side of his hood. "We destroy everything we touch. It was unconscionable to condemn the earth to go through it all over again."

"I don't believe you. Arakie told me—"

"Oh, you need not repeat his words," he says through a long exhalation. "I can recite his argument from memory: 'The archaic species will evolve along a different path. They will never develop a *Homo sapiens* brain, and without that brain the earth will be safe.'" After five long heartbeats, he adds, "He was wrong. And he knew it at the end. He'd already documented the mutations that would lead to modern humanity."

Jorgensen strides away into the growing darkness.

I watch him for as long as I can, until he disappears into the black weave of tree shadows. No one, especially me, should ever let Jorgensen out of his sight.

4

LYNX

The glare of sunlight reflecting from the Ice Giants is so brilliant this morning I have to squint as I make my way across the tundra. All around me, wildflowers wave in the sea breeze like a many-colored blanket, and the early morning air is intensely fragrant.

When I veer right onto the trail that slants down the cliff face and into the sea cave where Sky Ice Village nestles, I see a boy with huge blue eyes standing in the middle of the trail. His blond hair and big angular face make him unmistakable: Jawbone. Quiller adopted him three summers ago after his Rust People village was destroyed by a pride of lions. He's a curious child, small for his age, and weedy. I guess he weighs half as much as he should at thirteen summers. I can tell he's breathing hard.

Lifting a hand, I call, "Good morning, Jawbone. Is your mother in the village?"

Whirling around, he charges down the trail into the cave, shouting, "Mother! Mother! The Blessed Teacher has come for you!"

By the time I make my way down the narrow trail cut into the cliff face, Quiller is already hurrying across the village to meet me. In the background, I see women herd their children toward lodges. Even most of the elders hobble across the cave on their walking sticks and slump down in a circle on the far side, as far away from me as they can get. Only four people remain around the village fire: My brother, War Leader Mink, Quiller's husband RabbitEar, Elder Hoodwink, and Jawbone.

When I stand before her, Quiller affectionately says, "Lynx," and hugs me. "What are you doing here? I'm glad to see you. Come and have a cup of wildflower tea with us."

"Are you sure, Quiller? The elders are already whispering behind their hands."

"Of course I'm sure. Come on."

She links her arm with mine and guides me toward the fire.

"My wayward brother!" Mink leaps to his feet to embrace me and gestures to the bison hides spread around the fire. "What a surprise. Sit down."

People peer at me from behind lodge flaps.

"I won't be here long," I announce and can almost hear the sigh of relief coming from my relatives. "I just need to speak with Matron Quiller."

When I do not sit down, Quiller gives me an uneasy smile. "What about, Lynx?"

"May we speak in private?"

"Yes, of course."

I lead her to the lip of the cave, where I stare down at the zyme-covered waves splashing against the cliff barely twenty hand-lengths below me. When summer warms the water, the zyme grows so fast it creates vaguely human-looking mounds and pillars out across the surface of the ocean. They bob and sway for as far as I can see.

Quiller softly asks, "What's wrong? Do you need help?"

"No," I say with a smile. "But I thank you for asking. I'm hoping you have the time to come with me so that I may show you a strange cavern."

Red hair blows over her green eyes. She grabs a handful and holds it so she can see me. "What cavern?"

"Jorgensen calls it the Cavern of Blue Faces."

"Blue faces? What are they?"

"It's easier to explain if you see it for yourself. My words will be a poor substitute."

Quiller scans my expression. A long time ago, we were lovers, and she still looks at me with love in her eyes. She knows me better than anyone alive, including my brother. She asks, "Have you seen the faces?"

"Yes."

Quiller frowns. "All right. If you think I should see it, I will go with you. How far is it?"

"About four hands of time away, a little more if the trail is muddy from meltwater."

Quiller turns and heaves a sigh. "Let me gather my pack, quiver, and spear. Why don't you sit down for a few moments and speak with Mink while I do that?"

When I nod, Quiller trots across the cave toward her lodge, and I quietly walk back to stand looking down at my brother where he sits upon the hide. "It does me good to see you, Mink."

If it weren't for the fact that Mink has seen three more summers than I, we could be twins. He has a heavy-boned, blocky face with prominent brow ridge and dark, deeply sunken eyes. Long black hair hangs down the front of his hide cape.

Mink gives me a vaguely hostile look. "Why don't you come down the trails more often? You're always welcome."

As I glance around the village at the people peering at me from behind lodge flaps, I know my brother is just being kind. "You could come to my mountain cave, too, you know."

Mink nods. "True, but I'm War Leader. I have duties. You do not."

The words hurt. According to the traditions of the Sealion People, by now I should be married with three or four children. I should be a hunter bringing in food to feed people, and a warrior if we are attacked. In their eyes, I have abandoned my responsibilities.

"I know you do," I say softly. "How is everything here?"

Just above a whisper, he replies, "Well, not so good," and glances at Jawbone as though he doesn't wish to say more in front of the boy.

Jawbone watches me with a bizarre expression, as though he knows something I don't. I smile at him and he leans closer to RabbitEar, staying quiet as a mouse when an eagle's shadow passes over. RabbitEar puts his muscular arm around his son's back, murmuring, "He's just a man. Nothing more."

Jawbone blinks, but his wide eyes never leave me.

"Lynx," RabbitEar says. "Sit down. You're making Jawbone nervous, and me, too, if truth be told."

"Forgive me. I don't mean to make anyone nervous." I crouch beside Mink.

"You're peculiar," Jawbone says, "because you live with a spirit being. You can't help it. Mother told me."

"I suppose that's true."

Elder Hoodwink brushes gray hair behind his ears, and gently says, "All holy people are peculiar, Jawbone. Comes from constantly walking in the spirit world. Soon, you will understand."

Jawbone continues to stare at me.

Every time I see him, I sense something amiss, as though he's only partly here in this world. Despite the way he stares at people and things, his eyes are empty, as though his soul is off somewhere on a spirit journey. I wonder if that's what Hoodwink meant? Is the boy a shaman in the making?

I ask, "Jawbone, are you studying the ways of power with Elder Hoodwink?"

The boy shakes his head. "No, but I will after I've climbed the quest wall and gained a spirit helper."

The quest wall is a massive rock wall that rises one thousand hand-lengths into the sky. Handholds have been hacked into the wall to make it easier for children to climb. Generally, it takes a child four days to reach the top, where his parents wait in the parents' rock shelter, giant boulders that lean together. At regular intervals, caves dot the wall. That's where children camp at night to rest and wait for a spirit helper to come to them.

"Well, Hoodwink is an amazing teacher," I say. "I'm sure you will grow up to help our people. When are you supposed to climb the wall?"

"Three days from now," he announces with a look of pride. "After that, I will be a man."

"Yes, you will," I say.

Elder Hoodwink smiles at Jawbone. "Lynx would probably also be willing to serve as one of your teachers, if you asked him. Having many teachers is better than . . ."

A look of panic creases the boy's face. He leaps up and charges for his lodge as though fleeing a predator. When he throws back the flap, he almost bowls Quiller over as she steps outside with her pack and weapons. "Jawbone, what's wrong?"

"Nothing, Mother."

RabbitEar gives me an embarrassed smile. "Sorry, Lynx. It's not you. He's worried about this spirit quest. One of his friends fell last summer. Smashed his skull on the rocks below."

"What happened? I thought the quest trail was constantly maintained to make sure it's safe."

"It is, but a surprise rainstorm came through," Mink answers. "Little Gull's foot slipped on the wet rock, and as he scrambled to find another foothold, he lost his balance."

We are all silent, just listening to the zyme-muffled roar of Mother Ocean.

"I'm ready," Quiller calls and slings her quiver of spears over her shoulder, as she walks up to me. "We should be going. I want to be back before nightfall when the predators come out."

RabbitEar stands up. "I'll go with you. You'll need at least three people with spears, just in case—"

"No." I thrust out a hand to stop him. "Just Quiller. I mean no disrespect, RabbitEar. Once she understands the problem, I will leave it up to her to decide what should be done next."

Quiller looks at me, then back at her husband. "Thank you, RabbitEar, but we'll be all right. I'll be back before you know it."

"You'd better," RabbitEar says, and gives me a faintly angry look, "or I'll come looking for you."

5

LYNX

By the time we are halfway to the caverns, sunlight glitters through the wind-blown tundra flowers, creating a wavering yellow and blue vista all the way to the line of smoking volcanoes south of us.

It's a cold morning. Quiller walks with her hood pulled up and red hair streaming down the front of her cape. I smell the perfume of her body, mingled scents of campfires and womanhood, mixed with the faint pungency of zyme. Now and then her cape opens with the sweep of her arm and the blue dolphins painted on her knee-length shirt appear. She clutches her spear in her right hand while her gaze scans for danger.

For a few moments, I watch her in silence, my arms folded across my chest. Then I ask, "Are you well?"

"Well enough." But she gives me a guarded look.

To say her eyes are green is like saying the zyme is green, so inadequate that the word verges on being meaningless. In the brilliant morning gleam they are deep jade and enormous in her freckled face.

"You don't sound well, Quiller."

She hesitates, before responding, "I'm worried about my son."

"What do you mean? Is he fevered or injured? Perhaps I can bring some spirit plants—"

She shakes her head. "No, it's nothing like that. He's been hearing voices and having . . . spells."

"Spells?"

"Periods where he stares at nothing. Sometimes he shouts at invisible people. Hoodwink says Jawbone is being visited by spirits."

Veering wide around a glacially smoothed boulder in the trail, I let that sink in. Her eyebrows, slender lines of red gold, pull together slightly, telling me she's holding some important bit of information back.

"That's not unusual, Quiller. Children often hear voices just before they climb the quest wall searching for a spirit helper. I did. Didn't you?"

The lines at the corners of her eyes deepen. "No."

I give her a few moments before I say, "Why are you so worried about this?"

Quiller gestures her frustration with her spear. "I just have a feeling that Jawbone isn't telling me everything about these voices. There's more to this story, and I can't get him to open his heart to me. One summer ago, he would have told me everything."

I smile. "Boys on the verge of manhood start to pull away from their mothers, you know? It's part of the process of asserting independence. After he climbs the quest wall, he's not going to run into your arms like the boy you've known. In fact, I suspect he'll never do that again, Quiller."

Sadness fills her eyes. "This is different, Lynx. I have the gut feeling that these voices are hurting him, and if I just understood what's happening I could help him."

I place a hand on her shoulder. "Does Hoodwink think he needs help?"

She turns away from me, and I see her jaw clamp. In a

clipped voice, she answers, "He thinks the voices will go away once Jawbone finds a spirit helper."

I reach out to gently tug a lock of her red hair to get her to look at me. "First of all, he's probably right. Second, if the voices do not go away, it's because Jawbone is destined to become a very great holy man. Let him."

I watch something change in her eyes. As if relieved, she lets out a breath. "Even if my husband disagrees?"

A little taken aback, I drop my hand to my side. "RabbitEar doesn't want Jawbone to be a sacred elder?"

"He thinks we need warriors more than we do holy people." She frowns and glances down at the spear in her fist, then out to the towering peaks of the Ice Giants that cut a jagged blue line across the eastern horizon.

Carefully, I say, "Jawbone needs to choose his own path, I think."

Her gaze returns to me. "I'm so glad you came today. I needed to talk with a friend."

A concerned smile turns my lips. If she doesn't think her husband or relatives are friends, she must be feeling very alone.

"I'm here, Quiller, and I'm always on your side. Never forget that."

"Even if I make the wrong decision for my son."

I slip an arm around her waist and give her a hug. "The instant he reaches for the handholds in the quest wall, it will no longer be your decision. It will be Jawbone's. Besides, you've been my best friend since we were children. In all that time, I've never seen you make a decision without first turning it over and over in your mind to see it from every possible side. You've done that, haven't you?"

"Of course. A thousand times."

"Then I believe you've made the best choice for your son."

Clouds have blown in from the ocean, and erratic bands of

shadow and fallow gold flicker over the wet trail at our feet. Releasing her, I step wide around a puddle, and continue on.

Quiller reaches out to catch my hand and squeeze it. "It's not that easy, Lynx. RabbitEar has a say in what happens, as well. Jawbone is the only son he will ever have."

When a gust of wind throws her hood back, she shivers and draws it up again. I wait for her to continue. When she doesn't, I say, "I've wondered why you do not have children together yet. Is there—"

"I've been with child twice, Lynx." The words are cold and grief-edged. "My body will not carry a baby. And I'm not the only one. Four babies have been born dead in the past two summers."

"But Mink and Gray Dove—"

"Yes, they have a new son, but he's failing. Gray Dove spends almost all of her time in their lodge caring for him. I think they both know what the future holds, though neither will admit it."

Heartsick, I ask, "Why didn't Mink tell me?"

"How could he? You're never here."

The words are accusations.

To the east, I glimpse the tan ears of a dire wolf. They appear and disappear as the animal trots the dips and swells of the tundra. I try to keep track of him while my soul aches for my brother. She's right, I'm never there, but I have seen Mink since his son was born. Why has he never told me the boy is ill? Perhaps because each day I am less and less his brother, and more and more a strange hermit living in a cave with a bizarre creature he does not understand.

"I'm tired of speaking about me," Quiller says with tight eyes. "Tell me about you. Are you well? How is Quancee?"

"She's failing, too, Quiller." All the light and color suddenly disappear from the world, leaving it cold and gray and windswept. "I've known it for three summers, but as the moment gets closer, I find my blood turning to water in my veins. I keep telling myself it isn't happening."

She opens her mouth as though to ask me a question, but then seems to think better of it, and simply links her arm through mine. We walk in step for a long time before she says, "I wish we were children again and I could protect you from the world. I long for those lazy days in the northern Steppe Lands."

Under the spell of her voice, the tundra fades and the summers roll back, and we're laughing, running together through tall grass, hunting snowshoe hares with our children's spears. There is music in the air, drumbeats and flutes coming from a village that is no more, and my parents come walking back, smiling as though they've not been dead these many summers.

"I do, too, Quiller."

When she looks at me, there is a sweet sadness in her eyes that goes straight to my heart. "I wish you'd come home. I miss you."

"I can't. Quancee needs me now more than she ever has."

It's a beautiful morning, cold but sunny, bright but not glaring, and the breeze off the ocean turns soft as silk.

After another ten paces, a stern expression comes over her. "All right. Tell me about the blue faces. I assume there's a reason you wanted to bring only me here."

"There is. Jorgensen ordered me to bring our entire village."

She mulls that over. "You think he wants to use our village against you?"

"There's more to his request, Quiller, and he's smarter than I am. It's the truth. I thought if I just brought you here, maybe together we could figure out what he's after. If twenty other people were along—"

"I understand," she replies with a nod. "Too many opinions.

Very well, let's pick up our pace. I want to see this place and get back before dark."

She breaks into a run, pounding along the tundra trail ahead of me. I gratefully follow in her tracks as I have done for most of my life.

6

QUILLER

Two Days Later

I concentrate on the strange moans that ride the sea wind, rising and falling with the gusts that sweep this rare ice-free stretch of tundra along the shore.

"The dead are the source of the moaning?" Elder Hoodwink asks from behind me.

"I don't know the source, elder. It was late when Lynx and I arrived. We both wanted to get home, so I didn't have time to search the caverns. But I can tell you the moans crawl up from the tunnels deeper in the earth."

We keep our voices low, for it's unwise to speak too loudly this close to the chambers of the dead.

I gesture with my spear. "It's just over that rise."

Stepping wide around a puddle, I turn to look back at the three men and one boy who plod the game trail behind me. Mink guards the rear. Just in front of him Elder Hoodwink hobbles, using his spear as a walking stick. Long silver-streaked black hair sways around his wrinkled face. In front of Hoodwink, RabbitEar and Jawbone walk side by side. We all carry spears and quivers over our shoulders. "It isn't much farther."

"One hundred heartbeats?" Jawbone asks. His blond hair has a wild shine in the sunlight reflecting from the glaciers.

"A little more. Maybe two hundred."

Jawbone skips at his father's side, smiling, but RabbitEar barely notices. His gaze, like Mink's, constantly scans the shoreline. The tracks of saber-toothed cats, short-faced bears, and dire wolves are visible all around us. Only Elder Hoodwink keeps his gaze focused on his unsteady feet.

To the east, the Ice Giants are so brilliant and blue they could be carved from some turquoise stone. A haze of wind-blown snow obscures the tors, but lower on the slopes herds of mastodons and bison lumber along the sinewy game trails. I study them as I listen to the wind. The eerie cries ebb and flow, sometimes sounding far away, other times right beside me on the wildflower-strewn trail.

The wind has picked up, flapping my cape around my long legs. Because I am very tall I can already see the dark entry to the underworld caverns of the blue faces, but my companions can't.

I continue along the trail, happily listening to my son's soft laughter.

Hoodwink says, "Then perhaps wind flows through the tunnels and chambers and produces the cries, not spirits."

"Yes, perhaps. But I . . ." When I accidentally step into a puddle, I exclaim, "Blessed Jemen! And I'm already soaked."

Jawbone laughs. "We all are, Mother. The bottom of my cape is so heavy, it feels like I'm totin' rocks."

Like all Rust People, he tends to drop the 'g' at the end of words.

"It's good for you." RabbitEar ruffles Jawbone's blond hair. "Helps strengthen your shoulder muscles, so that you will be prepared to climb the quest wall day after tomorrow. When you return from your spirit hunt, you will be a man, and I'll be very proud of you."

"Thank you, Father." Jawbone gazes up at him and smiles.

RabbitEar props his spear over his shoulder, and his red hair and beard gleam in the late afternoon glow. He's seen twenty summers pass, two more than I have, but he looks much older. The stresses of war and starvation carve lines across his forehead and around his mouth. "Let's hurry, Quiller. We can't afford to waste time. It's been so muddy, it's already taken longer to get here than I thought."

"Yes, I know."

I turn back to the trail, sidestep another puddle, and head for the rise.

Early summer is always raw and wet along the seashore, but I appreciate the quietude of Mother Ocean this afternoon. Her voice is muted by the thick green hills of zyme that hug the shore and stretch in an unending blanket to the far western horizon.

"Lynx told you this place is what caused the rebellion one thousand summers ago?" Hoodwink calls.

"Yes."

Hoodwink pants the words: "And how does Lynx know this?"

"Jorgensen told him."

"Jor-gen-sen." Elder Hoodwink lets the name roll around his mouth. "A strange name for a strange man."

"Strange? That's a kind description," I answer.

Wild stories surround the man who calls himself Vice Admiral Steven Jorgensen. His devotee, Sticks the Dog Soldier, says Jorgensen is the last member of the long-gone god-like race we call the Jemen, and swears he saw Jorgensen change from a wolf into a man. I'm not sure I believe it, but I have seen long-dead legends come to life and walk in this world again, so I will not discount the possibility.

When a hare breaks from the wildflowers and bounds away across the tundra, I whirl with my spear lifted. The hare charges

toward the shoreline, where condors flap above the huge tubu-
lar thing at the edge of the water. Most of it remains buried, so
the top merely looks like a massive white ring upon the ground.
There are many more tubes out in the ocean, thrusting up
through the zyme like giants. I swear they are Jemen tombs,
but we've found no bodies inside, just strange symbols painted
over the walls from top to bottom. Not even Mother Ocean
can wash them away.

"Elder?" I call to Hoodwink. "What do you think the tubes
are made of?"

"Impossible to say. The material is nothing I have seen
before."

"Is it possible that they are iron?"

"Not likely." Hoodwink shoves wind-tangled hair behind
one ear. "Zyme loves iron. It gobbles it up as though it can't get
enough. If these were iron, they would have been eaten up
long ago."

Our old stories say that almost one thousand summers ago
the enemies of the Jemen cast crushed meteorites over the
zyme, and that's what caused zyme to change into a monster
and grow and grow—but zyme retreats from these tubes.

War Leader Mink frowns at the circles of open blue water
that ring the tubes out in the ocean. "Do you think the tubes
are poison? There are never fish near them, and I've never seen
a seabird land on one."

Hoodwink stops, breathing hard, and leans on his spear.
"Let me catch my breath before we continue on?"

"Of course, elder, but let's not linger here. My bones always
start to hurt when I stand too long near the white rings."

"Mine, as well, War Leader."

Jawbone takes the opportunity to charge off across the tundra to peer over the edge of the closest white ring. I love all four
of my children, but there's something special about this boy

who hears voices. The massive brow ridge of his birth people, the Rust People, is just beginning to form. I have the feeling he's going to grow into a powerful, muscular man. Today is a good day. He's acting like a normal thirteen-summers-old boy. I cherish these moments, for they will be gone before I realize it.

"This Jor-gen-sen . . ." Hoodwink gazes at me. "Did he tell Lynx what the blue faces are?"

"All he said is that they were innocents."

"Innocents?" Hoodwink grimaces and tilts his head, listening to the forlorn cries. "They do sound like children."

"There's a woman in there," Jawbone announces as he leaps around the tundra puddles and trots back to stand beside Elder Hoodwink, staring up with a knowing expression.

"Is she speaking to you?" Hoodwink asks as he pats Jawbone's shoulder.

"She's singin' to me."

"Right now?"

Jawbone's smile fades. "Can't you hear her, elder?"

"No. She sings only to you."

Jawbone slaps his ear. "I can't hear her very well."

Hoodwink says, "Can you ask her to sing louder?"

"I—I don't think she's really here, elder. I don't think she's human, either. She's singin' to me from far, far away in a vast, dark land."

Hoodwink smiles. "Then how can she be here in the caverns?"

Jawbone blinks, as though trying to reason it out. "She can be in two places at once, I think. Maybe four or five. She says she's comin' to help me." Jawbone's blue eyes narrow, as though he's not sure he wants this spirit to help him.

Hoodwink flexes his fingers and winces. "Well, then she's a good spirit. Let's continue on. My hands are already aching."

"Yes, elder." Taking a new grip on my spear, I climb over the rise and walk down the other side toward the dark opening in the earth. It's ice-rimmed and resembles a gaping maw ten hand-lengths wide. "It's narrow inside and patches of ice cover the floor. Be careful."

Ducking low, I enter the tunnel and reluctantly descend deeper. The darkness breathes cold, wafting the musty odor of the dead. The scent is cloying, nauseating, and fear tightens my chest. This is the sort of underworld den no one would enter by choice.

"Could we light a torch? I can't see my feet." Hoodwink leans on his spear, breathing hard.

"Oh, sorry. Should have already done that." RabbitEar reaches into his quiver and withdraws a birchbark torch. "Jawbone? Where are the coals we saved from our lunch fire?"

Jawbone pulls a soapstone bowl from his belt pouch beneath his cape. After removing the stone cap, he places it on the ground so that RabbitEar can touch the tip of the torch to the coals.

"You'll have light in just a moment, elder." RabbitEar blows on the coals until tiny flames flicker through the shredded bark, then he rises to his feet. "Recap the coals, son."

Jawbone quickly puts the stone lid back on the bowl, and tucks it back in his belt pouch.

"Cold in here." RabbitEar lifts the torch higher.

"And it's going to get colder. The passageways ahead are thick with ice." Bracing one hand against the wall, I cautiously lead the way through the wavering yellow gleam.

"Mother, what's that strange scent?" Jawbone asks. "Smells rotten."

"The dead."

"How can they smell after one thousand summers?"

"Don't know, but they do."

Hoodwink says, "The scent probably oozes up when they start to melt in the summer. I'll bet in the winter they have no scent."

As I approach the burial chamber, more tunnels veer off like crooked tree roots, heading deeper into the ground.

"The moans are louder down here," Mink whispers.

"Just wait. Very soon, you'll think they are coming from inside your own head." Stepping past the ghost of my own shadow that looms large on the wall to my left, I duck into the first cavern. As the light flutters over the ceiling and walls, it takes shape, spreading sixty hand-lengths across, but it has a low ceiling of solid ice. If I reach up, I can touch the faces.

The others quietly move into the chamber and gather around me to stare open-mouthed at the dead frozen in the ceiling. There are hundreds of them, thousands if you look into the adjacent caverns that veer off from this chamber and plunge into the depths.

"What is this place, Quiller?" Mink asks.

"A burial chamber."

"Doesn't look like a burial chamber," RabbitEar whispers. "All I see are heads. It looks like butchery."

"They are even more interesting than you think," I say. "Please, grind out the torch."

He frowns. "Grind it out? Are you sure?"

"Yes, it's all right now. You'll see why."

RabbitEar grinds out the torch on the floor.

When the yellow light dies, the faces begin to pulse and the cavern fills with soft blue light. The smallest faces pulse rapidly. The biggest are slower, but steady and bright, as though timed to the long-vanished heartbeats of the dead. If I listen hard, I can hear the faint staccato of thousands of hearts thumping. The sight is so stunning, it's like being clubbed in the head.

Gaping jaws and opaque eyes stare down upon us. For as far as we can see into the adjacent tunnels, faces flash.

"Blessed gods." RabbitEar breathes the words as he searches the ceiling.

Along the tunnel to my right, I glimpse what appears to be a small shadow trailing over the wall, as though pursuing the dancing phosphorescence down into the earth. "Did you see—"

"Look at their faces," RabbitEar interrupts as he reaches out to touch a woman's cheek directly above him. "They have oval faces and pointed chins. They are all Jemen."

The small shadow has vanished, but I'm getting a headache. The pulsing light suddenly feels like stilettos piercing my brain. When I squeeze my eyes closed to block it, Mink walks over to me.

"Feeling sick?"

"Yes."

"I feel it, too. We can't stay here for long. This place is evil."

"I agree." Opening my eyes, I see Mink massaging one shoulder.

Hoodwink says, "Pain is already working its way up my spine into my shoulders."

"Mine, too. Gods, it's hitting me harder and faster today than when I was here with Lynx. I'm not sure how long I can stand this."

"When it gets too bad, just go," Mink instructs. "We'll meet you outside."

Elder Hoodwink uses his spear to point at several faces. "Look at their eyes and mouths. They look terrified. What happened to them?"

"War," I reply.

Our people have many stories about the fate of the magical Jemen, the gods who breathed upon the ancient bones of our ancestors and brought us back to life—as well as bringing back long-horned bison, mammoths and mastodons, dire wolves, giant lions, and other creatures. They called us Reecurs, because they re-created us. At some point, warfare broke out. That was long before the Sky Jemen sailed to the campfires of the dead in ships made of meteorites.

Hoodwink hobbles a short distance away. "Did their shamans paint their flesh with a glowing paint? Is that why they pulse blue light?"

"I asked Lynx that same question. I memorized the word he used. He called it *cesium 42*."

Hoodwink nervously licks his lips. "What is that?"

"I don't know. It's something Jorgensen told him."

"Jorgensen says many things he fails to explain," Hoodwink softly replies.

"He thinks we're too dim-witted to understand." Mink scowls and shifts his spear to carry it across his chest. He has his black hair tied back with a cord, but wind has worked strands loose and they hang around his sun-bronzed face in tangles. As he edges forward to stare up at the face where Hoodwink's hand rests, he asks, "Even if their shamans painted them with glowing paint, why do they pulse?"

I shrug. "I don't know."

I'm staring upward into frozen eyes, when Jawbone says, "Mother, where are their bodies? I don't see any bodies."

"I haven't seen any, either." My gaze drifts down an adjacent passageway, following the shining faces for as far back as I can see. "But I haven't explored all the chambers."

Hoodwink smooths his hand over the face in the ice, tracing its shape. "The Dog Soldiers keep a fragment of a story about the great Jemen war. They say that the Old Woman of the Mountain, the leader of the Sky Jemen, rounded up the families of those who had rebelled against her and herded them like bison to a vast lake where they were slaughtered. It was known as Black Lake, because of the somber forests that surrounded the water. Over hundreds of summers, the Ice Giants consumed their bodies, but the Dog Soldiers say their faces are still there, buried deep in the ice. That's why we occasionally see Jemen skulls melting out of the glaciers."

"I wonder," RabbitEar says, "if the Jemen deliberately cast these heads along the shore."

"Why would they do that?" I ask.

"Maybe as a battle strategy to terrify the enemy?"

"If so, it was a poor strategy." Mink frowns up at the faces. "Such brutality generates the kind of hatred that makes people fight to the death to get revenge."

"True. But it would certainly terrify me if my family's severed heads started falling from the sky and bouncing around my village."

Hoodwink strokes the woman's face as though to ease her ancient agony. "By that time, I suspect the war was on its last legs, and all they had left between them was hatred."

In the tunnel to my right, something moves. I turn sharply and stare at it. Like a gauzy haze of darker blue, the shadow slips along, darting into cracks, then leaping out and flying away into the icy depths. "Did you see that?"

RabbitEar frowns in the direction I'm looking. "What?"

I massage my forehead. "Never mind. It's probably just my headache."

He puts a gentle hand on my arm. "You often see strange things when you have a bad headache: floating lights and zigzagging lines. That's probably all it was."

I nod, but I'm not so sure.

RabbitEar extends a hand to the garish ceiling. "Why do they still have flesh? Why haven't predators reduced them to gleaming bones? Are they, like the white tubes, poisoned and the animals know it?"

"I'm sure they must be." Hoodwink massages his jaw and looks at the rest of us. "We all hurt in here, don't we?"

Nods go around.

RabbitEar's feet grate on the floor as he steps closer to Mink. "Perhaps this wasn't about terrorizing the enemy. These could be war trophies. Taking the head of your enemy in battle is a sign of bravery. Maybe the Old Woman of the Mountain was trying to show her own people how brave she was?"

Mink slowly nods. "Maybe."

Almost mesmerized by the faces, none of us seems quite willing to acknowledge the darkness growing in the tunnel just outside the chamber. Father Sun must be resting upon the western horizon.

Finally, Mink turns to look in the direction of the exit. "We need to leave soon. As it is, we won't get home until full dark. There will be far more lions and wolves out hunting." He pauses and stretches his back muscles. "And I'm not sure any of us can stand this much longer."

Hoodwink shakes his head. "Can't leave yet, War Leader. I want to see how far the faces go down into the ice tunnels."

Jawbone grabs his parchment-like hand. "No, don't! The sad man doesn't want anyone to see him."

Hoodwink frowns down at him. "The sad man? Who is he?"

Jawbone blinks owlishly. "He doesn't want you to look at his scars."

"If he doesn't want me to, I won't."

Jawbone releases Hoodwink's hand and trots away down the tunnel where I saw the shadow.

"Don't go too far, son," I call.

"I'm not a baby, Mother. I won't get lost."

RabbitEar glances at me and grimaces. "He's a little surly today, isn't he?"

"Of course he's surly," Mink replies. "He's on the verge of

manhood. By the time he's seen fourteen summers, he will know far more than either of you ever will in your entire lives."

RabbitEar chuckles. "As you did?"

"That's how I know."

They laugh.

I do not. My gaze follows my son down the tunnel. Perhaps they understand my son better than I do, but I don't see an ordinary adolescent struggle. I see something far different. His taut muscles and clamped jaw tell me that fear lurks just behind that surly shield. He doesn't want the three most important men in his life—or his mother, the warrior woman—to think he's a coward, especially not just before he climbs the quest wall to become a man. But there's more going on inside him than I can fathom. Worries me.

As Elder Hoodwink walks toward a side tunnel, RabbitEar runs after him to grab his elbow to steady his steps.

That leaves only Mink standing beside me. All around, the walls quiver and flash.

"Did you notice, Quiller? Their eyes are all open. If they'd known they were about to die, at least a few would have closed their eyes. It's human nature. They must have died staring in wide-eyed horror at whatever killed them."

"I thought the same thing when I first saw them." I tip my chin toward the man with the startled expression. His blue-marble eyes have a chalky appearance, but tiny black dots glow. "See how small his pupils are? The horror must have been unbearably brilliant."

From somewhere down the tunnel Jawbone explores, a scratch-scratch sound rises. I glance in that direction and take a new grip on my spear. I call, "Jawbone? Are you all right?"

"No, I'm lying dead at the bottom of a cliff," he replies, as though exasperated. "I'm just exploring, Mother."

I start to say something angry, but Mink grabs my forearm and shakes his head.

"Not worth it," he says.

I sigh and nod.

We walk around together, studying the ceiling.

Finally, Mink says, "Did you also notice that while there are a few men here, most seem to be women and children?"

"I did."

It stirs in me again, the awful silence of the Jemen dead. I've never been able to shake the feeling that their mysterious war was savage beyond my understanding.

The scratch-scratch noise is louder, closer to Jawbone, who stands staring down the tunnel. I have the overwhelming urge to charge down there, grab my son, and bolt outside, just run and not stop until I get him safely home.

"It's just mice," Mink says.

"Doesn't sound like mice. Sounds like small feet shuffling—"

"Quiller?" Elder Hoodwink calls. "Could you please take a look at this?"

"Coming, elder."

Ducking low, I follow the tunnel until it opens into a new cavern. Womblike, it's circular, forty hand-lengths in diameter, and embedded all around with pulsing blue faces. More tunnels jut off and plunge downward.

"See here? This is an adult's body." Elder Hoodwink presses his nose to the ice.

RabbitEar whispers, "He was very tall, but thin to the point of starvation, and look at his terrible scars. Do you think this is the 'sad man'?"

"Possibly," I answer as I frown into the depths of the ice.

"I think he was a warrior."

"Why? I don't think these are battle wounds. See, here and here? Too perfect to be knife slashes. I think the designs were carved into the flesh while he or she lived." My finger traces the air above the ice, outlining the curling white ridges that cover the arms and legs.

"So you think he was tortured? Why would anyone have tortured him this way?"

"Maybe he did it himself. As a remembrance."

I struggle to see deeper into the opaque patches that obscure the body, trying to decipher the symbols. Like the white tubes on the shore, I have seen many rock-hewn cavern walls covered with ancient Jemen symbols. Lynx tells me they are letters, verses, and form-u-las . . . but this Jemen man's truths were not painted upon stone. They were inscribed like serpents slithering and coiling across his emaciated flesh. "Are you saying he lived through the battle and inscribed the events on his flesh? As we paint such events on hides to remember them?"

Hoodwink says, "RabbitEar may be right. If this was Black Lake, the man may have crawled from the water, sat upon the shore, and carved his flesh while he stared out at the floating bodies of his family."

"Gods, I can't imagine . . ." RabbitEar shifts his grip on his spear.

Hoodwink says, "Well, if this is Jawbone's 'sad man,' he does not wish us to stare at him. I'm moving on."

My gaze is drawn in the direction of our adopted son. Before we discovered our four children in a boat floating offshore, we walked through the corpses of their families, corpses that had been ripped apart and scattered across the decimated village. If anyone can imagine how the sad man buried in the ice feels, it's our son.

The tunnel where Elder Hoodwink walks is progressively narrowing until the shining wreckage of faces closes in around him, and the blue gleam bleaches the color from his wrinkled skin, making him appear as much a corpse as those poor people in the ice.

"Any more bodies?" Mink calls from the chamber above.

"Not yet," I call back. "But . . ."

"Mother!" Jawbone cries out and charges into the chamber breathing hard. "Let's go! We have to leave right now."

I stare at the tunnel he was exploring. "Why, did you see something that scared you?"

"I'm not afraid of the boy," he says and throws out his chest. "But he says it's time to go. Let's go!"

RabbitEar walks over to place a hand on Jawbone's back. "Actually, I agree. I hurt all over."

"*Elder?*" Mink calls down. "We need to leave here."

"Yes, I'm coming." Hoodwink hobbles up the tunnel. "I'm more than ready to return to the village and tell the others what we've seen. The council will wish to discuss it."

RabbitEar leads the way back up the tunnel into the main burial chamber where Mink still stands. "Are you guarding the rear again, Mink?"

"No, I'll take the lead." His eyes are focused on the tunnel where we heard the scratch-scratch noise. It's still there. It comes closer and closer, but never seems to arrive. "Come on. I don't want to stay here one moment longer than we have to."

Mink turns and strides for the exit tunnel, where he hurries up the incline. The amber gleam of sunset fills the maw.

"Let me help you, elder," RabbitEar says as he reaches out to support Hoodwink's elbow.

"Thank you, warrior. I'm very sick to my stomach."

I follow the men with my arm around Jawbone's shoulders. "Everything's all right, Jawbone. You don't have to be afraid."

"Stop treating me like a baby! I am *not* afraid!" he insists, but glances behind us as though trying to make certain we're not being followed.

7

QUILLER

When we duck out of the tunnel into the gleam of dusk, Jawbone whispers, "Mother, do you hear footsteps back there?"

Cocking my ear, I listen. "No. That's ice cracking as we walk across the tundra."

"It is not! You can't hear anything, can you?" Jawbone stalks ahead, leaving me far behind.

I know he's scared, but this hostility toward me is disrespectful. I'm about ready to slap him down just to get his attention. Instead, I keep my mouth closed. Lynx is right. I need to give him the time to find his own path.

Jawbone has already chosen his man's name: Kujur. It's a strange name, not a Sealion name, but something perhaps taken from ancient Jemen legends kept by his birth people: the Rust People. He will then be allowed to marry and be responsible for protecting his people and his family. He's told me how much he's looking forward to that.

As twilight draws close around us, the temperature drops. All of the tundra puddles are now skimmed with ice.

"Mother, I'm going to run over to the white tube buried on the shore."

"Why? We're trying to get home before midnight, my son. We don't have time to—"

"The sad man's head is down there."

I think about it before I say, "You just wish to look into the tube, then we'll keep walking?"

"No. I want to throw rocks at it."

"Rocks? What for?"

Jawbone lifts his shoulders. "To kill it."

The drifting clouds flame in the sky to the far west. "Why?"

"He hates us. He hates all Reecurs. I want to show him that I hate him back."

Before I can tell him no, Jawbone sprints away toward the tube.

I trot along behind him, afraid he's going to get into trouble.

When Jawbone reaches the tube, he grabs several rocks, then leaps up, and balances as he struts along the rim.

"Be careful," I shout at him.

"I am being careful."

I walk over and glower at him. The ring is gigantic, one hundred hand-lengths across, and bizarrely shiny. Everything else in our world tarnishes, but not these tubes. I suspect they glitter as brilliantly now as they did the day the Jemen created them.

As I peer over the edge into the darkness below, I say, "Hard to believe that Wind Mother has been trying to fill this tube for a thousand summers and we still can't see the bottom."

"There's probably a hole at the very bottom and Mother Ocean keeps washing it out."

"I suppose."

Jawbone hurls his biggest rock down into the hole, and yells, "Die! Die! Die! I hate you! Leave me alone!" Then he lets out a blood-curdling war cry, and follows the first rock with nine more in quick succession. Metallic clangs ring out.

"Is his spirit bothering you? Do you hear him talking?"

"Only his body talks. But I can hear his head movin' around down there, like it's wigglin' up through the dirt, trying to get to me."

"Well, that's strange, isn't it? His body talks, but his head doesn't?"

"Don't be silly, Mother. Mouths can't talk without lungs. They wouldn't have any air." Jawbone looks at me like he can't believe I asked such a stupid question.

Annoyed, I reply, "Are you finished? Can we go now?"

Jawbone dusts his hands off on his cape and tilts his head as though listening to see if he can still hear the head moving.

While we continue standing, mother and son, peering over the edge of the ring, the zyme blazes to life. The air turns emerald and the arms of zyme lying across the shore writhe and hiss. Once, a thousand summers ago, our legends tell us that the zyme rose out of the sea and walked upon the land like humans before the Jemen drove it back with balls of fire.

Jawbone jumps off the rim and lands with a thump. "If the caverns of the blue faces aren't burial chambers, how did the Jemen bury their dead? Did they place them on burial scaffolds covered with soft buffalo hides, like we do? Did they tie red and blue ribbons to the mammoth rib-bone posts? That's how I want to be buried."

"I know nothing of their burial traditions, son. Maybe. Though I recall Lynx telling me that his Jemen teacher, Arakie, wanted to be buried beneath a pile of rocks on the mountainside."

A shudder goes through Jawbone. "That's a witch's burial. Sounds awful."

"I think so, too, but . . ."

He charges after his father, forcing me to run to catch up with him.

Jawbone has his head down with his fists swinging at his sides. He seems to be concentrating hard on a barely audible sound inside his head, or perhaps on voices I cannot hear.

After a long time, he boldly says, "I'm going to marry that little Rust girl with the reddish-blond hair."

I'm searching my memory. "Which one? What's her name?"

"Hawktail. Will you speak with her grandmother about it?"

"Yes, but don't get your hopes up. The Rust People don't want us to marry into their clans."

"Because we're freaks and doomed?"

When I turn and glare at him, he lowers his eyes and kicks at a rock in the trail.

"Why did you say that? Sealion People are not freaks."

"We're doomed, though."

I swallow the words on my lips, because I know he's right.

———

Three hands of time later, we round the bend in the trail and Sky Ice Village comes into view. Two elders sit outside around the central village fire. The trail down to the sea cave appears as a gray slash angling down the zyme-lit cliff face.

As we follow it over the edge and slant down toward the sea cave, Jawbone says, "There is one thing . . . I want to talk about."

He hesitates and I frown at him. Hair falls over his face, so I can't see it. "What thing?"

"Promise you won't tell Father, or anyone else?"

"Of course I won't."

Jawbone turns slightly to glance at me and licks his lips before he exhales hard. "It does scare me . . . a little . . . when he comes out from behind my eyes."

"What? Who?"

Jawbone's face contorts and for the first time I see true terror glittering behind his blue eyes. "All right, I'm just going to tell you, so you stop asking. There's a cave in the back of my head where he lives. It's covered with a buffalo hide."

I don't want to scare him off this discussion, so I must choose my words carefully. "Who lives in the cave?"

"The other boy."

He's watching me and I can tell he's looking for any reason to stop telling me this secret. Softly, I ask, "Who is the other boy?"

He shrugs. "I don't know him."

Five paces ahead of us, RabbitEar speaks to Hoodwink and I see the elder point to the two people sitting before the central fire. They are little more than dark silhouettes, but I'm sure it's Elder Stone Bowl and Elder Crystal Leaf. My big black dog Crow sits on her haunches guarding them, which is odd. Crow should be guarding Little Fawn, Loon, and Chickadee.

When Jawbone almost steps over the cliff, I jerk him back. "Be careful, Jawbone! Mist has been blowing in all day and soaking the rocks that are now freezing over with nightfall."

"But maybe if I fall I could bash him out of my head?"

I stop dead in the trail with my heart thundering. "Don't ever say something like that again."

Jawbone suddenly grits his teeth and his head trembles. Slowly, steadily, the soul leaks from his body and his eyes go empty until they are little more than fixed blue moons in his head.

"Jawbone?"

He's staring straight at me, but I know one of his spells has chased his soul away, and he does not see me.

8

QUILLER

Jawbone? Can you hear me?"

Jawbone tightly clamps his jaw as his head is pulled back severely, seemingly against his will, forcing him to stare at the sky as though something up there amid the first campfires of the dead requires his attention. In the past he's told me that when we think he's having one of his spells, he's actually walking across the sky with ghost dogs trotting at his side. Is that where he is now?

Wrenching his head down, he starts walking toward the village, but he's gone deaf and mute.

I grab for his arm and hold tight to keep him away from the precipice. I never know what to do when this happens. Nothing seems to bring my son back to this world. I can't shake him, or shout at him, or coddle him. He stays gone for exactly the amount of time he needs, and then he returns. At least, so far.

"I'm right here beside you, Jawbone. Don't be afraid."

As we enter the sea cave, Crow rises and trots over with her ears pricked to lick Jawbone's white-knuckled fist.

I reach down to pet her head. "He'll be all right, Crow. He'll come back soon." These spells began on the twentieth day of the Moon of Wolves Pawing Snow. Neither RabbitEar nor I were there when the first one came upon him. The elders say Jawbone cried out and fell over as though speared through the heart. They tried to rouse him, but he did not wake for three days. When he finally opened his eyes, he was little more than a stuffed child-skin. He couldn't speak or move.

Crow whimpers and walks at our side toward the village fire where the elders wait for us. The squeal of an infant drifts from inside Mink's lodge. It's a bittersweet sound. Soon we will vanish just like the Mericans.

I lead Jawbone to the fire and pull him down atop a hide. "Let's speak with the elders."

When I sit down cross-legged beside him, he curls on his side and rests his head in my lap. His unblinking gaze fixes on my right knee as though nothing else exists in the entire world.

Crow stretches out at my side, hindquarters close to the fire, forelegs extended out in front, and gently licks Jawbone's arm.

"Quiller, how are you feeling?" Elder Crystal Leaf asks. Sparse white hair blows around her wrinkled face. "You were ill when you got back two days ago. Are you all right tonight?"

"Just queasy. It will pass."

Crystal Leaf's gaze shifts to watch Jawbone's leather boots waggle, rhythmically thumping the cave floor. I'm fairly certain my son doesn't know he's doing it. The elder looks more closely at his hollow eyes. "Is he gone again?"

"Yes." I stroke Jawbone's hair.

"That's three spells in the past quarter-moon, isn't it?"

"Yes."

RabbitEar heaves a disappointed breath. "I'm going to check on the girls. Should I bring back a hide for Jawbone so he'll be warm until he returns?"

"That would help, thank you."

RabbitEar strides toward Mink's lodge. Mink's wife, Gray Dove, always watches over our children when we are away. The girls must be asleep, or they would have come running out to greet us the instant they heard our voices.

"What was the cavern like, Hoodwink?" Elder Stone Bowl has seen fifty summers pass. A few wisps of gray hair cling to his age-spotted scalp; otherwise, he's bald.

"It's just as Quiller told us." Hoodwink leans forward and extends his cold hands to warm them before the fire. "Haunting. Hundreds of glowing blue faces are buried in the ice. Almost all are women and children."

"And they whimper?" Crystal Leaf asks.

"The childlike whimpering eddies up the tunnels from deeper in the earth, so it's hard to tell the source."

Crystal Leaf draws her collar more tightly about her wrinkled throat. "What does it mean?"

Hoodwink lifts a shoulder. "I think the old stories about the Jemen war are true. Our creators split into two factions, the Sky Jemen, led by the Old Woman of the Mountain, and the Earthbound Jemen. These poor souls may be the victims of Old Woman's wrath."

I say, "Lynx told me that Jorgensen and Arakie's families are both in those caverns, so I think that's right."

As though the Sky Jemen heard our conversation, far out over the ocean a ship of light sails westward through the green zyme light, leisurely winking in and out of the drifting clouds.

"No! I—I won't!" Jawbone's feet scramble for purchase against the cave floor as he curls up tighter on his side. When he finally settles, he's crawled half into my lap with his head limply hanging over the other side like a soaked string doll. Grabbing hold of my arm, he pulls it across his chest and keeps it there, exactly as he did the first time I witnessed one of these spells. Just before they strike, he tries very hard to get to me, so that he can curl up in my lap and ride them out. Beyond the cave, tufts of mist are being born above the zyme. Jawbone blankly watches them gather.

"Won't do what?" Hoodwink gently asks.

"Not goin'!"

I whisper, "Does the other boy want you to go somewhere?"

For a time, there is only the crackling of the fire and the far-off growling of lions filtering down from the Ice Giant Mountains.

Hoodwink reaches over and tenderly pats Jawbone's foot. "Ask the boy what he wishes to show you."

I feel my son tense before I see it. He's recoiling because someone has just crouched beside him, someone I can't see. Did the other boy emerge from the cave in his head and come to visit him in this world?

Jawbone retreats into the strange silence inside him like a turtle pulling his head and feet into a shell. His soul seems to have crossed over into the seductive darkness of the dead.

"When did this spell start, Quiller?" Elder Crystal Leaf's faded old eyes turn to me.

"On the trail just before we got here."

Jawbone sobs.

"It's all right, son." I examine his tormented eyes. "I'm right here."

He tucks his head into the folds of my cape. If he were awake and well, he would never allow anyone to see him lying in my lap like this. Especially not his father.

Mist has begun to fill the cave and turn the firelit air sparkling.

With one groping hand, Jawbone reaches up and grabs a lock of my red hair, then pulls my face down close to his mouth. His teeth gnash, but no words come out.

"You're very tired, son. Just try to rest. I'll be right here when you wake up."

Every muscle in his body quivers, then the seizure strikes.

9

JAWBONE

Why am I flopping around like a fish out of water?

Mother and Elder Hoodwink lean over me.

Hands clutch my shaking arms and legs so hard their fingers hurt me.

"Elders, I've never seen him do this before!" Mother shouts. Red hair shivers around her freckled face each time I jerk. "This is not one of his ordinary spells!"

Father charges across the village and kneels at my side, looking down in panic. "What happened?"

"Jawbone went rigid, then he started shaking."

Father grabs hold of my head and tries to hold it still, while he shouts, "Jawbone, can you hear me?"

His big hands, rough with calluses, can't hold my head still. It's bouncing up and down like a hide ball. Then . . . suddenly . . .

Flame shadows freeze on the cave roof. Strange patterns of orange and gray. Could be the back of a serpent. But dead. Not alive. Not slithering. Just lying on the roof above me.

Have to find mother's green eyes. There. There they are. Shiny. That's where home is. That's where I'm safe. The only place.

People rush out of their warm lodges to stand in the cold mist and whisper behind their hands, but all I see now are

Mother's eyes and her red hair flying above my face. If I had a free hand I could grab hold of it and it would tether me to this world. I wouldn't go flying off into the sky like one of the Meteor People sailing for the Land of the Dead.

Elder Hoodwink moves back, and Mother drags me into her arms and rocks me back and forth. She smells like campfire smoke and sweat. Comforting things. I think: this is the woman who adopted me after my real mother died.

What will happen if Quiller and RabbitEar are killed like my old parents in Great Horned Owl Village were? I will have to take care of my three sisters by myself. They'll need me. *They. Will. Need. Me.* More people come over and big eyes sway above me.

Jawbone. Jawbone. Jawbone.

The name crashes through the air.

Is that me?

My name?

"He needs to sleep," Elder Crystal Leaf says. "Why don't you take him to your lodge and cover him with warm hides?"

All the eyes come loose and bob away on a dark ocean. I remember another ocean with icebergs floating by. Somewhere there, the other boy cries and lions pant. Whiskers brush our silver lodge, and my little sister's fingers tear at my shirt as the lion drags her out by her feet. Mother shrieks, *"No, Racer, grab her!"* Father's arms swing like long ropes hanging from the sky as he leaps for my sister. Lion jaws clamp around his skull, drag him out. *"Jawbone, run for the boats!"* Mother screams. Red Calf. Her name was Red Calf. I shove out of the lodge and stare into the darkness and chaos. My relatives flee across the village, chased by lions. Run. Run. Leave them all to the lions. Save myself. Get to a boat . . .

"I think he needs to eat," Quiller says. "He hasn't eaten since lunch."

The words are rocks. Thuds. I jerk with each one. How long has my soul been walking in the past? Is this the same day that we visited the blue faces, or another day long ago when I'd only seen ten summers? Quiller is not my mother. But she is. I am in a big sea cave, on my back, with a man crouching beside me. RabbitEar. Yes. He's my father now. An old woman wobbles along past Father, her walking stick tapping the cave floor. She has a wolf-hide cape and white hair blowing. I throw my arms around Mother's neck and pull her down until our cheeks press together.

She lifts me into her muscular arms and hugs me tightly. "You're all right, Jawbone. I'm right here."

The old woman with the cape that sways bends over me. "His eyes have stopped rolling in his head. I think his soul has come back."

"Yes, he's fine now," Mother says.

Father sounds annoyed when he asks, "Can you sit up, son?"

I blink at my left foot and think: *This is not the other boy's foot. See, the toes wiggle when I try to make them.*

"Tired." I breathe the word against Mother's throat.

"I'm sure you are," she says. "That was a hard-fought battle."

"I fought a battle?" I ask, but no one hears me because the question tiptoed around and got swallowed before it reached my mouth. When I'd seen six summers, I swallowed two of my loose baby teeth and I could hear them clicking down in my belly.

Click. Clack.

Bat-tle.

I close my mouth to keep more words from falling out.

"I'm going to my lodge to get him a bowl of fish soup," Elder Crystal Leaf says.

"Thank you, elder." Mother smooths my hair. "How are you feeling, Jawbone? Are you hungry?"

When Elder Crystal Leaf returns with a bowl of warm soup, Mother takes it and slowly spoons it into my mouth as she would an infant. As my belly warms up, my eyes get very heavy. I slowly fall asleep against Mother's chest, listening to the rhythmic beating of the sea.

10

LYNX

Gauzy clouds scud just over my head as I carry my armload of wood up the bison trail through the fragrant pine grove. Smooth black boulders, taller than I am, cluster in groups amid the towering pines. In the light rain, they shine as though polished by the Ice Giants. Over the past one hand of time, the morning has gone from golden to dark gray. I need to get inside fast. The problem with summer thunderstorms is that water sheets down the faces of the Ice Giants in roaring torrents, washing away anything in its path. I don't want to end up being tumbled all the way to Mother Ocean.

Just before I walk through the square entry, I glance southward, trying to judge the severity of the oncoming storm. The volcanoes have been swallowed by a wall of rain, and lightning slashes the sky all the way to the horizon. The constant booms and grating shrieks of the Giants blend with peals of thunder to fill the air with an otherworldly symphony.

"It's going to drench the world," I murmur to myself and turn to walk through the entry into the Stronghold. There are an infinite number of caverns ahead of me. Some I've explored, most I have not. Like tree roots, they shoot off in every direction, boring deeper and deeper into the Ice Giant Mountains.

The first cave is filled with pale blue light. Doesn't matter how often I stand here, awe expands my chest.

Peculiar drawings curl across every flat rock face. I wish I understood all of these languages, but I've resigned myself to the fact that I will never learn Sanskrit or Hebrew, just to name a few of the oddly beautiful scripts that surround me. Some are love letters to people long gone: *Daniel, forgive me. I love you.* But most are mathematical formulas about mass and energy. I only understand some of the math, but better than I understand the written words. Though Quancee has taught me to read in several languages, I still have trouble with meaning.

To my right is an elegantly written German passage. I translate it and whisper, "Form is a revelation of essence." A few paces later, there's another that says, "The eye by which I see God is the same as the eye by which God sees me."

The words resonate, but I don't understand them. To me, the old Jemen gods are more like the evil spirits; they haunt my world, but they're just remote fanciful notions. They aren't real.

I've walked only a few paces before Quancee realizes I'm returning to her, and she begins to sing in a sweet high voice. The sound is ethereal in a way I cannot describe; it flutters inside me, gently touching my heart with featherlight strokes.

"I'll be there soon," I softly tell her. "I have all the wood we'll need until the storm passes, I think."

Along with her gladness to see me, I feel her loneliness. On occasion she has allowed me to walk the stillborn dreams of that emptiness with her, and her terror is epic. Even now, images coalesce and melt behind my eyes . . . threads of light traveling wastelands of darkness that go on forever . . . magnificent patterns colliding in folds of time . . . bell-like voices cascading from every cell in my body.

"Where did you go today?" I ask.

She continues to sing to me in crystal-clear notes that are more shapes than music, more pictures than words; it's a symphony of geometry that hints at bizarre relationships that can't be true, can they? She must just be theorizing. She does that, spins fantastic probabilities. Quancee maintains that if she can conceive it, it must exist.

In the middle of the cave, the first black handprints appear, blotting out the curling lines. Small prints. A woman's hands. The prints become stripes and circles. It isn't paint. The storykiller was trying to wash away the words and symbols with human blood, probably her own. Over the summers, the stone absorbed the blood and turned it black. I have always suspected the storykiller was the Old Woman of the Mountain, who, at the end, had lost all hope that these numbers and letters could save her or the Sky Jemen, but it could have been another woman, I suppose.

Before I leave the Storykiller Cave and duck into the round tunnel that leads deeper into the mountain, I read the last passage over the tunnel: "I shall be moving and yet it will be all one motion."

Form, essence, eternal eyes, one unifying motion . . . all pounding out a rhythm older than the campfires of the dead. Quancee tells me that motion *is*. Without motion nothing is real. But, she adds, that doesn't mean it exists. Reality is not the same as existence. She tells me that many things that are real—things that I can touch and see—do not, in fact, exist. I can feel the rightness of her words, but my mind can't seem to understand them. The concepts are like water flowing through my fingers. I can't hold onto them long enough to grasp what they're made of.

It takes another one hundred heartbeats before I enter the gigantic chamber with the ancient cages, and my gaze lifts to the broken rectangular boxes stacked atop one another all the way to the ceiling two hundred hand-lengths above me. Some of the cages look as though they were demolished with a stone ax. The bars of others were chewed through by whatever was inside.

Ancient legends drift through my head.

Sealion People tell stories of a time after the Jemen split into two factions—the Sky Jemen and the Earthbound Jemen—when the Earthbound Jemen hauled animals into a deep cavern to protect them from the growing cold. After they'd destroyed the Ice Giants, they planned to turn the precious animals loose in a warm and better world.

As I study the doors hanging at angles from the cages and the broken bars, I recall Arakie's words, saying there were many such sanctuaries around the world. This one failed. He didn't know what had happened to the others, but he feared that as ice crawled across the planet, the other Earthbound Jemen suffered the same fate.

I gently pet the chewed bars as I pass.

Since I was a child, I have dreamed of seeing bobcats and coyotes trotting along sunlit forest trails in the warm world to come. Now I'm sure that dream is dead. I have explored the frozen cities that glitter inside the glaciers, seen the dead Jemen with animals clutched in their arms, and peered for long enough to decipher some of the titles of the books that still line ancient library shelves. I know the sky will never again fill with huge flocks of songbirds. The sea will never erupt with leaping dolphins or magnificent whales. All that remains of them are fantastical stories about their grace and beauty.

When I enter the next tunnel, the temperature warms up. It isn't far to the drop-off.

At the end of the tunnel, I sit down on the ledge with my armload of wood and dangle my feet for a time while I gaze out upon the glittering paleo-ocean filled with trailing swirls of bioluminescent blue algae. Our greatest shamans say ancient oceans have always washed upon shores far beneath the Ice Giants. I try to chart the shoreline of this expanse of water to judge the size, but can't. The far horizon curves into infinity. It's a gigantic womb of blue light.

As I jump over the ledge and land on my feet, a few branches jolt from my armload of wood and thunk on the floor. I reach down to retrieve them, then carefully skirt around the edge of the slight waves.

The Jemen war ended here at the Stronghold.

Crisscrossing the air above me is a vast web of heavy black beams that hang like gigantic spears ready to plunge down into the heart of the ancient ocean, melding with the monstrous toppled beams that spike up from the water. The Old Woman of the Mountain and her warriors once took refuge in these caverns, sealing themselves and their unholy creations inside to escape the battle outside. It didn't work . . . the rebels, led by Arakie, found a way in.

As I duck low to enter Quancee's cave, I sense a yearning far beyond my comprehension. It pervades my body, clutches at my heart. Quancee is wildly happy to see me.

"The storm is going to be bad," I tell her. "I hope the cave entry isn't buried by rocks and debris in the morning."

Over the long moons since Arakie died, I have swept and cleaned Quancee's chamber, carrying away the rubble that in his vast age he could no longer carry. Even the small tunnels that branch off in every direction are spotless now. The only space I have not relentlessly scrubbed and organized is her chamber itself, and that's because I'm not sure what many of the things are. I'm afraid if I move something I don't understand, it may harm Quancee.

I brace a hand against the wall and plod another twenty paces to the ancient door that stands half open. Firelight flickers inside.

"Sorry it took me so long," I whisper.

I shoulder through the door and enter a chamber that is roofed, floored—even the walls are covered—with strange rectangular crystal panes. They are smooth and as translucent as ice, but clearer than any ice I've ever seen. Many of the panes are broken or missing. One pane winks. Three long red flashes. Three short green flashes. Three long red flashes. A pause, then it starts over. It keeps repeating.

Quancee has been crying for help for centuries. But no help has ever come, nor will it now.

Curious tools line the long shelf in the rear—clear tubes, metallic creations with no rust, ancient books with crumbling leather bindings. All are neatly arranged in a row. The volumes known as the Rewilding Reports lean against each other, the spines out so they're easy to read: Volume Alpha through Volume Tau. Volume Delta is the most interesting to me, for it chronicles the creation—re-creation—of Sealion People, Rust People, and Dog Soldiers. We were the Jemen's last hope for earth. Our ancestors had survived many Ice Ages before, and they prayed we would do so again.

Kneeling, I dump my armload of wood on the floor next to the crystal-lined fire hearth, and sadness fills me. There are twenty-two Sealion People left in the world, and seven Dog Soldiers. Only the Rust People's numbers are growing—well over one thousand—so I suppose that means *Neandertalensis* has proven to be the most adaptable re-creation. But the loss of my people, Denisovans, grieves me as much as the losses of bobcats and coyotes, for I see no purpose in it.

All along the base of the walls, I've collected and stacked some of the broken crystal panes that used to scatter the floor. They glitter in the flames.

Reaching out, I stroke the blinking pane. It blurs suddenly, like an eye filling with tears, and her timeless presence flashes around inside me.

". . . *If I teach you what little I know about her, will you care for her until the end? Will you tell her story? Her story is important.*"

Strangely, I don't know if I'm remembering Arakie's elderly

voice or Quancee is replaying it for me. Our memories so often bind together that I can't tell where mine end and hers begin. We are becoming one, melting into something very new and something very, very old. A symbiosis of consciousness as ancient as the Jemen themselves, I suspect.

"I will always be your caretaker," I say. "Don't worry about that. I'll be here for as long as I can."

Her gladness dissolves into dread.

"Why are you upset?"

A pause while I feel her questions. I understand the shapes that swirl around inside me. Her language is the symmetry of all symmetries, perfect and beautiful.

"Jorgensen was here?" I say in surprise. "How long ago?"

I glance back at the door, afraid he may be lurking outside, spying on me. I often find him waiting for me in places I never suspected I'd see him. More often I find the chevron patterns of his beaded boots embedded in the mud or ice from where he's been following me.

Patterns of circles flare and die inside me.

"Really? He must have been watching, waiting for me to leave this morning. What did he say to you?"

Braided globes spiral through my mind, growing fainter and fainter, until they spin down into a dark whirlpool. It's as though I can feel her flying away to hide.

My hand slowly trails down her panes and drops to my side. "I see. Well, he's wrong. I won't abandon you, even if my people move south in the autumn."

Nothing for a moment.

Then . . . I'm not here . . . I'm running somewhere in a dimly recalled world, running free across green meadows with Quancee at my side. I don't see her, but she's there, prancing deerlike with the wide sky overhead and curious flowering trees passing by. The air smells intensely green.

"Yes, it makes me happy, too," I say. "So forget about the things Jorgensen told you. They're not true. I wonder, though, why he wants you to think I will abandon you. Does he expect you will turn to him?"

Suddenly, bottomless blackness swallows everything. The death of motion . . . the death of all things . . .

My chest constricts and I shake my head. "No. No, Quancee. I don't care what he said. I won't let him kill you."

The tears slowly vanish from her panes, and she curls up in my mind like an infant in a cradle as though relieved and exhausted. I feel her breathing as pure glittering light.

"Just rest," I softly say. "I have a lot of work to do. I'm going to try to mend you."

I pull over the tripod and arrange the legs so that the pot hanging in the middle hovers above the flames, then I gradually began adding branches to build up the fire. The pot belonged to Arakie. It's about the size of two fists put together and as light as air. I think it's made from the same material as the giant tubes that line the seashore, for it gleams with the same unnatural luster and never tarnishes, never rusts. I accidentally dropped the pot once and watched in stunned awe as the dent repaired itself.

When the chunks of pitch in the bottom of the pot start to heat up, the fragrance of pine resin fills the chamber.

More shapes spin through me, and I feel warm and loved.

"And you're the only thing that matters to me, Quancee."

Reaching out, I pluck one of the broken panes from the stack along the wall and examine it, then I search for the other half and fit the broken triangles together on the floor.

"I don't know if this will help, Quancee," I softly explain, "but I don't think it will hurt you. Please tell me if it does?"

Using a stick from the woodpile, I stir the pine pitch, then I draw out the stick and drip the pitch between the broken halves of the pane, gluing them together.

While the pitch dries, Quancee carries me off on the flickering reflections of a sun that died billions of summers ago. On occasion, the reflections flash with faces as they pass by. At least, I think they're faces. They are so odd they may be words or mathematical symbols. I can't measure time when she takes me on such flights, but when I return the pitch has dried and hardened, and the fire has burned down to a wavering bed of red coals.

"All right," I whisper, or think I whisper. "Let's see if this works."

Clutching the first mended pane, I stir the barely warm pitch and pull the gooey stick from the pot. Just over the blinking pane there's a hole about this size.

"This looks right."

Carefully, I spread hot pitch along the edges of the mended pane and rise to tuck it into the hole. I have to keep it there until the pitch cools enough to seal the pane into the slot.

Then I return for another pane . . . and another . . .

As I rebuild the crystalline lattice that keeps her alive, I say, "Jorgensen told me there's a collapsed cave filled with parts to fix you. Once I've replaced all the missing panes, I'll go search . . ." My voice fades. "Why don't you want to discuss it?"

My heart quickens when unknowable gulfs of time hit me in waves, and my body seems to expand in all directions at once. For a while, I don't know how long, I cease to exist while my fingertips brush eternity.

I have to find my voice before I can say, "Your life has not lost all meaning."

Faint singing lies upon the darkness where I drift in a sea of glowing galaxies, drawing at my heart.

"I know you're lonely, but I don't want you to die."

Bowing my head, I close my eyes, allowing the painfully clear notes to tap against my heart like delicate fingertips.

"You're an exile sojourning in the wasteland of the godhead? What does that mean?"

When I open my eyes and look at the reflections of firelight flickering across her panes, I realize she's retreated and is sailing somewhere far away and a long time ago. She's left me far behind.

"Why do you have to walk the path alone?" I call. "Take me with you. I want to walk the wasteland at your side. Can't I do that?"

Darkness moves upon the face of the deep until I feel her thoughts seeping across time.

"What do you mean sometimes you guide others, and their paths are not my coordinates?"

There's a long pause, and the darkness smells faintly of alien rainstorms, of wet brush and trees that have existed in this world.

Reaching out, I gently stroke her panes. "I know I can't, but I'm trying to understand, Quancee."

11

QUILLER

Roaring wind shudders the mammoth-hide lodge over our heads, but RabbitEar and I barely notice where we sit together before the fire. I've tied the door flap back so we can watch the storm. It's been raining hard since dusk.

Lifting my wooden cup, I take a sip of tundra wildflower tea. The sweet tangy flavor soothes me. Jawbone still sleeps in the rear beneath a mound of bison hides with his sisters. Their four blond heads are like yellow ducks arranged in a row.

"This is a bad time to send a boy on a spirit hunt," I say. "We should tell him he can't go."

"He'll throw a fit if we do. He told me he's going no matter what. Besides, it's summer. The quest wall will be dry by noon."

"What if the rain turns to snow tonight? By noon, every handhold and toehold will be filled with water. He'll fall long before he reaches the first children's camp."

RabbitEar sloshes the tea around his cup. He hasn't taken a drink in a long while, but he keeps staring down into the pale liquid as though trying hard to see the future there. "He's more surefooted than you think he is. Don't try to stop him. He has his heart set on becoming a man."

"Fine, but why not wait a few days until we're certain there isn't another storm on the horizon? Surely a few more days won't matter?"

"It does to him." My husband reaches out to touch my arm. His red beard glimmers in the firelight. "Not only that, Elder Stone Bowl says if he doesn't go now, his next spell may kill him. And you know as well as I do that they're getting worse. He needs to find a spirit helper to heal him."

My gaze drifts to our children. Jawbone's spear rests right over his head in case he needs to grab it and rush outside to help his father fight off lions or wolves in the night. He is, truly, the bravest boy I have ever seen. I have witnessed him leap in front of his sisters with his spear to shield them from a short-faced bear that abruptly appeared in the brush while we were gathering berries. He would lay down his life to save them in a heartbeat.

RabbitEar pulls his hand away and sighs. "His last attack really scared me, Quiller. I've never seen him jerk about like a clubbed rabbit."

"Nor have I. But his spells don't scare me nearly as much as the stories he's started to tell about the other boy who torments him."

"Other boy?"

I suddenly realize I've just revealed my son's most closely held secret, but I can't stop now. Very softly, I say, "Don't you ever ask him about this. Do you understand? He told me this in confidence."

"Yes." RabbitEar waves it away.

Glancing at the hides where Jawbone sleeps, I feel like a rotten carcass, but I say, "He told me the other boy lives in a cave in the back of head. The cave is covered with a buffalo hide, but sometimes the boy sneaks out."

RabbitEar's eyes narrow. "A child's imagination."

"Are you sure?" I faintly hiss the words. I don't want any of our children to overhear this conversation, least of all Jawbone.

RabbitEar lowers his voice to match mine. "Do you think the other boy is an evil spirit that brings on his spells?"

I make a helpless gesture with one hand. "Maybe. Who knows? He's told me almost nothing."

"He wouldn't. He doesn't want you to think he's faint-hearted." RabbitEar bows his head to stare into his cup again. "Which is even more of a reason to send him on a spirit quest. Perhaps if he can face the other boy, speak to him, or maybe kill him, Jawbone's spells will vanish and he will become the man he should be."

"Kill the other boy? Why would he . . ."

We both flinch when the Ice Giants roar and the sea cave quakes around us. Our icy world is never quiet, never still. Even now, I can hear entire cliffs of ice cracking loose and splashing into the sea in the distance.

I watch Little Fawn's yellow hair drag across the hide as she rolls to her back. Is she awake?

Leaning close to RabbitEar, I whisper, "It's foolish to force our son to go on this quest now! Even if he can get a grip on the handholds and toeholds, the shadowed ledges could be covered with ice. Why can't this quest wait just a little longer?"

RabbitEar clutches his cup in both hands and gives me a resolute look. "If he starts early each morning, he'll make it to the next camp by midday. He'll be all right."

I don't respond. An eerie sense of disaster haunts me, as though something dark and hooded lives in the crevices of the quest wall and it's waiting to cast my son to his doom.

Taking a long drink of tea, I lower the cup and rest it upon my drawn-up knee. "If we start at dawn tomorrow, we won't even get there until noon. By then—"

"Do you think I'll let Jawbone start climbing if the wall isn't safe?"

"No. Of course not."

I study my husband. I've been so consumed with dread that I've barely spoken with RabbitEar. For days I've locked myself

in an internal prison where all I do is hear the sound of Jawbone's laughter, feel his arms around my neck, see the love in
his eyes. I've been so preoccupied that I've ignored the fact that
RabbitEar has been locked in a similar prison, and perhaps experiencing it with even greater agony than my own. Jawbone's
spells must make him feel just as powerless and alone as I feel.

I reach out and rest my hand on his bearded cheek. "Forgive
me. I know you'd never endanger our son. I just—"

"Quiller, he wants to do this. It's important to him. Let
him go."

"My greatest fear is that Jawbone will have one of his spells
when he's clinging to the wall. If he does . . ."

As RabbitEar stares at me, anger slowly fills his eyes. "You're
not the only one who's considered that possibility. I've imagined it happening over and over. Seen him go over backward . . ."
He turns to blink at Jawbone.

The hides move, and I fear our son is listening to us.

Setting my cup down, I wrap my arms around RabbitEar.
"Enough. I don't want to fight with you."

"I don't want to fight, either. Will you gather the things Jawbone will need for the climb, so we can walk him there at
dawn?"

"Yes," I say and immediately regret it.

12

JAWBONE

My eleven-summers-old sister Little Fawn reaches her hand across beneath the sleeping hide and pats my arm. I'm breathing so hard my whole body is throbbing. Like pouring water into a cracked wooden bowl, it doesn't matter how hard I suck at the air, my lungs won't hold enough. I'm light-headed and afraid one of my spells is coming on.

"You'll be all right, brother," Little Fawn whispers. "You're strong."

Her words float in the firelight that fills the lodge.

"Of course I am." I snuggle deeper under the hides to stare at her eyes. Tangles of blond hair frame her small face. She's biting her lower lip, squeezing my arm hard, trying to will her strength into me. "I'm very strong. I'll be all right. You'll see."

"I know. You'll find a very powerful spirit helper." Little Fawn smiles and yawns before she closes her eyes and braces her forehead against my shoulder. "Every other boy who's climbed the quest wall has found a helper."

"Little Gull didn't find a helper, or he'd still be alive."

"I know, but you will."

Far back in my head, the buffalo hide sways, and there's the glitter of snow or the campfires of the dead falling around me, so shiny it hurts. Claws clicking on rock. A woman singing in a chirp-chirp voice that stabs at the backs of my teeth.

Little Fawn slides closer and drapes an arm across my chest to hold me. "Mother and Father won't let anything hurt you. Try to sleep."

I pull the hide down to look at our parents holding each other before the fire.

No words come out of their mouths, just daggers of breath puncturing the firelight.

I squeeze my eyes closed so tight all I see are sparks flying through chunks of darkness. There are thousands of them, so I make sure to catch the closest one and hold on while it drags me spinning down, down into the smooth black depths where Father doesn't speak to Mother through gritted teeth.

13

LYNX

Dropping my pitch stick into the pot, I step back to examine my work. The black pitch lines create a mosaic that zigzags across Quancee's face, but all of the empty squares are now filled with glued-together panes. I feel her smiling at me. "Do you feel a little better? Stronger?"

The sensation is like the languid fluttering motion of autumn leaves falling to the ground . . .

"Glad to hear it." I smile and stroke her panes.

As I look around, I realize it's darker in here than I've ever seen it. When I first entered this chamber with Arakie three summers ago, the entire upper portion of one crystal wall was gone, lying in shards at my feet, which allowed the cerulean gleam cast by the paleo-ocean to fill the chamber and flicker from Quancee's panes. It was stunning, like translucent blue wings beating all around me. With the shards glued back in place, however, the only illumination now comes from Quancee herself. Her sickly yellow glow reminds me that she's slowly fading into oblivion before my eyes.

As grief constricts my chest, invisible tendrils of emotion reach out and touch my heart. Her presence is feather-light but filled with love.

"I'm all right," I whisper. "Just worried about you."

When I turn to walk back to the fire, I hear boots shishing in sand along the shore of the paleo-ocean. His steps are unmistakable, for he moves like a hunting wolf, each step carefully placed and barely audible. How long has he been out there?

When my shoulder muscles go tight, the firelit air quivers.

"No," I softly answer. "I'm not going to run away with you. I'm staying right there."

Quancee vanishes, and I sense her melt into the vast distances between now and then. Her abrupt flight leaves me lightheaded for a moment.

As Jorgensen enters the tunnel outside and stealthily approaches the doorway to this chamber, I call, "What do you want?"

"I just want to talk, Lynx."

I walk over, grasp my spear where it leans against the wall, and carry it back to my fire. Kneeling, I rest the spear on the floor at my side and stir the simmering pot of bison stew that rests in the coals.

When Jorgensen stands in the doorway, he's frowning. He shoves his hood back and examines the panes I glued back into Quancee's face. "Well, that's appalling. You've made an ugly mess, haven't you?"

I continue stirring my stew. The rich fragrance of bison meat rises with the steam. "Maybe, but Quancee says she feels stronger."

"It just says that to coddle you. That pine pitch you're using as glue restricts the flow of energy."

"Well, it has to feel better than having pieces of her body lying broken on the floor."

"I doubt it." Jorgensen leans one shoulder against the doorframe and crosses his arms over his chest. "Have you learned nothing about how this computer entangles superpositions to create qubits? By now, you should at least have a basic grasp of how energy—"

"Quancee wouldn't lie to me. She does feel better."

He laughs. It's a low, demeaning sound, as though I am even more dim-witted than he assumed. "I thought you'd read the Rewilding Reports? Of course it would lie. It's been deceiving humans for centuries."

He has the strangest blue eyes. The color mimics nothing in nature.

"That's not true," I reply. "Volume Epsilon speaks about Quancee's kindness and sense of wonder. It never says—"

"That's a very early volume. The detailed discussions of her ability to hate and punish those who opposed her were chronicled in Volume Omega. Have you read Volume Omega?"

Angrily, I reply, "You know I haven't. It's been missing for centuries."

"Well, I have read it. Do you want to know what it says?"

I use my spoon to dip up a chunk of bison, and blow on it to cool it, before I say, "I'm not sure I can believe anything you tell me, Vice Admiral."

"I'm going to tell you anyway. It was the subject of a great deal of discussion just before the war, because no one could explain Quancee's shift in behavior. At one point, the device was innocent and childlike, joyous to learn everything it could. But toward the end of the war, it grew into something absolutely terrifying. It began to wield its powers in monstrous ways. For example, when it became displeased with Premier Elektra, her advancing army simply vanished into thin air."

Startled, I say, "Vanished?"

"Just disappeared from the face of the earth. Arakie speculated that Quancee had moved the army to a different time and place, but Elektra said they were all dead."

The blood pulsing in my ears is deafening. "If Quancee did that, she was trying to stop something horrifying before—"

"It was done to punish the Premier for ordering Quancee to be reprogrammed."

"I don't believe it. Quancee is incapable—"

"You're a fool." Jorgensen throws up his hands. "Well, I've done the best I can to warn you. I suppose it's up to you now."

I blink down at my stew pot. "You are free to leave at any time, Vice Admiral."

Jorgensen does not leave. Instead, he flicks a hand at me and chuckles. "No wonder John Arakie liked your species so much."

"Why is that?" I reach for my wooden cup and dip it full of stew.

"Your intelligence level, huge eyes, heavy brow ridges, and long cranium reminded him of his long-dead pets. He was very fond of pets. Dogs especially. He was a true sentimentalist. He always gave Quancee the benefit of the doubt, which turned out to be a cataclysmic error that cost billions of lives."

Cautiously, I take a bite of the hot stew, and let the delicious flavor of long-horned bison distract me from Jorgensen's smirk. He enjoys tormenting me when I don't agree with the 'truths' he reveals, particularly when it concerns my beloved friend, Arakie.

Jorgensen strolls across the chamber and sits down cross-legged on the other side of the fire. His protruding chin shows a slight stubble of gray whiskers. I've never seen this before. Ordinarily, he uses a sharpened iron knife to clean his face. Not only that, his graying brown hair hangs over his cheeks in greasy strands.

"Will you be staying long?"

"Depends, Lynx. Did you ask Quancee about her death wish?"

I leisurely chew a bite of stew and swallow, forcing him to wait. "Not yet."

Faint amusement turns his lips. "I am not your enemy, Lynx. We could be the best of friends if you would allow it. After all, we both want what's best for Quancee."

"Do we?"

"Yes." He props one fist on his knee. "Remember when you asked me if I could repair it? Here's the thing, Lynx. If it wants to die, I may be able to salvage enough parts to reconfigure—"

In shock, I blurt, "You want to tear her apart? Is that why she's afraid of you?"

The fire crackles suddenly, and sparks whirl toward the ceiling.

"It is not afraid of me."

"She is! She flees every time you are close."

Jorgensen exhales in frustration. "Listen, I don't know if you can understand this, but it's impossible for Quancee to be afraid. You're imagining it."

"How could you possibly know—"

"Try to concentrate," he orders. "Fear is about the future, and Quancee knows time doesn't exist. Everything that ever was or ever will be is happening right now. They're just different coordinates in space-time, and it uses those coordinates like stepping stones to understand and calculate probabilities."

"Yes, I kn-know," I stammer. "Arakie taught me that reality is a four-dimensional space where everything, past, present, future, is just there. But I—"

"Look." Jorgensen leans forward. "Quancee is a conglomeration of parts put together in a way that allows it to be useful to humans. That's all it is. But it's malfunctioning. If I can dismantle it, I may be able to construct a smaller version—"

"You mean she—she's sick. Yes, she's told me. I'm trying to heal her."

His jaw vibrates with grinding teeth. "It's not 'sick.' Quancee requires error correction. It's hanging on the precipice of quantum decoherence, and there's no way I can explain to your species what that means. You simply don't have the brain capacity to understand such complexities. You have to trust me. I know what's best for her. You don't. But you're the caretaker. You need to grant me access to her systems, or I can't stop it. You must let me salvage what's useful before it's too late."

At times like this, I fear he's right. I don't have the same mental abilities that he has. Arakie taught me everything he could before he died, and Quancee has taught me infinitely more, but I still struggle with concepts like entanglement, time, and decoherence.

Setting my cup down, I draw up my knees, prop my elbows atop them, and massage my temples. Where is Quancee? I can't feel her at all. It's as though she's passed beyond the wasteland to whatever lies over the next hill. Is that where qubits hide—in the geometry of infinity just beyond eternity?

I look back at Jorgensen. "I won't let you kill her."

"It's not alive, Lynx. You just think it is. Your animistic worldview is the problem. You think everything has a soul and it will love you back if you only—"

"You can't tear her apart!"

He sits back and firelight flickers over his curious expression. "Tell me something? Are you and Quancee 'lovers'?"

My mouth gapes. "I don't even know what that means. Of course I love her, and I know she loves me, but it's impossible for us to be lovers."

"It seduced Arakie, too, you know."

An eerie sensation of danger comes over me. "No, I don't know. He never told me that, though I'm fairly sure he loved her, but—"

"You simple-minded fool. You're in love with an illusion, and it's going to kill you and every other archaic hominin on the planet."

Vice Admiral Jorgensen rises to his feet, gives Quancee a speculative glance, then turns and walks to the door.

"Why don't you just kill me?" I call to his back. "Then you'd have unfettered access to her."

The ancient hinges squeak as he props a hand on the door. With his back to me, he answers, "Honestly? I'm afraid to. Even in her weakened state, there's no telling what Quancee might do to me."

"Meaning?"

"Meaning"—he turns and glances at me—"it's a weapon. Understand?"

He walks away, and I hear his feral steps softly moving through the sand outside.

This is our relationship: he comes, tells me I'm inferior and stupid, and leaves.

I listen until the sound of his steps fades entirely before I relax enough to pick up my cup of stew and try to finish eating, but my hand shakes as I lift my spoon. Dropping it back into the cup, I exhale hard and study the dimly lit panes that surround me.

I have read every reference I can find about Quancee. I realize my understanding of her is limited, but my experience tells me far more than a book ever will, for I *feel* her goodness. All of my decisions are based upon that perception.

But I am not blind. Deep inside me questions hover, I just refuse to ask them. To do so would be unforgiveable treachery. She is absolutely vulnerable with me. I will not betray that. She has been betrayed by so many humans in her long life.

"Where are you?" I softly inquire.

Nothing.

Then, slowly, images glitter . . .

Here.

From the coordinates of a long, long time ago, the lids of silver eyes slip open, and I hear the scrape of scales as she gathers together all the golden threads that curl in the darkness around her and shapes them into wings to fly home to me.

I smile. She knows I love these fanciful creatures she invents.

When her crystal panes flicker and brighten, I know she's returned to me, and I feel warm.

"I missed you."

The chamber suddenly feels very old. I sit for a moment, listening with my ears and soul. Every book on the rear shelf is outlined in brightness, every dark corner quivering with shadows, as they have done for centuries.

"Yes," I answer with a nod. "He scares me, too."

14

QUILLER

Thunderbirds rumble in the distance, but for the most part the sea cave is calm and quiet this morning. Father Sun has not yet risen, so there's still a faint green glow in the air. As I warm my hands before the village fire, I absently let my gaze drift over the soft bison and mammoth hides spread around the hearthstones. The longest hairs glint golden in the flickering light.

Last night, in my dreams, I found myself standing on top of the quest wall watching Jawbone climbing up below me. He was small and looked like he was having trouble. His fingers kept slipping from the handholds. Far below him, snow mounded the shore but the tops of the black boulders that killed Little Gull were visible. As I watched, my son cried out my name, started jerking, and fell straight down. He didn't make another sound until his body struck the rocks.

I keep living that dream. I can't get it out of my mind.

Behind me, conversations drift as people move about in their lodges. The voices of sleepy children ask about breakfast. An infant whimpers.

I glimpse RabbitEar when he ducks out of our lodge and heads toward me. He has a burly swagger, which makes the red salmon painted on the exterior suede of his cape appear to be leaping.

As he sits down on the hide beside me, he gives me a faint smile. "Did you get any sleep at all?"

"No. You?"

He exhales hard. "Couldn't. After I crawled beneath the hides with Jawbone, he begged me to stay, so I just held him in my arms until he finally fell asleep. That was a couple of hands of time ago."

"Was he asleep when you left?"

"I think so. Not sure. When I got up, he rolled over and buried his head deep beneath the hides."

I hug myself. "At least he stopped crying."

"Yes," he says and clamps his jaw tight while he squints out at the ocean. "He wouldn't tell me what his nightmare was about."

I've felt cold before, but it's nothing compared to the icy sense of foreboding that congeals in my heart at this moment. I stare at him. The flames have turned his eyes into amber gems. "I'm sure he dreamed the same thing I did. All night long, I watched our son fall off the cliff."

He starts to say something consoling, but I raise a hand to stop him. "Don't. After you say those words, you'll just tell me we have to do this, and I have already agreed."

RabbitEar clasps my fingers and draws them back to hold them over his heart. "When the time comes, I'll wake our son and get him dressed. If he starts crying again, I'll take care of it."

"By telling him to be a man?" The question cuts.

He squeezes my hand so hard it hurts. "It will mean more coming from me, Quiller."

Pulling my hand away, I clench it into a fist and rest it upon my drawn-up knee. I feel like all my veins have been opened and my strength is draining away into the crevices in the cave floor.

Quietly, my husband asks, "Did you pack the charm Elder Hoodwink made him to keep the evil spirits away?"

"Of course I did." The tiny buffalo carved from gray soapstone is about the size of my thumb. "I tucked it in his belt pouch with an extra pair of bison-wool socks."

I keep telling myself Jawbone can't die, not after all the horrors he's gone through in his life. Unfortunately, I've stood over the bodies of too many dead children to believe it.

War Leader Mink ducks out of his lodge carrying a pack and walks across the cave toward us. His long black braid hangs over his left shoulder. As he crouches across the fire, he sets the pack aside and his gaze goes back and forth between us. "Is there a problem?"

"No," I answer coldly.

"Then why do you two look like you're walking to your own executions? This is just a spirit quest. He'll be all right."

RabbitEar smiles. "In a couple of summers, when your sons are preparing for their first quests, I'm going to come out here and sit before the fire with you and remind you that you said that."

"I certainly hope so," Mink answers with conviction.

RabbitEar chuckles and gestures to Mink's pack lying on the stone floor. "What's in the pack?"

Mink drags it over and loosens the ties. "You've both been so obsessed with death, I know you're unprepared for the trip."

"We are not unprepared," I say.

"Of course you are." Mink pulls out a flat chunk of sandstone and two stilettos made from splits of mastodon femurs. They're as long as his forearm. "When I'm done sharpening these, I want you to tuck them into your belts, just in case you need them. Most of the predators are up high in the mountains feasting on newborn mammoth and bison calves, but you'll be hunted by a few."

I suppress a smile. "Thank you."

Mink arranges the sandstone on the hide before him and picks up the first stiletto. As he draws the tip across the stone, sharpening it, the stiletto makes a sharp grating sound. "Are you packed?"

"Yes, we're packed."

"Jawbone's belt pouch is filled with the things he'll need? And it's not too heavy? You don't want to off-balance him when he's climbing."

RabbitEar's mouth quirks. "Is he your son or mine? Of course his pouch is correctly packed. Quiller packed it herself."

"Ah, then I feel better. Quiller definitely did it right. Now, what have you forgotten?"

"How would I know? If I've forgotten it, it's forgotten."

"Did you put extra pairs of boots and gloves in his coat pocket in case he gets wet?"

"Quiller did."

While they banter, I watch Elder Hoodwink walking across the cave with his walking stick. As though his hip hurts, he winces with each step.

"Pleasant morning to you, elder," I greet.

"And to you, matron. It's a beautiful morning, isn't it? It will be a good day to walk your son to the quest wall."

After inhaling a deep breath, I reply. "I hope so. Thank you for making him a protection charm."

Hoodwink slumps down beside Mink and rests his walking stick at his side. "Did Jawbone cry in his sleep? Children usually do before a quest."

"Yes. None of us slept. RabbitEar finally crawled beneath the hides and held him in his arms. It was the only way our son could rest."

"Well, don't worry about it. That's normal."

"I'm not sure the gods agree. The Ice Giants have been

grinding and thundering against one another, and I have the feeling they're telling me to pick another day for this spirit quest."

Hoodwink fiddles with his walking stick, laying it out straighter at his side. "You're not afraid to let Jawbone become a man, are you?"

"Of course not," I say, but the question affects me strangely. The truth is, if I could keep Jawbone as a little boy for the rest of his life, I would. Just so I could hold him close and protect him. Once he becomes a man, he'll have to face those dangers alone. "What scares me, elder, is that he'll have one of his spells and lose his grip."

"He won't. Jawbone is a special boy. His spirit helper has been waiting for many summers to find Jawbone climbing the quest wall. You must let her find him."

When I don't respond, Hoodwink gives me a sad smile. "I remember your first quest, Quiller. We were far north in the Steppe Lands. You were younger than Jawbone, twelve summers. Your parents didn't think you were old enough to undertake a quest, but you demanded the right to seek a spirit helper. Your mother wept the entire time you were gone."

That makes me smile. "Yes, Father told me."

I miss my mother and father. They were killed in one of the last raids by the Rust People, before we established an uneasy peace alliance.

"When you returned with two spirit helpers, Bull Bison and Sister Moon, she was so proud of you she could barely stand it." Hoodwink exhales a white cloud of breath that drifts away in the breeze. "You will feel the same way in a few days."

"The quest wall was different in the Steppe Lands, elder. It was gritty limestone, not slick basalt. It required less skill."

"Please trust me. I promise you that a helper will find your son and take care of him. When he steps off the trail onto the cliff top, he will run into your arms cured and so happy you will . . ."

We all stiffen when we hear boots on the cliff trail that leads down into our sea cave. Rust People steps, heavy and rhythmic, pounding the trail with intent. In contrast, the steps of Sealion People are quick and light.

"It's early for visitors." Mink grips the stiletto he's been sharpening and watches the three people in silver capes march out of the darkness. "Is that Sticks in the lead?"

"Yes," I whisper. "With two Rust warriors to guard him. They're carrying spears. I can see the polished spear points flashing in the zyme light."

Sticks lifts a hand. "Greetings!"

No one responds.

Mink softly asks, "What's he want?"

"We'll know soon enough," RabbitEar answers.

Sticks is the youngest Dog Soldier, almost twenty-four summers, but his strange alliance with Jorgensen has made him an influential man among the Rust nation. Lynx says this has caused a great deal of resentment among the six other Dog Soldiers, for Sticks has not even been initiated into the Dog Soldier society yet. He is considered a soldier in training. Thanissara, the eldest Dog Soldier at forty-five summers, leads the society.

As I examine Sticks, I'm struck again by his extreme height and the low dome of his skull. Truly, Dog Soldiers appear half-human. Around his neck he wears an ancient lump of rust suspended from a leather cord. My adopted children tell me it is an ancient weapon. As he walks, the lump sways, leaving a reddish-brown arc across the trayalon fabric of his silver shirt. I have learned this is a mark of status. Other Rust People come up and reverently touch that arc to gain some of its power.

Under his breath, Mink says, "I don't like this."

We all straighten when Jorgensen strides out of the darkness, walking ten paces behind the others. His eyes glow in the fire-light just like a dog's.

"Does he look older to you?" I say.

Elder Hoodwink answers, "His brown hair has far more white in it than the last time I saw him three moons ago. A lot more. His temples have gone entirely white."

"Blessings to you." Sticks marches directly to Elder Hood-wink and bows. "May we share your fire?"

"Of course." Hoodwink gestures to the hides. "Please sit and warm yourselves."

Sticks remains standing until Jorgensen sits down beside Hoodwink, then he seats himself just behind the Jemen's shoulder. His eyes fill with awe when he looks at Jorgensen. He obviously worships the man.

Mink's intent gaze follows the two warriors as they walk five paces away and stand overlooking Mother Ocean. "Why don't they sit down by the fire with the rest of us?"

"They are not a necessary part of this discussion," Sticks explains.

"I see. And what exactly are we discussing? Since our peoples made peace, we haven't seen much of you, Sticks, and we've only seen Jorgensen from a distance at ritual celebrations."

Sticks replies, "We came to speak with you about the blue faces. May we do that?"

Mink returns his attention to sharpening the stiletto, dragging the tip over the sandstone. "What about them?"

"The Blessed Jorgensen, the last of the Jemen, wishes to know if you visited the cave."

I study Jorgensen, who seems happy to allow the Dog Soldier to speak for him. "Yes, I took a few people there. Why?"

"The evil there is very great. If any of you still feel ill, the Blessed Jorgensen wants to—"

Annoyed, I say, "Has Vice Admiral Jorgensen lost his voice? Is that why he can't speak for himself?"

Jorgensen puts a hand on Sticks' arm, and gives me a condescending smile. "Forgive me, matron. It's the way of Rust People; they allow Dog Soldiers to act as intermediaries in all formal discussions."

Suspicious, I tilt my head. "I thought this was a friendly visit. Is it a formal one?"

"Let me rephrase that." Jorgensen pulls his cape forward to cover his knees. "It's an important visit. If you are still ill, I have a . . . a spirit plant . . . that might help you."

Mink gives the man a hostile look. "None of us are ill, so if that's the only reason you're here, I'll have someone escort you back the way—"

"Actually," Jorgensen says, "that's not the reason I'm here."

"I thought not," Mink says.

The wrinkles across Jorgensen's forehead deepen. When the wind gusts, he flips up the hood of his cape and clutches it closed beneath his chin. "War Leader, I came here to speak with you about your brother."

"What about him?"

"Lynx is in desperate trouble."

Mink's brow furrows. "And he sent you to tell me?"

"He did not. For the simple reason that he doesn't know he's in trouble."

Mink fingers the stiletto and waits for Jorgensen to get to the point. The longer the two men glare at each other, the more the feeling of danger grows.

I ask, "What kind of trouble?"

Without looking at me, Jorgensen replies, "The War Leader's brother is falling into the trap of the evil device that killed all the people you saw in the blue caverns."

I exchange a glance with Elder Hoodwink, who seems to be fascinated by this discussion.

Hoodwink asks, "What evil device? Are you talking about Quancee?"

The conversation dies as villagers begin to emerge from lodges, dragging children by the hands. The adults glance at us, then lead the children to the far side of the cave where they can empty their night water. The constant ocean spray that bathes that place keeps it tidy. One little girl skips at her mother's side, laughing, but most of the children glance worriedly at us, as do their parents. They have, of course, been listening to the strains of conversation carried to the lodges by the wind. Not only that, Rust People make all of us nervous. It has not been that long since their last attack killed many of our loved ones.

"Yes, I am," Jorgensen finally answers.

Mink's brows lower. "How do you know Quancee killed them?"

"I was there when it happened. My wife and children are in the caverns."

"Really?" Mink smiles. "So you truly are over one thousand summers old? I know that's what Sticks and the other Dog Soldiers believe, but—"

"When Quancee tires of your brother," Jorgensen cuts him off, "it's going to swat Lynx like a gnat. I'm sure you don't want that any more than I do."

"Lynx says Quancee is as gentle as a mouse."

"He's a fool." Sticks leans forward, and his dark skin gleams with firelight. "Please, listen. I lived in Quancee's cave. Believe me, the device is malignant and deceiving Lynx into doing its bidding. In the end—"

"And when did you last see Lynx?"

"Well, it—it's been several moons, but the Blessed Jorgensen saw him just a few days ago, and he's definitely under the device's spell."

"Spell?" Mink's black brows lift. "Sounds like you're accusing Quancee of witchery."

"We are. The Blessed Jorgensen says the only way to break the spell is to drag Lynx away from it and force him to accept the spirit plants offered by the Vice Admiral. We all want him to be cured."

Lowering his stiletto to the sharpening stone, Mink grinds it across the surface again. The sound is so ragged, it makes my teeth ache. "I'm not dragging Lynx anywhere."

"But he's your brother. It's your duty to care for him."

I can't help it. I raise my voice to shout, "I'm quickly tiring of this game you're playing. Tell me what you—"

Hoodwink reaches out to lightly touch my arm. "They are our guests. Let's hear them out."

Mink turns to Hoodwink. "Elder, I agree with Quiller. It's time they get to the point. I want to know how they benefit. If I bring Lynx back here against his will, what does Jorgensen gain?"

Elder Hoodwink peers at Sticks and Jorgensen. "Can you answer the War Leader's question?"

"Gain?" Sticks looks mystified. "The Blessed Jorgensen doesn't gain anything."

Mink balances the stiletto on his knee. "The Vice Admiral obviously needs to get Lynx out of the way so he can achieve some goal. What is it?"

Jorgensen sits so still his unnatural eyes catch the flame reflections and hold them like mirrors. "Honestly, I need to dismantle the computer, but your brother won't allow it."

"Why do you need to dismantle Quancee?"

Jorgensen pauses. "Quancee must cease to function."

"You mean you want to kill Quancee?"

"It's not alive," Jorgensen says as though exasperated. "It can't be killed. I know Lynx has told you it's alive, but it isn't. I assure you, it's nothing but a conglomeration of mechanical components."

Mink starts flipping the stiletto in the firelight. It's a gesture full of meaning. The bone glints and flashes and ends up in his fist vaguely aimed in Jorgensen's direction. "Why is it so important to you that Quancee 'cease to function'?"

When a gust of wind flutters my hair over my face, I have to tuck it behind my ears before I can see Jorgensen staring at Mink through half-lidded eyes.

"It's more evil than I can possibly explain to—"

"To someone like me?" Mink asks.

"Not just you, War Leader. Trying to explain quantum phenomena to anyone among your species is difficult at best. Every time I try, you think I'm talking about magic or witchery. You can't grasp even the most rudimentary elements of the discussion."

I gruffly slam a stick of wood onto the fire, which makes everyone jump when sparks whirl toward the cave roof. "Then try again."

"Matron, I assure you it would be a waste of my efforts."

Affronted, I reach for the war club tied to my belt beneath my cape, draw it out, and rest it across my lap.

Mink glances at me, smiles. "That's fine, Jorgensen, but I'm a little confused. Why would you think I'd help you?"

Jorgensen seems to be rethinking his approach. Finally, he gives Mink a solicitous nod. "I understand. You see me as an ancient god fallen to earth. You're afraid—"

"You're mistaken." Mink shakes his head. "No one among the Sealion People sees you as an ancient god. As a matter of fact, we don't know what you are. Despite the fact that this Dog Soldier"—he offhandedly gestures to Sticks—"thinks you are some kind of sacred relic, to Sealion People you're just a mildly interesting curiosity wandering through our world."

Jorgensen casually spreads his hands. "That's acceptable, so long as you believe that I mean you no harm. All I want to do is repair Quancee so that it functions again."

"Repair her? But I thought you wanted to dismantle her," I say.

Jorgensen clutches his hood beneath his chin and nods. "Yes. I have to dismantle it, find the parts that work, and reassemble the device into something functional. I'm trying to fix it."

"Then why is Lynx an obstacle? He must want Quancee to be repaired, as well."

"No. He doesn't. Lynx knows that after Quancee murdered all those people in the cavern of blue faces, it shut down, but he believes it's because the device was heartsick over the deaths. I assure you that's wrong. Quancee malfunctioned. It thought its job was done. That's why it shut down. Since that day, its systems have continued to deteriorate. You must understand, Quancee is the most powerful weapon my people ever created. As it deteriorates, it 'thinks' incorrectly. It can't distinguish between a threat and an innocent act. If I can't dismantle it . . . well, there's no telling what it might do."

Mink studies Jorgensen, then his brow furrows, as though considering the words. "The only reason I can think of that Lynx would oppose you is that he believes you're lying."

"I am not, War Leader. He just doesn't understand the device as well as I do."

In the uneasy pause, Elder Hoodwink shifts his sore knee to a more comfortable position and massages it. It's ten heartbeats before he says, "As I understand it, Lynx is Quancee's caretaker now. It's his decision, isn't it?"

The two warriors standing out on the lip of the cave turn to look at the fire, and I see their hands clutch their spears more tightly. Is this discussion taking longer than they'd thought it would?

Jorgensen's nostrils flare. "Lynx is an incompetent caretaker. None of you realizes how dangerous Quancee is. In the wrong hands, its powers can be wielded to kill everything alive on this planet, and he refuses to turn over control to me—"

"Well, you're right about that," Mink says with a hard-edged smile. "Lynx is incompetent. He's the worst hunter and warrior I have ever seen. On the other hand, the last person I'd want to wield Quancee's powers is you, Vice Admiral."

"War Leader . . ." Jorgensen bows his head and starts lacing and unlacing his fingers in his lap. "If you don't listen to me, your brother is going to die. Along with the rest of us."

The silence stretches while the men glare at one another.

Finally, Mink flips the stiletto to point directly at Jorgensen's chest. It's no longer a thinly veiled threat, and Jorgensen knows it; his strange blue eyes narrow. "I've listened to you. Now I want you to listen to me. Make no mistake, *Blessed Jorgensen*, if anything unfortunate should happen to my brother, I will find you."

The muffled roar of waves rises from the ocean below the sea cave.

Jorgensen lets out a chilling laugh. "You have no idea what you're saying. Quancee, as a personality, is crumbling. It must be eliminated before it completely decoheres. If I don't act soon, our world is doomed."

Mink looks around at the other people in the circle. None of us has any notion of what 'decoheres' means, and Jorgensen shows no signs that he's planning to explain. "Well, I'm done. Anyone else wish to comment?"

RabbitEar and I shake our heads and turn to Elder Hoodwink.

"Yes," Hoodwink says. "I have one more question for the Blessed Jorgensen."

"Of course," Jorgensen answers.

Hoodwink says, "I don't understand. Why has it taken you so long?"

"What do you mean?"

"Well, it's been a long while since Sticks claims he saw you change from a wolf into a man. In all that time, you've never before come to ask anything of Sealion People. Why now? If Quancee is as dangerous as you say, why didn't you seek out our help to destroy her two summers ago?"

"I didn't realize until recently how close Quancee is to falling apart. Lynx never allows me to get close to the device. Now it's almost too late."

Mink gets to his feet and gestures to the trail that angles up the cliff face. "All right. Thanks. Do you need help finding your way home?"

Jorgensen rises with wind whipping his cape around his body. He takes time to meet the eyes of each person sitting around the fire. "Remember that I warned you. When reality starts to flutter before your eyes, it will be too late."

"What does that mean?" Hoodwink asks.

Jorgensen turns and stalks up the dark trail. Sticks leaps to follow, and the two guards trot to fall in line behind them. We can hear Jorgensen speaking hoarsely to Sticks as they vanish beyond the halo of firelight.

I wait until they are beyond hearing range. "Sounds like they're plotting."

Mink sighs and tests the stiletto's sharp point on his thumb, then tosses it to me. "You might want to keep that close."

I catch the weapon and slip it through my belt. "I think that's a good idea."

At the top of the trail, I glimpse four dark shapes standing against the glittering background of the Ice Giant Mountains. The glaciers have turned pale yellow with the rising of Father

Sun, but black veins of crevasses carve the slopes. Along one of the lower game trails, dire wolves lope. I faintly hear their howls above the crackling fire and roar of the waves. "What do you think his next move will be?"

"I'm still trying to figure out what he really wants," Mink says. "Did anyone else notice that he seems desperate? He hid it well, but—"

"Yes. Why?"

"Just wondering if Lynx is somehow responsible."

"How could Lynx—"

"It's not Lynx." Hoodwink frowns toward the figures still standing at the top of the cliff. As the sky brightens, the men are clearer, huddled in a circle. Jorgensen waves his hands in wild gestures. "It's Quancee. One of us has to warn Lynx."

"I'll be happy to do it," I say with a huge sense of relief, "but it means delaying Jawbone's qu—"

"It's my responsibility." Firelight reflects in Mink's unblinking eyes as he watches the man waving his hands on the cliff top. The drifting clouds are shading pink. "I'll do it, though I suspect my brother already knows."

Hoodwink tightens the fingers laced in his lap. "What I don't understand is why Jorgensen came to us. He could simply enlist a few Rust warriors to drag Lynx away from Quancee and kill him."

"Perhaps Lynx could kill them with a word, as Sticks claims he can," RabbitEar says.

"Nonsense. Sticks tells such lies because he wants people to fear Lynx."

"I do fear Lynx." RabbitEar makes an awkward gesture. "Don't you?"

I don't reply, but the answer must be clear on my face. We all know Lynx has changed. None of us can be certain what Lynx might do if attacked. In the old days, I could imagine him throwing up his hands and scurrying for the high country as fast as his feet would carry him. But today? Each time I see him, I shrink away. I know it hurts him, but I can't help it. There's something uncomfortably alien about him. It's as though my soul senses a predator hidden behind his eyes. A predator watching me, sizing me up, planning how to hunt me.

I've always wondered if it's really Quancee looking out through Lynx's eyes. At the thought, a chill goes through me.

RabbitEar says, "I need to go wake Jawbone and get him dressed. We have to be at the quest wall by noon at the latest."

"Thank you," I reply.

As I watch RabbitEar swagger toward our lodge, my concerns shift to our sick son. My nightmare replays: I hear Jawbone scream my name and see him fall.

"Quiller?" Mink shakes a finger at me. "Don't be surprised if you see Jorgensen or Sticks on your journey to the quest wall. Capturing and holding you hostage would be a powerful incentive for Lynx to give him what he wants."

"No one will ever take me captive again, Mink. Not alive, anyway."

15

QUILLER

Early afternoon sunlight glitters on the snow-dusted trail. The black rocks and boulders that line the path have melted out into circles, creating a mosaic of light and dark that's very pleasing to my eyes. As the tide comes in, a narrow strip of water has escaped the zyme and waves rush back and forth over the shore.

Ahead of me, Jawbone and RabbitEar run hand in hand through the surf, leaping slithers of zyme. Jawbone is laughing.

"Good jump," RabbitEar praises. "I swear your legs are longer than they were one moon ago."

"And I'm much taller."

"Yes, you are. And stronger. You're not going to have any problems climbing the wall."

Jawbone casts a frightened glance over his shoulder, and at first I think he's looking at me, but he's not. He's looking past me, as though he sees someone walking behind me.

Turning, I search for anything that might have scared him. "Did you see someone?"

"No, Mother."

But he quickly reaches into his belt pouch. When he pulls out the buffalo charm Elder Hoodwink made for him and holds onto it, I search the trail again.

"Father, look, a dire wolf's tracks!" Jawbone races ahead to bend over the snow.

"I see that," RabbitEar responds. "Does he have his pack with him?"

Jawbone searches each mark in the snow that might be a track, and at last shakes his head. "No, he's a lone wolf."

"That's right. Why do you think he's alone?"

Jawbone straightens and thinks about it. "His paws are smaller, so he's a yearling. His mother must have new pups, and she won't let him nurse anymore."

"Yes, but there's another reason, too." RabbitEar looks down expectantly, and the crow's-feet around his eyes deepen.

"Probably . . ." Jawbone seems to be considering his options. "The bigger males in the pack beat him up. Just like the boys in the village beat me up, because I'm smaller."

RabbitEar ignores the comment. He's taught Jawbone how to fight, but Jawbone is too small to hold his own with the bigger boys. "It's mating season. The other males don't want any competition, so this young wolf is off on his own until he can find another pack who needs a strong male like him."

"And he'd better be a good hunter and prove he can drag home something to eat, or his new pack will kick him out, too."

"Yes, they will." RabbitEar's wolf-hide cape flaps with the sea breeze as he ruffles Jawbone's blond hair.

Jawbone looks away, as though he can't bear to look into his father's eyes, and conscientiously blots out the wolf's pawprints with the toes of his boots. "Without his pack, I'll bet he's scared. There are many prides of lions who will hunt a lone wolf."

"That's true. But don't worry about him. I'm sure he'll find a new pack soon."

When we round the curve in the shoreline, the quest wall

looms ahead of us, and Jawbone stops dead. I'm watching his back when he starts to breathe hard.

The sheer basalt cliff rises one thousand hands-lengths high. Snow frosts the ledges, but the steps chopped into the stone are filled with shadows. The trail is clear, slithering up the cliff face in a line of black dots, heading for the three gaping cracks where children sleep each night.

Jawbone turns and gives me a panicked look. I can taste his terror, like a copper pebble in my mouth.

"Mother?" Jawbone trots back to me and whispers almost too low for me to hear: "Take me home, Mother. Please, take me home. I've changed my mind. I don't want to do this today."

RabbitEar, who's overhead, calls, "You're going to be a man in a few days. Your mother and I will be waiting at the top to greet the victorious Kujur."

"But Mother—"

"I can't wait for you to become a man," RabbitEar tells him. "Then you will be initiated into the warrior clan, and I will be able to tell you all of the secrets that only warriors know." He gives Jawbone a proud smile.

"Come on." I stroke his back. "Once you start climbing your fears will vanish."

With my arm around his shoulders, we march forward, listening to the blended melody of waves, roaring Ice Giants, and the distant playful trumpeting of infant mastodons drifting down from the high mountains.

At the base of the quest wall, RabbitEar places his hand in the first step, then the next step, making sure they're not filled with water, then he crouches in front of Jawbone. "Son, we've already discussed everything you need to know, but don't forget, if the steps fill with ice or snow, you can use your ax to chop them out."

Jawbone doesn't seem to be breathing. He's rubbing the charm in his hand. "I remember."

I add, "And don't forget, if you rise in the morning and it's storming, stay put. There's plenty of wood and food in each children's camp. You don't have to climb that day. You can just wait out the st—"

"Mother," Jawbone blurts, "let's just go home? Please?"

RabbitEar clasps Jawbone's shoulders and stares hard into his eyes. "Don't you want to become a man? Don't you want to get well? The elders say that only a spirit helper can heal you."

"This will make me well? The spells will go away? Are you sure?"

"If a spirit helper comes to you, you will be well." RabbitEar holds him out and gives Jawbone a stern nod. "And a helper will come to you. I'm sure of it. Someday, you are going to be a great leader of our people."

"But, Father, I don't want to be a great leader. I just want to go home."

Jawbone turns to gaze at me with pleading eyes, and I say, "RabbitEar, perhaps we can—"

"No." RabbitEar turns Jawbone around to face the quest wall, and rises to his feet. "Now, put the charm back in your pouch and get going, son. You need to reach the first camp before it gets dark."

For a few heartbeats, Jawbone stands looking up with silent sobs puffing his chest. Snow gusts over the top of the wall, but the highest crags of the Ice Giants are visible, shining blue against a background of white clouds. While he tucks the charm into his belt pouch, he asks, "You'll be up there on top in the parents' shelter waiting for me? You promise?"

"Of course we will."

"No matter how long it takes me to climb up all the way?"

"We'll be there, son. Don't rush. Take your time." Rabbit-Ear gives Jawbone a gentle shove toward the wall. "See you in a few days."

Then RabbitEar marches back, grips my hand, and pulls me away with him as he heads south along the shore.

Barely audible, he says, "Don't look back, Quiller."

16

JAWBONE

I watch my parents until they disappear around the curve in the shoreline, then I turn back and stare upward at the sheer vertical wall. It's terrifying. My gaze lingers on the first children's camp high above me. From down here it's a shallow half-moon-shaped darkness. As I reach for the first handhold and pull myself up, dream memories whisper through my soul, as if I've looked down from up there and seen Father Sun setting over the distant ocean.

"Just c-climb," I whisper through gritted teeth.

I haul my weight up another body-length, find the footholds, and try to calm my nerves. As I climb higher, the winds gets stronger and the stone is increasingly slick beneath my fingers. But Father thought it was safe. It must be safe for me.

The Ice Giants rumble constantly, sending odd reverberations through my body. Here and there ghost-pale stalactites of ice hang from ledges. The higher I climb the more frightened I become. I expect to peer into the next crack and see a malignant blackness seeping out, coming after me. There is spirit power here, stronger than any I've ever known. In spite of my thundering heart, I can't help but look around. Is my spirit helper here yet?

By another fifty handholds, I'm starting to get tired. It shocks me. Am I truly such a weakling?

When I sweep my hand across the cliff over my head searching for the next handhold, all I feel is smooth stone. Tilting my head far back, I try to see above me, but the rock curves outward here, blocking my view. "Has to be there."

Stretching out as far as my arm will reach, I shove up until I'm perched on tiptoes in the footholds.

"There!"

I sink my fingers into the hole and groan as I climb another step.

I climb for what seems forever, but as Father Sun descends toward the western horizon, I know I'm in trouble. The sunlit reflections off the cliff blind me.

Have to pat the ice for any depression, feel for it.

Don't stop. Climb!

Dig my fingers in and pull myself up another step. As I pant, the white clouds of breath that freeze in front of my face turn glittering and deadly. I can't hang in one place for too long or they freeze on my eyelashes, welding them together, and I have to let go of one handhold to bat the ice off.

Above me, the children's camp now resembles a golden sunlit maw. It's only about twenty hand-lengths away, but all around me the Ice Giants rumble and laugh, and I'm certain they're waiting for their chance to throw me to my death.

"Keep . . . goin'. Almost there."

My lashes click when I blink. Where's the next handhold? That faint shadow? The reflections sink far back into the depths of the blue ice where they leap and dance as though alive. It's mesmerizing.

"Stop lookin' and climb."

Pat the ice. Sink fingers into the only hole deep enough to support my weight, take a good grip, pull upward, and then scramble to find the foothold that must be there below me.

"B-Brace your toes."

My legs are shaking, but the camp is just above me!

Hanging like a shivering spider on the wall, I realize that Father Sun has sunk so low on the western horizon that soon, I'll no longer be blinded by the cliff reflections, but I don't want to be here when twilight begins to settle over the shore and the temperature plunges.

"Hurry. Hurry."

My knees wobble as I shove up, grab for the lip of the crack, and pull myself over the edge into the first children's camp. My relief is so great I'm lightheaded. For a time, I just sprawl on my belly and gasp air into my lungs. The crack is seventy hand-lengths long but just twenty deep. Folded bison hides rest in the back beside a driftwood pile and a tripod with a boiling bag. A short distance farther, I see the cluster of boiling stones, bags of food, and a single wooden cup. Elder Hoodwink always makes certain the children's camps are fully stocked.

Gods, I'm so happy tears blur my eyes.

When I've finally caught my breath, I roll to my back and realize I can see all the way up to the top of the cliff.

What is that?

Rubbing my eyes, I stare harder.

A man waving.

It's Father! He's too far away for me to see his face, but I know he's smiling. He's proud of me. I smile back, and wave, then let my arm thunk to the floor. Hardly able to move, my eyes half snow-blind, I'd like nothing better than to lie here for a full hand of time to rest, but I know I'll die if I do. I must get up and make a fire before my body starts to cool off and my fingers get so cold they stop working.

"Get w-wood."

Dragging myself up, I stagger over to the rear of the cave and gather an armload of twigs and larger sticks, then reach for the tripod and boiling bag and place them on top of the sticks, before I grip the edge of the bison hide. As I stumble toward the hearthstones, dragging the hide, a soft shishing trails behind me.

"Shouldn't have tried to carry so much. Have to . . . be more careful."

I drop the bison hide, then dump the wood beside the hearth and set the tripod and bag down before I collapse to my knees.

My fingers are stiffening. I search my belt pouch for my firesticks—one is a sharpened hardwood stick and the other is a punky stick with half-drilled holes down the length. Doesn't take long to arrange the wood into a tent, and mound twigs in the center, then I lower the sharpened stick into one of the punky holes and start spinning it between my palms. When the wood in the hole starts to glow, I empty it onto the twigs and blow gently until flames lick up.

It's a huge relief, but now I have to chop ice and fill the boiling bag, so I'll have warm tea to drink when the temperature plummets with nightfall. It's already much colder than just moments ago, and the zyme has started to glow. As the waves push the blanket of zyme up and down, green flashes mix with my firelight and flicker over the walls and ceiling of the ice cave.

"See? You—you're all right," I tell myself, despite the fact that I'm shivering so hard it's tough to make my mouth say words.

Pulling out the legs of the tripod, I arrange them so that the hide bag hangs in the center, and search around the hearth for boiling stones.

"Where . . . ? Oh, gods." Rising, I stagger back to the rear of the cave and pick up two from the pile of boiling stones. When I return, I slump before the tiny fire and tuck the stones into the fire to heat.

"Tired . . . really tired," I whisper as I drag up the bison hide and wrap it around my shoulders.

Far out across the luminous vista, I watch towering pillars of zyme soar up on wave crests and plunge into troughs. One of the pillars has twisted arms that swing as it walks toward shore.

Some of our oldest stories say that when the Jemen realized the zyme had given birth to the Ice Giants, many of them walked into the ocean as punishment and became zyme. We see them out there, towering human-shaped pillars that rock upon the waves. Since I was a young boy, I've tried to see eyes or noses in the pillars, but never have. Nonetheless, they do have strange, hissing voices. Someday I plan to study their language with our greatest holy people so I can learn how to speak with zyme-Jemen. They must have amazing stories to tell.

When I yawn, my whole body aches. Do all children feel this exhausted when they reach the first camp?

"Probably not. I'm just pathetic," I whisper miserably to myself. "Isn't as bad as one of my spells, though."

My muscles suddenly feel like they're shrivelin' into my bones, trying to find a place to hide, and I wish I hadn't thought about my spells. The bison hide behind my eyes sways . . .

Don't look.

Concentrating, I focus on the quake moving through the cliff. Ice Giant children play hide-and-seek as night falls. Their laughter and squeals resonate from deep inside the cliff to the north, then chitter past me and run southward.

It's a curious feeling, sitting here alone. In Sky Ice Village, there are always people around to protect me and teach me the things I will need to know once I become a man. I feel hollow without them. I especially miss my sisters. Little Fawn may only have seen eleven summers, but she is the bravest person I know. When I'm scared, I just have to look at her, and my fears go away. We were both born into the White Foam clan of the Rust People, so we cannot marry . . . but she's my best friend and I love her. I have to marry a Rust woman, hopefully Hawktail. There are just five Sealion girls left, and they are all promised to other young men. Mother says she may take me to the autumn equinox celebration held by the Rust People in a few moons and try to broker a marriage with Hawktail's grandparents. When a man marries, he has to move to his wife's village. I don't want to, but it is the way of our peoples.

Gradually, I add more wood to the fire, building it up. Takes another finger of time before I stop shivering. And yet another finger of time before the thick bison hide has absorbed enough warmth to finally drive the cold from my bones.

"See? You're all right." I exhale the words. "You didn't have a spell while you were climbin', did you?"

Leaning, I peer over the edge of the cliff to gauge how far I climbed today. It's a long way down.

It occurs to me that I haven't chopped ice for the tea bag . . .

Pulling my ax from my belt, I hack three chunks from the floor and stuff them into the bag, then I return my gaze to Mother Ocean.

The color of the zyme is odd tonight, more jade green than emerald, and a black wall of clouds hovers in the distance.

"That isn't another storm, is it?"

If it rains or snows tomorrow, my caribou-hide clothing will get wet and be immensely heavier. Wet leather boots also slip more on ice than dry boots do, and they freeze to ice when the temperature drops.

"It's not goin' to rain. Stop scarin' yourself, you coward."

Yawning, I turn when an enormous iceberg rounds the curve in the shoreline. Like a knife, it cuts a swath through the zyme.

The boiling stones won't be very hot yet, but I need to start melting the chunks of ice.

Using two sticks of driftwood, I pull one heated stone from the fire and drop it into the hide bag. Ice cracks and sizzles as the warm stone melts it to water. When the sizzling stops, I pull out another stone and drop it into the bag. This time, an explosion of steam gushes into the air.

I haven't had anything to drink since noon. I'm very thirsty. Dipping my wooden cup inside, I draw out a cup of water, but I don't gulp. I sip slowly, letting its warmth seep through me. Father says warriors do not gulp water, especially not if they've been running or climbing all day.

I take one small sip at a time.

When I've drained the cup, I curl onto my side and blink dreamily at the flames. I'm too tired to eat. I'll eat in the morning. I know I'm going to need my strength tomorrow, but I'm exhausted.

Closing my eyes, I watch firelight flicker on the backs of my lids as my soul drifts.

Sometimes, I think of my old family and our silver lodge on the shore far north of here in the Steppe Lands. I had a big dog named Barker who slept beneath the hides with me to keep me warm. But oftener, I remember Quiller pulling me out of the boat where I hid with Little Fawn, Loon, and Chickadee. Then I think of RabbitEar teaching me to make bone tools and to hunt mammoths. Since they adopted me, I've tried very hard to learn the ways of Sealion People. I listen carefully when Sealion elders tell their strange Beginning Time stories, which are so different from the stories of my old people. I'm not sad. That old life is dim and distant, and such memories growing fainter by the day, but I can't help but wonder what would have happened if that pride of giant lions had not attacked our village and killed my family. I'd still be Jawbone of the White Foam clan of Great Horned Owl Village. Right now, I'd be sleeping before another fire with another family.

Images flit about as my breathing grows deeper and my eyes fall closed.

In the blackness, ships of light leap from the earth and sail upward, hundreds of them streaking for the darkness where the campfires of the dead blaze. I'm awake enough to realize I'm dreaming the story about the Jemen leaving the earth in their ships made of meteorites. But there's something different tonight. I've never seen those eyes before. Big shining eyes up there. I squeeze my eyes tightly closed.

I'm in the children's camp. I'm all right.

The eyes bob along the sacred Road of Light. There's a sound coming from the eyes.

What's that?

Like . . . claws. Claws scratching at ice.

The hair on my neck and arms stands straight up. I slit one eye open.

The darkness wavers in the firelight. I want to touch it, but my body won't move. The sound is clearer now. Not claws. Talons. Huge talons ripping at ice. Terror turns me inside out.

Scrambling up in my bison hide, I call, "Hello? Is someone there?"

The fire has burned down. I swiftly pull another piece of driftwood from the woodpile and place it in the center of the flames. How long was I asleep? Sparks crackle and pop into the air where they wink toward the pale green ceiling.

"You were dreamin'," I whisper angrily at myself. "Try to go back to . . ."

Suddenly, big wings thump the night air beyond my camp, and I gasp when a bizarre winged creature lands on the lip of the crack and peers at me with gleaming eyes. It has a snowshoe hare clutched in its talons. Though I see no bird droppings, it must perch here often to hunt the shore and eat.

I'm afraid to speak, but I mouth the words, *What are you?*

The creature ignores me, bends down and tears off a chunk of hare, which it bolts down, and then lazily gazes out across the zyme to the far horizon where the black clouds resemble domed lodges. Above its long, toothy snout it has an almost human face.

Finally, I gather the courage to whisper, "I've never seen a bird like you."

The creature inspects me with one liquid silver eye. Its skull is three times the size of my head, and it has wide cheekbones like shelves upon its jaws. Scales cover its short wings, tiny round scales that come to miniscule points thinner than the tips of pine needles. I wonder if they're sharp? Even the slightest movement makes the wings glitter as though aflame. We are always discovering curious new creatures in this country far south of the Steppe Lands, but usually they're dead, washed ashore after being smothered by the zyme. Less than one moon ago, we found a giant fish that we'd never seen before. It was especially strange because not even our elders could imagine how it had gotten there. It must have tumbled around beneath the zyme until it made landfall. Around the fire later that night, the elders told stories of giant fish that had traversed great blue oceans in the long-ago days before the Jemen were born.

The creature utters a low shriek, as though conversing with the dead hare, and I wonder . . .

There are old, old stories about Flame Birds. The elders say that just after the enemies of the Jemen cast crushed meteorites upon the zyme, it began to spread over the ocean like wildfire. The world got colder and colder until the Ice Giants were born. Then the Jemen split in two and fiery birds soared across the skies engulfing the entire world in flame. Is that what this is? A Flame Bird straight out of our legends?

"Are you a thousand summers old?" I softly ask.

The Flame Bird bends forward and uses sharp teeth to break

off a chunk of ice soaked with hare blood, which it chokes down whole. Then it tilts its head sideways to eye what remains of the hare carcass in its talons. Must have needed a drink, and now it's going to eat again.

I've heard the Blessed Teacher Lynx speak of deep caverns where grotesque mummified corpses lie in heaps. He says they are monsters, unholy creations that could not have existed in a real world, so they must have been created by the Jemen. Or perhaps re-created, as Sealion People were.

The Flame Bird gobbles down two more chunks of snow-shoe hare.

"I'm sorry," I say. "I didn't mean to disturb your dinner. You must be hungry. Want me to go back to sleep so you can eat in peace?"

The creature just blinks out at the glowing ocean. In the zyme light, its big silver eyes now appear faintly green. As though unconcerned by my presence, it grips the last chunk of hare in its teeth, playfully tosses it into the air, then snatches it and gobbles it down.

I'm awestruck by the way the creature's silver talons gleam. It's the first living creature I've seen since Mother and Father left me, and I wonder if they saw it earlier sailing over the cliff top.

Twin white streamers drift before the creature's nostrils as it tilts its head to stare at me, silently asking a question.

"I don't . . . understand," I begin and stop, for it has suddenly occurred to me that I dare not mistake this creature for something ordinary.

I pull myself up straighter. "My name is Jawbone," I say in a reverent voice. "Of the Blue Dolphin clan from Sky Ice Village. Are you my spirit helper?"

The creature flares its nostrils as though scenting me, maybe trying to decide if it likes my smell.

"I'd be honored if you would be my spirit helper. I think you're amazin'. I give you my oath that I will try very hard to learn whatever you wish to teach me."

The creature tips its glittering scaled head back to gaze upward at the point of light slowly traveling through the campfires of the dead. The Sky Jemen appears and disappears through the thin layer of clouds. The creature watches the ship of light very closely.

Trying not to disturb the bird's concentration, I whisper, "Were you alive when the Jemen walked the world like giants?"

As though my question made it sad, the Flame Bird lets out a deep sigh, hangs its huge head, and slowly blinks at the shore far below.

"I'm sorry, I didn't mean . . ."

Spreading its taloned wings, the Flame Bird drops over the edge of the cliff and plummets downward. Moments later, I spot it in the distance gliding just above the luminous zyme with its wings flashing like faceted emeralds.

A sense of wonder expands my heart until I fear it might burst.

The Flame Bird flips in midair, dives into the zyme and comes up with something in its talons, then it swoops upward and vanishes over the top of the cliff.

Holding my breath, I watch for a long time. "Please, come back?"

I feel strangely empty, as though the creature took part of me with it when it left. Pulling the bison-hide around me, I stretch out on my back and stare at the rocky roof over my head.

Waiting.

She's coming back. I know she is.

17

QUILLER

Thank the gods, he made it." RabbitEar stares down into his tea cup as though he finds his own reflection a little curious.

We sit before the fire inside the parents' shelter that perches on the lip of the cliff overlooking the quest wall. The shelter, a natural lodge, is formed by seven big black boulders that lean inward against one another. The only way in or out is through a gap barely big enough to slide through sideways, which means it's defensible if we're attacked by predators. Not only that, there's a blocking stone to the right of the gap, just in case we need to roll it over the entry to seal ourselves in from wolves or lions.

"He'll be all right now. He knows he can do it." RabbitEar swirls the tea in his cup.

"Hope so." My dream has not left me for an instant. Behind my eyes, all I do is watch my son falling toward the rocks below.

I rip off another hunk of mammoth jerky, and chew it while I peer through the gap at the evening outside. I can see all the way to the far horizon. If our son cries out, it's five heartbeats to race out and get to a position where we can look down upon him. Which may or may not be useful. After all, Little Gull's parents heard their son screaming for help, but they didn't have time to climb down and reach him before he toppled to his death.

RabbitEar shoves hair behind his ear and turns to me. "But why did it take him so long? He should have made the first children's camp a full hand of time before he did. Were the handholds slick? Did he pull a muscle on the climb?"

"Maybe he was just being careful, taking his time like you told him."

"I thought his legs were trembling. Did you?"

Reaching out, I touch my husband's hand where it clutches his tea cup. "Jawbone made it. That's what counts. He'll do better tomorrow. He just needs a good night's rest."

I toss another chunk of bison dung onto the flames. There's very little wood up here on the cliff top, and dung is a slow-burning, efficient fuel, but our stack is dwindling fast. "We'll have to gather more dung tomorrow."

RabbitEar nods and sips his tea.

We sit together in companionable silence for a long while, just gazing absently at the fire, before I say, "I have a strange question for you."

He frowns. "What is it?"

"When we were in the cavern of blue faces, were you counting how many voices Jawbone heard?"

RabbitEar shakes his head. "No. Why?"

Sparks pop and glitter as they float upward.

"I think he heard three voices that day. The singing woman, the sad man, and the other boy."

RabbitEar lifts a shoulder. "He's a power child, Quiller. Spirits speak with him."

"It doesn't worry you?"

"Well . . . a little, but I assume they are friendly spirits. If it were a problem, Hoodwink would tell us."

My heart lurches suddenly as wingbeats thump the darkness outside the lodge. RabbitEar and I turn simultaneously to look up at the lodge peak. There's a tiny crack between the stones that lets the campfire smoke out into the night air. When something passes over it, disturbing the flow of smoke, RabbitEar lunges to his feet and runs out into the freezing cold.

"What is it?" I call, grabbing for my spear.

"I don't see a thing. There's nothing out here."

I sink back to the floor with my spear across my lap. "Probably just a big owl skimming over the lodge."

RabbitEar slides back inside the shelter and gives me a puzzled look as he sits down again. "Sounded bigger."

"Magnified by the seriousness of our conversation, I suspect."

He chuckles. "Yes, probably."

Despite our smiles, an uneasy feeling has taken hold of me. The night itself seems to be straining to hear, holding its breath, waiting for the creature to return. It's like waiting for a small voice to pick up the words of a broken song, but the song simply drifts into unearthly silence—the ghostly calm of things passing away and never to be seen again.

RabbitEar reaches for his cup and props it atop his drawn-up knee. "Why are you worried about the things our son hears?"

I swallow my jerky, rip off another bite, and around a mouthful answer, "Never mind. I probably shouldn't have said anything. You're right. He's a power child."

His red brows draw together over his nose. "I know that tone of voice. Tell me."

"Oh, it's just . . . It's something Hoodwink said to me when I'd seen five summers."

"What was that?"

Lionlike, the roars of a bison bull echoes down from the Ice Giant Mountains and seems to rumble in the spirit bag that hangs around my throat. Is the bull trying to catch my attention to tell me something?

"Do you remember the battle in the Steppe Lands where the Rust People attacked in the middle of the night and wiped out half our village?"

He leans back. "Of course I do. I can still hear the screams and war cries. Two of my uncles died in that fight."

"My favorite cousin died, as well. She was a beautiful little girl. Always smiling and teasing me." Behind my eyes, I see shrieking women and children flooding out of our lodges, trying to get to the boats to escape, while our warriors are dying around us. "Afterward, my soul fought the battle over and over. Not just at night in my dreams. Even in the day I was terrified. Hoodwink found me one afternoon where I'd wedged myself beneath an ice shelf to feel safe. He sat down beside me and started talking softly."

"What did he say?"

Flame shadows waver over the boulders. I squint at them, for they seem to be alive, moving in some pattern I don't understand. "He told me he knew why I was hiding. He said there is a part of us that is only innocent when no one is looking."

RabbitEar gives me a curious smile. "That's a strange thing to tell a child. What did he mean?"

"He explained that I was too young to have fought in the battle, and I shouldn't feel guilty for not saving my family."

"Were you feeling guilty?"

I nod. "And Hoodwink knew it. He was very kind to me that day."

RabbitEar sets his half-full cup down and reaches over to the bag of jerky to pull out a strip. "I don't understand what this has to do with Jawbone," he says as he uses his teeth to rip off a piece.

"It's probably nothing, but each day he seems to hear more and more voices and he's more and more terrified. I don't think he's slept through a night in moons. I suppose I'm wondering if his terror is guilt turned inside out."

RabbitEar chews jerky while he considers my words. "You mean because he watched his family hunted down and torn apart by lions?"

"Of course. How would you feel?"

Before he answers, he swallows his bite of jerky. The lines across his forehead deepen as he grimaces out through the narrow gap to the luminous night beyond. "Guilt is part of the warrior's burden, Quiller. It never goes away. We all feel guilty for the people who died, people we should have protected and couldn't. Jawbone will have to get used to it. It's life."

"For adults, it's just life, because we've learned how to use it as a weapon to keep us wide awake, but when I was a child, it was a monster lurking in the dark inside me. It watched me all the time."

His eyes narrow. "What do you mean it 'watched' you?"

"I could see it moving behind my eyes. It was a dark shape."

RabbitEar shrugs. "A scared little girl's imagination."

"Maybe, but it sounds a little bit like the cave Jawbone sees in the back of his head, the place where the other boy hides."

A softness comes over my husband's face. He gazes out at the wavering curtains of deep green that eddy and flash as Sister Sky begins her nightly dance. "Why has he never told me about that cave?"

"I'm not sure why he told me."

He swallows his last bite of jerky, and cleans his hands off on his boots, where the oil will help waterproof the leather. "Because you're his mother. You'd never tell him it was silly or cowardly."

When the wind picks up, the air outside is alight with twinkling particles of frost. I study them as they blow and whirl. "You wouldn't, either."

RabbitEar tilts his head uncertainly. "I hope that's true, but I'm his father. It's my duty to teach him how to be a man. On occasion that requires hard lessons, like pointing out when he's acting like a baby." When I start to object, he holds up a hand, and adds, "I don't think the other boy is just a childish fear. That's not what I meant. I'm only saying that Jawbone trusts you more than me, because you're his mother."

Frowning, I watch the flame shadows. They've changed. Now, they resemble hunching creatures moving around the lodge in a circle, bobbing and weaving, as though conjuring spirits from the black boulders.

"What are you thinking?" RabbitEar softly inquires.

"Just . . . I wonder if the cave behind the buffalo hide is the one place no one is looking. The one place where's he's innocent."

RabbitEar goes quiet for a long time, and I fall into memories of my childhood. I couldn't find a place inside where I was innocent. I had to hide outside, beneath ice shelves and in tangles of brush.

"Did you hear me?" RabbitEar asks.

"No, sorry." I reach out and slip my arm over his muscular shoulders to hug him. "What did you say?"

"I changed the subject and asked you about Lynx. He hears voices, too. Do you think it's guilt for the times he ran in battle and people died?"

I give him a curious look. "So far as I'm aware, he only hears one voice. Quancee's. Are you aware of others?"

Father Sun long ago disappeared into the underworld, but a vague glow persists, a thin pale line that rims the verdant ocean.

"No, but I find it odd that he hears Quancee even when he's

far from her cave. You've seen it. He speaks back to the air all the time."

"She's his spirit helper, RabbitEar. That's normal. I hear Bull Bison and Sister Moon, too. Are you suggesting there's something wrong with me?"

"No, no, of course not. I've just been thinking more and more about what Jorgensen said, and I wonder if he's right about Lynx."

"What do you mean?" I ask in a hostile voice.

"Don't get angry." RabbitEar lifts a hand to fend off my attack. "Let me just say this: I know he's been your best friend for most of your life, but each time I see Lynx now, he's a little less like the person we grew up with. A little more—I don't know—distant. As though his soul is leaking from his body a little at a time."

"You're afraid Quancee is sucking the life from him? Killing him? Is that what you mean?"

RabbitEar nods. "And I'm not the only one worried about it. Mink has tried to speak with him about it, but Lynx just smiles beneficently at his brother and tells him not to worry. It's as if none of us really exist anymore. Quancee is the only thing that matters to him."

A loud *whoosh* sounds in the sky beyond the cliff edge and we both stiffen.

"What was that?" I whisper.

RabbitEar stares at me. "Don't know, but it was much bigger than an owl. Sounded huge."

I stare upward and listen, but the creature doesn't return. All I hear is the deep subdued roars of the Ice Giants and the snapping of the fire.

"Getting back to Lynx. He's struggling to learn everything Quancee can teach him. I'm sure it isn't easy. He says Quancee is dying, and he doesn't have much time. Right now, she has to be the most important thing in his life."

"Then you think it's impossible that she's extending her life by feeding off his soul? Killing him bit by bit?"

"It's impossible. He'd tell me if he thought that was true."

RabbitEar hesitates, seems to consider whether he ought to say what he's thinking, then, with trepidation, says, "You love Lynx, Quiller. Not so long ago, you were supposed to marry him. Are you sure that isn't blinding you to the truth? Think about—"

"Listen to me, my husband. One day Lynx plans to return to our people. I'm convinced he will become a great teacher and leader. Quancee is helping him to do that. That's the truth I see. Now I'm going to sleep." I flop onto my back and glare at the firelit smoke hovering on the ceiling, waiting its chance to escape through the smoke hole into the night beyond.

"This is important, Quiller. Are you sure you don't want to finish discussing—"

"I'm tired, RabbitEar. We have to gather fuel tomorrow, and I must be standing on the cliff at dawn. I want Jawbone to see me when he starts climbing up. Don't you want your son to see you waving at him?"

RabbitEar gives me a tight smile. "Of course I do."

He rolls up in his cape before the fire and turns his back to me.

Fifty heartbeats later, I hear RabbitEar softly say, "You should start considering what we will do if Lynx returns to us as a soulless monster."

18

QUILLER

A pale pink halo has begun to swell over the peaks of the Ice Giants, blushing color into the long fingers of mist that creep down their flanks toward the ocean.

I keep an eye on the mist as I wander across the cliff top near the parents' shelter, gathering bison dung and stacking it in the crook of my left arm. The morning smells damp and earthy, as though a rainstorm is drenching the glaciers somewhere out of my sight. Occasionally, I think I hear thunder, but it could be the quiet voices of waking Ice Giants.

RabbitEar collects dung five paces away. He's balancing a large stack in his arm. We've barely spoken this morning, but it's more than our unpleasant discussion about Lynx last night. We're both worried about Jawbone.

"Let's head back," RabbitEar says. "My armload is getting precarious."

To illustrate his point, a frozen bison patty slides off the mound he carries, thuds upon the ground, and rolls in a circle at his feet.

As he reaches down to pick it up, movement catches my attention. To the north, a red shape steadily moves along the rim. Slowly, I lean down to pick up my spear where I left it lying on the ice. "RabbitEar? Wolf."

Quickly, he snatches his spear from the ground and whirls to face me. "Where? Show me."

Using my chin, I gesture northward to the lone dire wolf. The big animal has broken into a lope with his tail wagging. He's happy to finally see breakfast, meaning us.

If we run, the wolf will chase us. We'd never make it back inside before we were in a fight for our lives.

We both dump our armloads of bison dung, brace our feet, and glower at the oncoming animal.

The dire wolf continues to lope toward us with his tail wagging. They are so unlike dogs. This young wolf weighs half again as much as I do and has massive front legs. His reddish fur glints in the pre-dawn glow.

"Dire wolf strategy," I say and raise my left arm to flare out my cape to make myself appear larger and more threatening than I am.

RabbitEar does the same. "I doubt he'll be stupid enough to challenge two of us."

"Depends on how hungry he is. Do you think that's the same young wolf that's been trotting the shoreline?"

When the wolf gets to within twenty paces, we both shout and wave our spears. The dire wolf stops, pricks his ears. As he sizes us up, he licks his muzzle.

"One more step and I'll spear your heart!" RabbitEar yells and ferociously growls back at the wolf.

The animal backs up two paces. He seems to be weighing the taste of our flesh against the danger we present. While he thinks about this, he bares his fangs, and his gaze moves back and forth between us.

"He's a young beautiful animal," I say. "Be a shame to kill him."

"Won't, unless he makes a childish mistake."

As Father Sun edges closer to the horizon, the red tip of each wolf hair shimmers like it's been dipped in liquid gold. His gaze has fixed on me. RabbitEar's stout body is packed with muscles. I'm tall, but willowy. I'm the weaker target, and the wolf knows it. If he decides to lunge, it will be straight at me.

RabbitEar whispers, "He's coming."

I take a new grip on my spear. "Give him a little more time to work this out."

"I will, but not too long."

When the dire wolf lays his ears flat and snarls, I lunge forward, my feet pounding across the ice while I roar like a crazed lion.

The young wolf's eyes fly wide open in shock, then he bounds away with his tail between his legs, casting several glances over his shoulder to see if I'm still pursuing him.

Chuckling, I prop my spear over my shoulder and walk back.

"Blessed Jemen! I wish you wouldn't do things like that," RabbitEar shouts. "What if he'd decided to meet your challenge and leapt for your throat? You were directly in my casting line. I couldn't have speared him if I'd wanted to."

"I would have speared him myself." As I pass him, I say, "Come on. It's almost sunrise. We need to see if Jawbone has built a breakfast fire."

RabbitEar places a hand to his chest. "I'll be there as soon as I can get my heart out of my throat."

19

JAWBONE

Slowly, I become aware that yellow light paints my closed eyelids.

Is it dawn already? My arms and legs still ache from yesterday's climb. I don't want to get up. I roll to my side, pull the bison hide tight against my throat, and listen to the sounds of the cold morning.

Down along the coast, right below me, condors hiss and snort.

I almost fall back asleep, but Wind Mother shifts and fills the air with the happy bleating of bison calves. Makes me smile. They only bleat like that when they're kicking up their heels and tossing their heads in utter joy. I suspect they're flying across the ice in a game of chase.

"Have to rise."

Groaning, I sit up with the hide around my shoulders and yawn.

The zyme light has faded enough that the distant streaks of falling rain are dark purple. Like long-legged creatures, the streaks walk across the horizon, heading south. Doesn't look like the storm is pushing inland, but once Wind Mother starts gusting, there's no telling which way the Thunderbirds will carry the storm.

My fire has burned down to a bed of gray ash.

Tugging a piece of driftwood from the woodpile, I start sorting out the biggest coals and piling them in the center of the hearth. Then I gather the smallest sticks and add them. Faint heat touches my face as I bend over and blow until the coals redden and start to smolder. When tiny flames lick up around the new wood, I remain huddled in my warm hide, adding more driftwood until my fire really crackles, then I roll my boiling stones into the coals and heave a tired breath. The morning smells of smoke and the pungency of zyme.

I'm sad the Flame Bird didn't return. I waited for her half the night, which means I'm tired, but I'm sure she probably had to hunt more food. A single hare couldn't possibly have filled her stomach. She's a big bird.

Turning, I look at the food bags stored in the rear of the cave for hungry children. Should I have fed her a bag of jerky? Have other children fed her? Was I supposed to? I've never heard any child mention feeding Flame Birds while on their quest, but it worries me that my ignorance may have offended her.

"I'm sorry," I call out, hoping she can hear me. "I didn't know any better!"

Hopefully, I'll see her gliding by today as I climb, and I can apologize in person, but for now . . .

I walk away to empty my night water over the edge of the cliff. This is the place where the Flame Bird perched, but I don't see any tracks. Of course I wouldn't. A dusting of snow blew in last night and coats everything. I kick at the spot where the Flame Bird tore up the snowshoe hare. The ice is clear and blue. There isn't even a drop of blood or tuft of fur.

"It *was* a spirit creature," I whisper in awe as my heart seems to expand. "That's why there's no trace. Spirit creatures don't eat live animals, so it must have been a spirit hare."

Amazement fills me. I so long to see the Flame Bird again that's it's a physical ache in my chest.

On the shore, a woolly rhinoceros lumbers along at the water's edge with his long tusk shining in the morning gleam. Maybe twenty-five hand-lengths long and thirteen tall, I guess he weighs as much as fifty or sixty grown men put together. Hopefully one of the hunters from Sky Ice Village will see him. He would nourish our people for the entire summer. We'd just have to find a good hole in the ice to store the meat and then protect our stash from hungry lions, bears, and wolves.

Just thinking about food makes my stomach growl. I was so worn out last night, I wasn't hungry, but I'm suddenly starving.

Trotting to the rear of the cave, I retrieve a jerky bag and walk back to sit down before the fire.

As I loosen the ties and reach in for a strip, the rhinoceros bellows. The lonely cry carries on the wind.

I rip off a hunk of jerky and chew it, saying, "I know how you feel."

I've heard the other boys tell stories about climbing the quest wall, and one of the worst things for them was the loneliness. Children are never allowed to walk away from the village alone for fear that they'll be caught and killed by predators or attacked by mammoths or bison protecting new calves. Bison are extremely fast. No boy could outrun a bison or a mammoth. And they're very strong. If they see you crawl into a hole to hide, they can dig you out with their horns or tusks and kill you just for spite.

I prod my boiling stones with a piece of wood. I'm sure they're just barely warm, but I need something to wash down the jerky. Using two driftwood sticks, I pull one rock out of the fire and drop it into the tea bag hanging from the tripod. It clunks on the ice in the bottom, then steam hisses as the stone melts down.

Before I drop in the other stone, I stuff the rest of the jerky stick in my mouth and chew it up, while I listen to the Thunderbirds rumble in the distance. Is that rainstorm pushing inland or trailing southward out over the zyme? I can't tell. Seems to be going both directions at once.

"Have to get movin'." I dip my cup into the bag and pull it out dripping. Warm, it tastes earthy. "Father says I have to make it to the second children's camp by noon."

Gulping the entire cup of water in five swallows, I stand up and carry the bison hide back to the rear, where I carefully fold it up for the next child to use on his or her quest. Then I tilt the boiling bag over the fire and dump the contents on top of the flames. Finally, I carry the tripod, bag, and wooden cup to their former places beside the hide. Everything is now exactly as I found it. The next exhausted child will be thankful to find them.

When I walk over to the edge of the crack and peer at the trail chopped into the cliff, my shoulder muscles go tight. Blessed Jemen, it's steep. Just for good measure, I pull the stone ax from my belt and chop out the thin rime of ice that glitters in the first handholds and footholds. After tying the ax back to my belt, I reach into my pocket for my leather gloves and put them on. They're warm because they've been close to my body, and they feel good against my icy fingers.

Bravely, I lean out over the sheer precipice to dig my fingers into the handholds. That grip will have to support my weight while I swing out and catch the footholds.

"Gods!" I blurt as I let my body slide over the edge and scramble for the footholds.

Panting in terror, I hold tight to the cliff and look up.

High above me, Mother and Father stand on the edge, waving.

They're still there.

Tears blur my eyes. Blinking them away, I work up the

courage to let go of one handhold to wave back, then I swiftly grab for it again.

The second children's camp is about three hundred hand-lengths above me. From here, it looks like ten thousand.

Climb.

Just climb.

20

LYNX

A layer of blue fog wavers across the surface of the paleo-ocean, but it's thickest in the far distance, just at the point where the water seems to curve into infinity. There, the fog is a solid blue wall stretching from the water to a ceiling so high above me it fades to darkness. The gigantic black beams that hang down from the ceiling are so drenched with moisture, they drip constantly. It sounds like rain falling, but more magical, for the patter echoes through the endless caverns, coming back to me a thousand times. The air is alive with it.

These are ethereal mornings. I love to stand here on the shore and listen. Sometimes, I swear I hear the ancient voices of the Jemen underneath the rain, jabbering in a language I do not understand. I wish I could. One of them might be able to explain Quancee to me.

She was gone most of the night, finding the path across the wasteland for another, she said. I don't know what she means when she says 'another.' Arakie mentioned them once, but I didn't really understand at the time, so I paid little attention. All I recall is that he speculated the 'others' she guides are actually her own quantum waves that, as her consciousness fragments, she mistakes for 'others.' He said it must be a little like seeing your own multiple reflections moving around you in a mirrored room. The room, of course, is the vastness of time.

All I know is that when Quancee returns from these voyages she instantly goes to sleep to conserve energy. She was so feeble this morning her presence felt thin and faint.

Sighing, I watch the drops send ripples across the surface. The bioluminescent algae is being beaten to shreds out there. I see the clumps separating and dispersing across the ocean, becoming luminous pinpoints that resemble bouncing blue stars. It's beautiful here, but I must get back to Quancee.

I glance over my shoulder at the corridor that leads to her chamber. A faint yellow glow pulses there. She's still alive. If only I were smart enough to repair . . .

"*Lynx?*"

"Mink?" I call back in surprise.

"Up here."

I whirl around and see him silhouetted on the ledge above me. He waves as he sits down on the lip of the drop-off and dangles his feet over the edge.

"What are you doing here?" I call.

"There's something I have to show you. Come outside with me. This is important."

21

LYNX

As we step outside, the morning is so bright I have to lift a hand to shield my eyes. To the south, bleak gas clouds drift down the slopes of the volcanoes. Here and there, flames lick up from red lava flows, then extinguish.

"To the west," Mink says and points.

I study the large procession of Rust People moving through the tundra wildflowers in the distance. "When did you first see them?"

Mink holds his spear across his chest. It's such a warm day, he's not wearing a cape, just his red-painted war shirt, a tailored mammoth-hide garment that hangs to the tops of his knee-high boots. He ran all the way to get here, and a sheen of sweat covers his face.

"At first light. Elder Stone Bowl heard a rhinoceros bellow. I took three people and trotted north to hunt it. We cut the Rust People's trail along the way, and started tracking them. They're headed to the cavern of blue faces."

"I'm surprised Jorgensen didn't take them there long ago."

Mink watches the procession winding along the game trail toward the entry. They all wear silver capes that flash and glitter in the sunlight. The man leading the procession is identifiable by his unique marching gait: Vice Admiral Jorgensen.

Mink asks, "What do you want to do about it?"

I lift a shoulder. "Nothing."

The trees rustle in the cold breeze blowing in off Mother Ocean, and the pleasant fragrance of pine fills the air.

"What do you mean, nothing? Don't you realize he's gathering allies to drag you out of Quancee's cave? Perhaps even to murder you?"

"I'm sure he is. He always recruits other hands to murder for him."

"And you don't want to do anything?"

I consider the possibilities. "Do you think I should do something?"

"Of course you should do something. To start with, you should trot back to Sky Ice Village with me, where I can protect you."

"Quancee needs me, Mink. I'm not going to abandon her at this stage."

I can feel my brother staring at me, but I keep my gaze on the group of elders moving toward the entry to the caverns.

More than a little annoyed by my apparent lack of alarm, Mink spreads his feet and props the butt of his spear on the ground with an authoritative thunk. "I came here to tell you that Jorgensen and Sticks visited Sky Ice Village yesterday before dawn."

"Gathering allies from my own relatives?" I ask with trepidation. It would be a heartbreaking betrayal.

"Don't be ridiculous. None of us will help him. But it wasn't pleasant."

"What did he say?"

"He told us Quancee was responsible for killing all the people in those caverns, and that she had seduced you into doing her evil will." He uses his spear to point to the triangular entry where, one by one, Rust People are disappearing into the glowing blue underworld. "And that's exactly what he's telling the

Rust elders right now. Not only that, Jorgensen is saying that Quancee is about to do the same thing to everyone else, and you won't let him fix her."

"He doesn't want to fix her, brother. He wants to turn her into a tool that he alone can control."

"I know that. So does everyone else." Mink gives me a sidelong glance. "We're not stupid, you know?"

I smile in relief. "Yes. Thank you."

"Although," Mink adds, "I worry about your stupidity. I think he wants to turn Quancee into a weapon, not a tool. Why don't you?"

"I do, actually."

From far, far away, Quancee whispers to me, or perhaps it's the wind through the forest or distant Ice Giants murmuring. If it's Quancee, I can't hear her well enough to understand her meaning.

Mink says, "Why can't Quancee help you to defeat Jorgensen? I mean, she's powerful, isn't she? Jorgensen said she is the greatest weapon the Jemen ever created."

The faint breeze feels like spiderwebs against my face. I let the sensation pass through me before I add, "They used her as a weapon, Mink, but that was not why she was created. Quancee was supposed to be the greatest teacher ever."

"I'm not sure those are different things. But since you are, tell me how she became a weapon?"

"That, brother, is a long story."

I'm not sure he wants to hear about theories of consciousness, the idea of self as separate from being. Sealion People and Rust People believe that dreams are real. If you dream you walk in the Land of the Dead at night, then you do. Voices heard inside the head are invisible spirits, sometimes good, sometimes evil. There is no difference between reality and existence. I assume Dog Soldiers think the same thing, but I know so little about them, I can't be certain.

Mink punches my shoulder and glares at me. "Then you'd better get on with it. I'm not standing here all day."

"All right. It's complicated. The truth is that Quancee's abilities developed so quickly she transcended the Jemen's mathematics—the numbers they used to understand her."

"I have no idea what you're saying, but go on."

I make an airy gesture with my hand. "They hoped she would help them break the bonds of time and death. Instead, she became a complete mystery to them. They only grasped a tiny part of her personality, but they learned how to manipulate it to destroy their enemies. When she realized what was happening, she shut that part of herself down and found a way to lock them out. That's what Jorgensen is trying to 'fix.' Don't you see? That's why I must protect her from him. At least for as long as she will allow it."

Mink's black brows draw together. "Allow it?"

"She says she must help a few others, but after that she wants me to let her die in peace." Grief strains my voice.

Mink glances back at the Rust People, watching the procession funnel into the ground. "Are you in love with that device?"

"What? Of course not. Is that what Jorgensen told you?"

Mink lifts a brow. He knows I just dodged his question. "Something like that."

"Well, it's an odd question. Yes, I love Quancee, but I'm not 'in love' with Quancee."

"What's the difference?"

The last of the Rust People ducks into the cave, and I can imagine their frightened voices as they proceed deeper and deeper into the underworld burial chambers.

"The difference? Quancee is not a person. I can't be 'in love'—"

"You call her by name. You say she's female. If not a person, what is she?" He's sounding more and more annoyed, as though he suspects I'm just spouting nonsense to avoid answering him.

I search the ground until I find a small pool of glacial melt-water. "Could you please come with me? I have to show you."

"I will, but don't make me regret this by spouting gibberish, brother," Mink says as he follows me to the pool.

When I kneel down at the edge of the clear water, he kneels opposite and grimaces at me expectantly. As the summer day warms, trickles of meltwater run down the mountainside in a musical babble.

Dipping my fingers in the pool, I lift them and let the water drip back into the surface. "See the waves on the pool?"

"Yes."

"Pretend the pool is the ocean. Quancee is, at once, the drops and the waves."

Mink glances down at the concentric circles bobbing out-ward each time another drop falls from my fingers into the pool. "Drops? Waves?"

Drying my wet hand on my cape, I frown up at the deep blue sky where clouds drift. "What I mean is that I experience Quancee as drops and waves, but that's not what she is." I ges-ture down to the pool that now reflects a puff of cloud. "Do you see the cloud?"

"Uh-huh." He says it through gritted teeth.

"The drops and waves are like the puffs of cloud, reflections passing over an ocean. The cloud doesn't exist in the water, does it?"

Mink lifts his gaze and stares unblinking at me. "What's your point?"

"I'm trying to tell you that, if you look beyond the drops and

waves, you will see a perfectly still ocean. A place of no reflections. That's why I can't be 'in love' with Quancee. Do you see?"

Mink stands up and grips his spear with both hands. He
glares at me for an eternity before he says, "What I see is that
Jorgensen is going to lead hundreds of Rust warriors against
you, drag you out of Quancee's cave and murder you, and you're
fiddling around with drops and waves."

"I'm sorry. I'm trying to learn to explain these things better,
but my current skills are inadequate. I know that."

Mink's face hardens. "Let me try another path to reach you,
brother. She's an ocean, correct, and you want to protect her
from Jorgensen? How can you, a mere man, protect an ocean?"

As usual, Mink hit the target perfectly.

Feeling drained, I softly reply, "I'm not sure I can, but I have
to try."

"Let Jorgensen have Quancee!"

"No." Standing up, I stare at him. "She's so afraid of him,
Mink. I don't really know why, but I have to give her the last
moments she needs to finish her life."

"Even if it costs you your life?"

"Yes."

He swings his spear up and rests it across his left shoulder,
where he clutches it with both hands. "Sticks said he stopped
studying with you because you spent more time with Quancee
than teaching him."

"Not true. He . . ." I hesitate, consider the ramifications, and
look up at Mink. "Sticks refused to listen to Quancee. He was
too terrified."

Mink's fingers play along the spear shaft as he takes a new
grip. "Terrified of what?"

"I'm not trying to make you angry when I say this, it's just
not easy to explain. The ocean I spoke about? It's not really
here. Not as Sealion People understand 'here.' Quancee rests—"

"If you're going to spout nonsense, I'm leaving."

He turns to go, and I leap up and catch his sleeve. "Mink, wait."

My brother clamps his jaw. "Go on. *But make sense.*"

I suck in a deep breath before I continue. "The thing that scared Sticks the most was the 'ocean.' You see, Quancee is a vast realm of silence where nothing is certain. That's how she teaches—in silence, while cradling her student in the palm of things neither this nor that. Not everyone can hear words that aren't spoken."

Mink throws up one free hand in exasperation. "Are you aware that none of that—I mean *none* of it—made sense?"

I feel so empty. I long to go find Quancee and let her lead me through lightless mazes filled with songs played by strings of light.

After a long pause, I gently say, "There is a threshold, Mink. That's the only way I can describe it. Once you step across the threshold into the place where you are at once alive and dead, true learning begins. Sticks could not step across. Letting go of certainty is terrifying. And he is certain of so many things. He thinks he has absolute truth. The most dangerous people in the world believe they possess absolute truth. It gives them the freedom to commit any act in the name of that truth. Both Quancee and I tried to show him the error—"

"Jorgensen says you are the one in error. He says you believe Quancee is alive, but it's really just a dead 'thing,' and you're too much of an imbecile to realize it. I'm beginning to think he's right."

I don't know what to say, so I just smile at him. "I love you, brother."

Mink's expression contorts. "I swear, you have become a dimwit. Jorgensen told me it was my duty to drag you home before it's too late. He says Quancee is broken and dangerous."

"She's sick, Mink."

He props a hand on one hip and clamps his jaw. "How can an ocean be sick?"

I tilt my head, contemplating what I should and should not say. "I—I'm not sure, but I think she helps others find the path through the wasteland, and it's part of the way she heals herself. She tells me there is one final journey she must make."

Mink's gaze goes over me, apparently noting the way the wind blows my long black hair around my face, and how my ratty bison-hide cape hangs over my shoulders. "Your soul has flown away, my brother. You're completely mad."

"It's possible, I admit it. But I . . ."

My words trail away as one pure note, unbearably sweet and resonant, rings out. It's as if the universe itself has struck a perfect bell. The timbre moves through every cell in my body, and fades to an otherworldly glitter. I'm experiencing Quancee's name. Her true name, which cannot be spoken, for it's both alive and dead, neither this nor that.

Reaching out, I put a hand upon my brother's shoulder. "Thank you for worrying about me, Mink, but you need to go home now. Take care of your family. I'll be all right."

Mink shakes his head, and his heavy brow ridge shadows his eyes.

When he doesn't leave, I heave a sigh and look southward. Two of the volcanoes have streams of red lava running down the sides and cutting swaths through the tundra all the way to the ocean. Long ridges of cooled lava vein the water. Oddly, the zyme seems to like them, for enormous, many-armed pillars of zyme perch on the older ridges like the monsters from our Beginning Time stories.

"Lynx, let me help you," Mink says. "I can at least bring a few warriors up to guard you and Quancee."

Our gazes hold.

"No, but thank you. Truly. I appreciate the offer. So does Quancee."

"Our dead parents would never forgive me if I let you face this alone. Keep that in mind."

Before I can answer, he trots off, following the winding mammoth trail down to the sea.

22

JAWBONE

When I have good footholds, I use my teeth to pull the glove from my right hand and tuck it into my pocket. Meltwater has been draining down the cliff and filling up the handholds. With gloves on, I can't feel the subtleties of texture, and I must know the instant the water freezes. I pull off the other glove and stuff it in my pocket, then dig my fingers into the next handhold. The ice has a grainy texture now.

Not good.

The next camp is still far away. Too far. Father Sun stands just over the western horizon, and it's getting colder.

I pull myself up to the next handhold. Then the next. As I reach for another with my right hand, a wedge of ice cracks off beneath my fingers and my grip shatters. In an instant, my right arm is flailing in thin air.

"No!" I throw myself against the wall, trying to regain my balance. Thank the spirits my footholds and one handhold are steady.

"Mother? Father?" I cry out. "Can you hear me? I need help!"

My gaze shoots upward, praying they heard me and are rushing to climb down and rescue me . . .

But there's no one standing on the rim. All I see is a haze of snow gusting down from the mountains. They must have gone back inside the parents' shelter to get warm or cook lunch.

Easing my right hand down, I pull my ax from my belt and chop out the rotten handhold. The ice is still soft, so it chops easily, but if the temperature continues to plunge, that's going to change soon. I slip my ax back through my belt and take a good grip on the handhold.

And climb. Keep climbing.

A rumble shakes the cliff. At first I think it's the Ice Giants talking, but then I see towering thunderheads edging over the cliff top, moving due west out to sea. A solid wall of black clouds follows behind them. In less than fifty heartbeats, misty rain drifts out of the sky and shrouds the cliff. The quest wall turns into a shining black monster.

My wet fingers slip from the next handhold.

"No! Father? Mother, where are you?"

When the rain falls harder, every handhold and foothold starts to fill with water. I can't get a good grip. While I'm hanging there trying to decide what to do, my left foot slides out of the foothold as though it's been greased with hot bear fat. Frantic, I shove my boot into the foothold again, and manage to climb up three more steps.

If I live long enough to make the next camp, I must start climbing at night when the cliff is frozen!

Trembling, I look up again, searching the sky for the Flame Bird, then the cliff top for Mother or Father. The rain is falling harder, pelting my upturned face like small rocks.

For the first time, I notice there's a slight bulge in the stone above me. Even if mother and father were up there, they might not be able to see me. The trail curves leftward around the bulge and angles upward toward the next camp.

Suddenly, I understand where I am.

This bulge is the place where Little Gull lost his grip.

I watched my friend topple over backward with his hands and feet extended above him like a dead dog. His shriek echoed up and down the shoreline, growing louder and louder until he crashed into the boulders at the bottom.

Blinking rain from my eyes, I reach for the next handhold and struggle to pull myself up.

Climb!

23

QUILLER

Light drops patter against the black boulders, and water drips through the smoke hole over our heads to sizzle in our fire. I frown upward at the place where the boulders come together in a peak. The sky beyond is empty of the campfires of the dead. Instead, faint zyme light reflects from a ceiling of solid clouds.

"It's raining!" RabbitEar lunges for the gap, shoulders his way outside, and rushes to the cliff's edge.

"Do you see him?" I'm right behind him, flipping up my hood to shield my face from the icy drops borne on the gusting wind. Thunderbirds rumble and flash as the storm rolls westward, pulling a black wall of rain with it. When I stand on the precipice, I lift a hand to shield my eyes from the onslaught. I see the dark dots that mark the handholds and footholds on the cliff face, but I can't see every part of the trail from this angle. "I—I don't see him. RabbitEar, answer me! Do you see our son down there? Anywhere?"

"No, I don't see him, but it's almost sunset, Quiller. By now, he must have made it to the second children's camp."

"Maybe, but he could just be holding on somewhere, clinging to the rock. The last time we saw him, he looked exhausted. Did you notice? I thought his arms were shaking. Didn't you?"

"He was too far away for me to tell. Let's see if we can glimpse him from different places on the rim."

RabbitEar's green eyes are huge as he turns and runs southward along the cliff.

I trot northward, but I don't see our son hanging to the cliff anywhere. Fearing the worst, I dash headlong to the curve in the rim where I can look down at the base of the cliff clotted with huge rain-slick boulders.

If he fell, I'd see him lying down in the rocks or sprawled on the ground. All I see is rocks and wet sand streaked with green filaments of zyme that have just begun to glow.

RabbitEar calls, "I don't see him! Do you?"

"No!" I shout into the gale, then whirl to look at RabbitEar where he stands fifty paces away. "But I have a clear view of the base of the cliff. He's not there! So he did not fall."

"Are you sure?"

"Yes. Absolutely!"

RabbitEar trots back and I run to meet him at the edge of the cliff, looking down at the slithering trail of dots again.

"Then he—he must have made it to the camp," RabbitEar stutters. "Do you agree?"

"Probably, but we can't be certain, so I'm going to climb down and find him."

"You can't climb that cliff in this downpour! No one can!"

"But you know as well as I do that he could be beneath one of the bulges and we wouldn't see him. I'm going down."

"No, Quiller!" It's an order. "I'm not risking your life on a hunch. Jawbone made it to the camp. He must have."

I shake my head as though to will away his words. "We don't know that."

When I turn away and stride for the cliff, he grabs my arm hard and swings me around to face him. "Think. This. Through."

"How can you just stand here? Don't you care that he may be desperately clinging to the cliff waiting for one of us—"

"Of course I care. But this is not a moment for rash decisions! In all likelihood, he's sitting before a fire, sipping warm tea and eating jerky to build up his strength after today's hard climb."

As the rain intensifies, half-frozen drops clatter upon the ground around us, then water begins to flood down the flanks of the glaciers. At first, they're just trickles, but in a matter of heartbeats they become streams, and finally raging rivers. The roar is deafening.

"We have to get inside or we're going to be swept over the edge!" RabbitEar shouts in my face to make sure I hear him.

Grudgingly, I nod, and we both run back. I watch RabbitEar slide through the gap into the parents' shelter, but I remain outside in the drenching rain, feeling like huge hands are tightening around my lungs.

For as far as I can see, waterfalls cascade over the cliff edge.

24

LYNX

As I silently make my way through the darkness to a hill overlooking the Rust People's council fire, the rain turns to snow, falling in a whirling haze across the huge village. Their campfires, spread across the tundra to the south, glitter like a huge overturned box of amber jewels. I came here to speak with the elders in private, but now I see there is a council meeting underway.

Six old men and six old women—the Rust People's council of elders—are seated around the flames. They all have gray hair and deeply wrinkled faces. Sticks stands before them with his silver cape shining in the firelight. He's clearly telling a story, but I can't make out any of the words, just the deep rich drone of his voice. I monitor the twelve elders around the fire, then my gaze moves to the people who've gathered to listen. Maybe two hundred are visible in the fire's halo, but many more stand out in the darkness. As Sticks speaks, they transmit his words from one person to another so that even those far away will know what was just said. Like a wave rolling through the crowd, whispers rise and I see eyes widen and heads shake in disbelief as the story moves.

Instinctively, I search the crowd for Jorgensen, but I don't see him here.

Sticks extends his hands to the assembly and raises his voice until I can hear him, as can the entire gathering: ". . . *Then the Blessed Teacher Lynx reached down and breathed upon the hand of the evil Old Woman of the Mountain, and she woke from a slumber of a thousand summers and rose from the dead covered in the blood of the prophet. Her power shook the world. With each word she spoke, the earth quaked and the Ice Giants trembled.*"

Gasps and moans erupt out in the darkness, and my stomach knots. This is a new part of the story I haven't heard before. In only three summers, Sticks has revised so many elements of the true tale that the Rust People and Sealion People now have very different versions of this historical event. At the winter solstice ceremonial six moons ago, a number of fights broke out over whether or not I can change into a giant bird and fly, as Sticks claims.

The leader of the council, an old man named Ganmor, rocks back and forth. Many elders appear lost in a catatonic reverie. Sticks bows his head as though reverently awaiting the council's words. Occasionally a villager glances out into the darkness, toward where I stand cloaked by the falling snow twenty paces away, but I don't think they actually see me. Just an odd shape amid the pines, perhaps.

Sticks was my student. Did he learn nothing? Feeling betrayed, I fold my arms tightly across my chest.

Ganmor finally looks up and asks, "You actually saw this?"

"I saw it with my own eyes, elder. Just as the ancient Jemen breathed upon the bones of giant lions, dire wolves, and mastodons to bring them back to life, the Blessed Teacher Lynx breathed upon the hand of the evil Old Woman of the Mountain and brought her back to life. I will remember it to my dying day . . . the expression on her hideous face . . . her blond hair dripping the blood of the Blessed Prophet Trogon."

An unpleasant eddy of conversation passes through the circle of elders.

Then Ganmor asks, "Why would the Blessed Teacher Lynx bring the evil Old Woman back to life? Is he evil?"

"He is not, elder. The Blessed Teacher was being deceived by the strange device called Quancee. It devoured his soul, leaving him an empty husk that could be controlled, just as it did so many of the ancient Jemen. That's how it keeps itself alive. The same thing happened to the dead with the blue faces. It devoured their souls and then destroyed them."

"And the Blessed Jorgensen says it will do the same to us?"

"Yes, elder."

An old woman with thin gray hair asks, "How can he be sure of this?"

"Elder Indona, it's happening this instant to the Sealion People. When it finishes with them, the last of the Jemen, the Blessed Jorgensen, says we will be next."

Two of the elders stop rocking and lean their heads together to converse in soft voices. A short while later, nods go around the campfire as though the council has come to some quiet decision.

Leader Ganmor says, "How powerful is the Blessed Teacher? Will Lynx fight us if we try to destroy the evil device?"

Sticks bows his red head and blinks thoughtfully at the fire. "He will fight, and he's very powerful. I have seen Lynx wave his hand and cause condors to fall dead from the skies."

My mouth drops open in astonishment at this absurdity.

Sticks continues, "But it doesn't matter. I read the ancient Rewilding Reports. I know the Jemen considered Quancee to be the pinnacle of their civilization and their greatest achievement. The device had monstrous magical powers. That's why both sides fought so hard to get their hands on it during their legendary war. Quancee could kill from vast distances or simply make entire villages disappear into thin air."

"Then we have no choice, we must destroy the device," Elder Indona says.

Ganmor listens respectfully while the council discusses the issue in hushed tones, then he holds up a hand to get the council's attention. "Despite what the Blessed Jorgensen tells us, I am not sure this is a prudent decision. Lynx is the greatest holy man of the Sealion People. We have a peace treaty with them."

"Doesn't matter," Indona calls. "If we have to kill Lynx to get to the evil device, there's nothing they can do about it. There are only twenty or so Sealion People left, and half are women and children. A handful of our warriors could sweep them into oblivion."

A tremor goes through my muscles. Why did I even come here hoping to speak with the elders? Sticks and Jorgensen have already poisoned them against Quancee. If I reveal myself now, they will never let me return to her cave. There's no use trying to tell them about Quancee's gentleness and wisdom, or the fact that she tries to help anyone who calls out to her.

My gaze shifts to the darkness beyond the halo of firelight, where a shadow sways amid the black trunks of pines. My dread is so great, I suspect a short-faced bear.

No. Human. Very tall. So . . . Jorgensen watches from a distance, letting his surrogate, Sticks, lay the groundwork for whatever he plans to do next. Does the Vice Admiral know I'm here? He has the eyes of a wolf, but he's made no move toward me.

Sticks has adeptly convinced the Rust People of the righteousness of Jorgensen's cause. Once their warriors have removed me from Quancee's cave—and they're right, they will have to kill me to do it—he will have free access to Quancee.

Nonetheless, I'm puzzled. Jorgensen could shorten the process by telling the council that I'm standing right here.

If I had any sense, I'd flee this instant. But I must wait until I know the council's final decision.

An unknown elder leans sideways to speak with Indona, then nods and turns to Sticks. "If Quancee has great magical power, what will it do to those who attack the Blessed Teacher?"

I wonder the same thing, just as Jorgensen does. Neither of us knows.

Sticks lifts a hand in the direction of the shadow in the pines. "Jorgensen tells me that Quancee is too weak now to fight back. It will be easy."

Another old man asks, "Once the task has been completed, what happens next?"

"Jorgensen will kill Quancee's heart and dismantle the device so it can no longer hurt anyone."

The council members lower their voices. I can no longer hear what they're saying.

I'm ready to leave, but I stop when, from the darkness, a deep voice calls, "Elders? May I address the council?"

Ganmor looks up and respect slackens his face. "Of course, Blessed Thanissara, leader of the sacred Dog Soldiers. Step forward."

A dark-skinned man with a shock of white hair strides out of the shadows with great dignity and bows to the circle of elders around the fire. His silver cape is painted with red geometric symbols, and he wears a lump of rust on a cord around his neck. Though he leads the Dog Soldiers, I've heard that his influence has waned somewhat since Sticks' alliance with Jorgensen. "If it please the council, I have questions."

"Yes?"

The old Dog Soldier's gaze moves quietly around the circle before he asks, "I am confused, I suppose, but if the 'evil device' is too weak to fight back, why does Jorgensen need us? He is, after all, the last of the gods to walk the earth and supposedly a man with extraordinary powers." Thanissara gestures to Sticks. "Sticks the Novice claims to have seen Jorgensen change from a wolf into a man, is that not correct?"

In a dire voice, Sticks answers, "It is, Thanissara. I saw it with my own eyes."

"Then perhaps you can answer my question, Sticks? Has Jorgensen lost his powers?"

The shadow in the trees goes still.

"No, no," Sticks insists. "Of course not. It's just that the last of the Jemen does not wish to interfere in our earthly affairs."

"I see." Thanissara nods and pauses as though to consider the idea, before he continues, "And why is that?"

Firelight reflects from faces as people whisper behind their hands.

Sticks looks upset at this apparent challenge to his authority. He has ascended to prominence because of Jorgensen's support, but he is still the youngest Dog Soldier. "The Blessed Jorgensen is above this debate, Elder Thanissara. He cares little about the puny affairs of men."

"Puny? After hearing your words tonight that strikes me as an odd description. You have just told us that the device is monstrous and about to destroy us all, and Jorgensen has beneficently offered to kill its heart to save us. That does not seem puny to me. Further, if Jorgensen is truly above this puny matter, why would he be willing to slip in after we've dispatched the Blessed Teacher and kill Quancee's heart? Why not allow us to use our axes to demolish the device?"

"Axes may not work, Elder Thanissara." Sticks has adopted a superior tone. "Only the Blessed Jorgensen knows how to kill its heart. You see, once Lynx is out of the way—"

"What I see, Sticks, is that Jorgensen's bravery is as nonexistent as his powers."

A wave of gasps and shocked voices roll through the gathering.

Thanissara just set himself up as a target, for if Jorgensen truly does have godlike powers, the elder Dog Soldier will soon be dead. Stunned, I watch people leap to their feet and flee across the village, trying to get away before the sky falls.

A slow smile of admiration creeps across my face. I suspect Thanissara's words were designed to test exactly that hypothesis, which means Elder Thanissara may be the bravest man here.

Elder Ganmor leans close to speak with Elder Indona. For a long while, the council talks amongst itself.

My gaze moves to the shadow in the trees. Jorgensen stands dead still. I wonder what he's feeling. Outrage? Amusement?

At last, Ganmor grips his walking stick where it rests on the ground beside him, and uses it to shove to his feet. The night goes quiet. "And what is your recommendation, Blessed Thanissara?"

Thanissara straightens. "Elders, the Dog Soldiers recommend that we do not break our treaty with the Sealion People, at least not until we have more information about this device."

"By then, elders," Sticks calls and glares at Thanissara, "we could all be dead. The Blessed Jorgensen says we must act now."

Ganmor clutches the head of his walking stick, listening to the elders who whisper around the circle.

When Elder Indona rises and hobbles over to Ganmor to speak into his ear, the remaining villagers close in around the fire, awaiting the council's final decision.

Nodding, Ganmor heaves a deep breath that frosts in the snowy air. "The council has debated the issue and reluctantly decided to dispatch warriors to drag Lynx away from the evil device so that it may be dismantled."

"I understand." Thanissara bows deeply to the council, turns, and walks away into the crowd.

Sticks' voice stops him. "I wish to address the Blessed Thanissara."

Thanissara turns where he stands in a group of warriors.

Sticks calls, "You were lucky tonight, elder, but in the future you would be wise to temper your words when you speak of the last of the Jemen. His patience with you wears thin."

The old Dog Soldier bows again, this time so deeply it almost seems a mockery, then he continues pushing through the whispering crowd.

Jorgensen's shadow detaches itself from the pines and glides toward me along the trail that circles the village.

Perhaps he does know I'm here . . .

I turn and hike away up the trail as fast as I can.

25

LYNX

Now and then, I hear twigs cracking on the trail behind me. When I step into a cluster of head-high black boulders, the dark place echoes with my tortured breathing. I try to see through the snowfall to pick out the shapes.

My own impotence is strangling me. I must protect Quancee, but I can't fight a hundred Rust warriors, and I will not doom Sealion People by asking my brother for help. They'd all be slaughtered in a heartbeat.

From just a few paces behind me, Jorgensen calls, "They'll be coming for you, you know. It's only a matter of days."

Scrutinizing the shadows, I think I see his dark silhouette among the weave of branches.

"Lynx, why don't you simply step aside? By all rights, I should have been its caretaker anyway. It was created by my people, not yours."

I stare for a moment at the snowy trail before I decide to get this over with and walk back down the trail to face him.

Jorgensen has his hood flipped up. His white temples shine. "Why are you aging so quickly? I asked Quancee and she won't tell—"

"It won't tell you because it doesn't want you to know how petty it is."

I prop my hands on my hips, and my cape sways across the blanket of snow. "What are you talking about?"

"It's very vindictive, Lynx. The device has assumed the role of my executioner."

"Explain."

He runs a hand over his cape shoulders, brushing away the snow. "It's a long story. I'm not sure you'd understand, anyway."

"That's always your excuse. You never explain because Sealion People, Rust People, and Dog Soldiers are too small-brained to understand. How convenient."

Jorgensen walks closer to me and gives me an unpleasant smile. "All right. Here's the story. I'll try to make it simple: When Quancee shut down during the last battle, our forces overwhelmed the stronghold and captured Premier Elektra. But we were still greatly outnumbered. We had to make a deal to end the war."

My thoughts are jumping through images. "What does that have to do with the fact that you're aging—"

"You already know most of the answer to that question." He tilts his head to peer at me, and his eyes give off that inhuman shine. "We agreed to keep Elektra alive in stasis if they agreed to establish a consortium of scientists from both sides who would work tirelessly to find a way to warm the planet again. We agreed that once that was accomplished, we would wake Elektra and restore her to her position as Premier. Isn't that what your oldest Sealion stories say?"

"No. We don't have that story."

"Well, then," he says in a bored tone. "Enlighten me."

"Our sacred stories tell us that one thousand summers ago most of the Jemen sailed to the campfires of the dead in ships made of meteorites. We still see them at night traveling along the Road of Light that leads to the afterlife. We call them the

Sky Jemen. A handful of heroes, the Earthbound Jemen, remained behind to carve out a great hollow in the heart of the glaciers, a place where they hid cages of animals and plants, and vowed to continue their search to find a way to kill the Ice Giants. One day, when they've won the war with the Giants, they will release the animals and plants into a warm and beautiful world." Taking a breath, I continue, "While I know she was kept in stasis, guarded by you, we have no story that specifically names Premier Elektra."

He walks one step closer to me. "I suppose that makes sense. No one has the whole story, except me, and I know it because I lived through it. But the Rust People apparently have more coherent fragments than your people. At any rate, I was ordered to guard Elektra until the consortium found a solution, and Arakie volunteered to become Quancee's caretaker. Though she would obey no battle commands, Quancee was still functioning at a reliable level for other tasks."

"Why are you—"

"Don't you understand, Lynx?" He sounds angry. "They left me and Arakie, and a few groups of wildlife biologists, behind. All we could do was watch the glaciers advance around the world, and pray the consortium would return with a solution to the problem caused by the introduction of the zyme to the ocean. We were condemned men, kept alive by Quancee to wait for a day that never came. It's been the worst prison sentence any man could imagine."

I clench my fists at my sides. "Is that why you killed Elektra?"

"I did not kill her. *I could not kill her.* Quancee was programmed to kill me or to kill Arakie if either of us tried to break the treaty by ending her life. When Sticks stabbed Elektra, I was as shocked as you were."

Down in the village, the council is breaking up. Elders rise from around the fire and walk across the snowy plaza toward their silver lodges.

"Listen to me." Jorgensen lifts one finger, as though about to make a critical point. "I obeyed my orders until I knew for certain Admiral Arakie was dying, then I had to take action." He spreads his arms wide in a pleading gesture. "Who could blame me for recruiting other hands to do what I could not do?"

His voice sounds so reasonable. He expects me to give him absolution for recruiting Sticks and Trogon to kill Premier Elektra.

"And that's why you are aging?"

"No." He runs a hand over his white temples. "This is punishment from Quancee. I did not technically break the treaty, so it can't kill me outright, but it's stopped extending my life." He hesitates, before adding, "And it has taken away my other 'gifts' as well."

"Then your legendary powers are now nonexistent, just as Thanissara said?"

Jorgensen smiles. "All you have to do is step aside, and I'll tell the Rust People to let you go home to Sky Ice Village. Do you understand? They'll set you free."

"And you will kill Quancee and create a new device that will continue extending your life or . . . or even give you back your godlike powers?"

His face is expressionless. "You don't want to die, do you? Right now, you are a marked man. Forsaken and completely alone."

Standing there with my heart pounding, I suddenly hear Quancee calling and calling to me. I hang my head and listen. Her words drift like cloud shadows from the profound silence of the wasteland.

We are all alone and forsaken.

"That's not true. I will never forsake you."

Jorgensen's eyes narrow. My answer doesn't make sense, of course. "Are you talking to me, or . . ."

I walk away through the falling snow, heading back to be at her side when the end comes.

"What did she say? Was it about me?" he asks.

I leave the questions to die on the wind and march up the slope, shoving branches out of my way, trying to get to the mammoth trail that cuts across the mountain ahead.

"Lynx, stop! This conversation isn't over."

"Yes, it is."

26

JAWBONE

C-cold . . .

Heavy snow falls through the zyme light in shining green veils. I've been hanging here for hands of time, waiting for night to come and the handholds and footholds to freeze solid. I found a place near the bottom of the bulge where I'm slightly protected from the waterfalls cascading over the cliff, but I'm drenched and shaking hard. Won't be long now. I can feel my handholds freezing up, though my footholds are still filled with water. My hide cape and shirt cling to my body as though made of sculpted granite. They're so heavy it's hard to lift my arm to feel for the next handhold.

When I look up, I see gaps in the clouds, so the storm has broken. For the moment, the campfires of the dead blaze in the open patches of pale green night sky. I have to start climbing again or very soon my fingers will be too numb to feel the ice.

Concentrate. Probe the glacier beneath my fingertips. Find each dimple and crack. Hook my fingers over the tiniest ice ledge. I can't see it in the flickering zyme light, but it feels like a handhold. Just another hair's breadth. I drag myself up the frozen wall toward the second children's camp that nestles inside the crack fifty hand-lengths above me.

Shaking. Really shaking hard.

The crack in the glacier grins like a toothy maw for as far as

I can see to the north and south. If I can just get to it, I'll crawl to the rear, find the hides, and rest. Start again tomorrow when my strength returns. Or maybe even wait until day after tomorrow.

When I try to pull my foot from the foothold, it won't budge. My wet boot has frozen along with the puddle. Grunting, I have to wrench it loose before I can reach for the next hand-hold, then my fingers break through the skim of ice and sink into slush. Gods, I'm freezing, but the cliff face isn't as slick as it was. Zyme-light has turned the blue ice into a shimmering jade-colored wall, veined with tiny black cracks. The quest trail is almost invisible—just pockmarks of shadow. I shove upward and reach for the biggest shadow.

"M-Must be a hand h-hold," I whisper through chattering teeth and keep climbing.

Gripping the ledge of the ice cave with my left hand, I hold tight with my right and shove with my feet until I can drag myself over the lip and into the second children's camp.

Lightheaded with relief, I just lie on my belly and breathe as I look around. Wood is neatly arranged in the firepit, and several pieces of driftwood are stacked beside it. As well, the hide bag hangs from the tripod and below it are two boiling stones. Strange. Usually, all the things a child needs are stocked in the rear of the cave. Perhaps the last child who made it to this camp prepared the fire and teabag for the next child? I can't remember who was here last. My brain seems as frozen as the rest of me, but I'm so grateful it brings tears to my eyes.

I stagger toward the hides stacked in the rear. It's not an easy journey. Ice stiffens my pants. With each step I take, chunks crack off and shatter on the floor.

"G-gods, just l-let me make it back to the firepit." Gripping a hide with half-frozen fingers, I pull it over my shoulders and turn to make my way back.

This cave overlooks the zyme-covered shore and the towering cliff as it winds northward toward the highest peaks of the Ice Giants. The entire cliff is alive with reflections. From where I stand, they could be an endless troupe of dancing ghosts.

Dropping to the floor beside the dead fire, I close my eyes, trying to will myself to stop shaking, but it's not going to happen until I warm up. I fumble with the ties on my belt pouch and remove my firesticks. I can't even feel my fingers as I spin the hardwood stick in the holes drilled in the punky stick . . . but finally the punky wood reddens and I dump it out atop the dry kindling. Blowing softly, I wait until flames lick through the wood, before I allow myself to suck in a deep and relieved breath. In the frail light, I can see into the tea bag. It's already filled with chunks of ice. Just have to heat the boiling stones.

I panic slightly when I realize my boots have frozen to my legs.

"Get th-them off."

I have to jerk hard to complete the task, then I discover my bison wool socks are solid ice. Stripping them from my feet, I carefully place them on the hearthstones to warm.

"Ev-everythin's all r-right now. Just have to . . . warm up."

All across the ocean, hundreds of icebergs cut swaths through the luminous zyme, shining like enormous green sails.

"Never s-seen so many at once." Talking aloud makes me feel better, not so alone.

The arrival of summer always brings surprises. As the zyme closes in and creeps over the shore, Sealion people turn from fishing to netting birds and hunting the big game that grazes the tundra grasses and wildflowers. One moon ago, when the ice floes first started to break up, we found a bizarre bear floating through the zyme on a sheet of ice. It had a pointed snout and hump on its back. When the bear finally got desperate, it dove into the zyme and tried to swim for shore, but the zyme dragged it down and we never saw it surface again.

My fingers start to tingle wildly. I can feel my hands! It's thrilling. Finally, I pull my extra boots and socks from my pockets and shove my numb feet into them, then I huddle close to the fire with my hands extended to the flames.

I'm so exhausted, I barely notice when the sea breeze picks up and snow drifts out of the sky. It's just a few big flakes at first, but then powerful gusts strafe the cliff and the snow turns to a blinding wall of white.

"Just a squall," I whisper. "It will pass."

With a stick of driftwood, I shove my boiling stones into the coals and toss the stick on the flames. Holding tight to the hide around my shoulders, I curl up on my side facing the fire and watch the snow fall while I wait for the stones to heat.

One moment, I'm just lying there, staring at the flames, and the next I'm shaking so hard I'm afraid one of my spells is about to come over me. I don't know what to do. Crying out for Mother or Father would be pointless. They'd never hear me in the roaring wind.

"Be a m-man," I tell myself and curl into a tighter ball, trying to will it to go away.

Besides, I know that when a person is really cold, shivering hard is a good sign, means his muscles are warming up. That's all this is.

I tuck my head beneath the hide, and breathe warm air into the cocoon. I can still see a slit of firelight around the curly buffalo fur and I try to stay with it. Don't let go. Stay here! No flying to the stars.

The flames sizzle and snap. Our greatest shamans can understand the language of flames. Someday, I hope to be among them. Strange. The sizzling sounds oddly rhythmic. Like the beat of a pot drum or . . . wings beating against the storm.

Shoving aside the hide, I look around.

"Hello?" I call out. "Flame Bird? I'm right here!"

Flap, flap, flap . . .

I sit up and smile into the darkness, waiting for silver wings to appear out of the snow. This is the hardest moment, the waiting, the being alone in the dark and spinning snow.

Listening harder, I try to separate the wingbeats from the sounds of wind and distant groans of the Ice Giants. Sometimes it's perfectly clear, other times gone.

When I hear it again . . .

I realize it's not wings.

My eyes are drawn to the lip of the cave, where snow has accumulated in a firelit rime. Ice crackles down below. Something's climbing the trail.

Rising to my feet with the hide clutched around my shoulders, I stagger to the edge of the precipice and look down. "Hello? Mother? Father?"

It's impossible that they could be climbing up from the shore. The last time I saw them they were standing just outside the parents' shelter on the cliff top, waving to me. Besides, this doesn't sound like an adult climbing. The panting is too rapid. The steps not heavy enough.

Leaning out over the snowy lip of the cave, I struggle to see anything. The only visible handholds are right beside me to my left and they're quickly filling up with snow. In a little while, they will be invisible. By tomorrow morning, the cliff face will be a smooth white wall. I'll be trapped here until the snow melts.

Soft breathing from below. Then muffled weeping.

Sounds like . . . a child.

"Hello!" I cry. "Who are you?"

A dark splotch appears and disappears through the snow.

Like a huge black spider, it's hanging on the wall twenty hand-lengths below me.

Boots scrape for purchase as it climbs closer. The splotch congeals into a human shape.

"Wait!" I cry and rush to flatten out on my belly on the rim with my arm extended as far as I can. "Take my hand. I'll help you!"

The shape sways, looks up. He's so close, his face flickers with firelight.

The other boy reaches for my hand, and my heart stops. The knowledge of centuries shines in those blue eyes.

27

LYNX

Lynx, wait!" Jorgensen yells. "We must discuss this!"

His heavy steps crunch snow behind me as I veer wide around an icy fallen log and keep pushing up the mammoth trail. The Ice Giants have been rumbling constantly and shaking the ground. Clumps of snow routinely shake loose from the pine boughs and thump the ground around me.

"Quancee is gone more and more often, isn't it?" he shouts. "Even your primitive brain should find that worrisome by now."

Leaping off the trail, I thrash through a grove of willows, taking a shortcut I've used many times; it winds up the mountainside. It's a difficult climb. Surely, he'll give up and return to the Rust People village.

He shouts, "At least let me tell you where Quancee goes when it's gone. Aren't you curious?"

My steps falter. Does he know what the wasteland is? I desperately want to understand where she goes. I've studied every book in Quancee's chamber but find no reference to it.

I turn halfway around to gaze down the slope at him. He stands in the middle of the mammoth trail looking up the hill at me, clutching his cape closed beneath his chin.

"She's already told me," I call.

"What did it say?"

"She told me she's walking along the standing stones of time that dot the wasteland of the godhead."

His loud laugh echoes through the trees. "Good God. Does it actually say that? How poetic. Did it say why?"

I hesitate, feeling like I'm revealing private conversations. "She's looking for the place where she casts no shadow. The healing place where no light falls."

Jorgensen chuckles as though greatly amused. "Decoherence has turned it into a mystic. Who would have thought? Must be trying to make sense of the gaps in its memory as its identity leaks into the environment."

"Leaks?" I shift my weight to my other foot.

He hesitates as though trying to find words I will understand. "Let me see. How can I explain in a way that . . ." He sighs. "Quancee's soul is seeping from its body and flapping around in the air. Isn't that what Sealion People believe causes insanity?"

Swallowing hard, I answer, "Yes, but she's not insane."

"Not yet. Right now it's just dementia setting in, but soon it will be. That's the danger."

"She is not dangerous. She's the kindest and gentlest—"

"This affection you have for it is bizarre and unnatural."

"I don't care what you think!"

Jorgensen weaves through the willows until he's two paces below me. "Please, let me tell you the unvarnished truth. Quancee is losing more and more of itself and trying to figure out why. You must have seen the same thing happen in elderly Sealion people. As their souls seep away, they begin to believe things that are not true. They think their family is stealing from them or hurting them. When Quancee completely loses itself in madness, there's no telling what it will believe. In a worst-case scenario, Quancee could mistakenly wipe out every human village on earth."

My mouth gapes in disbelief. "You just told the Rust People council that Quancee is so weak she can't fight back."

"I did. At this point, Quancee can still control itself. But in two days or ten? No guarantees. I could write out the problem for you mathematically, if you want."

I shake my head. "Equations are nothing but magical supplications to the quantum-wave gods."

Jorgensen's brows lift. "Magical?"

"It's the same thing as Sealion shamans begging the Thunderbirds for rain. If we get rain, we believe our prayers worked."

Jorgensen bows his head and chuckles. "My, my. That's so pessimistic, Arakie must have told you that."

"Yes." I nod. "He did."

"Did he also explain that those magical supplications predict Quancee's 'absences' will become longer and longer until the wave collapses, and Quancee simply isn't there at all?"

Stubbornly, I say, "Doesn't mean she'll be dead."

"Is that what Arakie told you? He was wrong, Lynx. When the wave function at the heart of her identity collapses, Quancee ceases to exist."

"You can't prove that!" My voice echoes through the night. "Her wave function may still exist. She's just stepped into a realm beyond measurement."

"Ah. Another Arakie-ism." He gives me a condescending look. "You don't even know what that means."

"Actually, I do." My lungs feel like they're starving. "It means you can't prove she's dead, and I can't prove she's alive."

His laughter trails across the slope below me. "Better start praying to your primitive gods, Lynx. When it gets to that point, you'll be just as dead as Quancee is."

28

JAWBONE

Screams ring out—but I don't know if it's the other boy or me. Scrambling sideways, I leap for the handholds on the cliff wall. Gods, they're filled with snow! I scoop them out and weakly start hauling my body up the quest trail, trying to reach the cliff top where Mother and Father can protect me.

The other boy no longer pants, but I know he's still there. When I glance down, I can see a blackness methodically moving beneath me.

Wait for me.

"Leave me alone!"

Reaching over my head, I sink my fingers into the next handhold and struggle to pull my weight up. Keep climbing! It's snowing hard. Giant drifts must be piling up against the cliff far below.

Wait for me. I know the way. I'll show you the way.

My hand slips out of the next handhold, and I cry out as my body swings outward, but I have good footholds. I manage to brace myself enough that I can dig snow from the slick handhold, and grip it tight. Gods, the blizzard is getting worse. I can't see anything now.

Feeling for the hole that will tell me I've found the next handhold, I try to listen for the other boy. It's a mistake, and I know it the instant I make it. I lose focus. Just as I grab the handholds, my feet slip from the footholds. The Ice Giants let out a deep-throated belly laugh that pounds through the heart of the mountains.

Gasping, I flatten my body against the wall and dig my fingers deeper into the handholds while my toes rake for purchase.

Is my spirit helper watching? Maybe judging me? This could be a test of courage.

"Please, Flame Bird, help me!" I cry out.

I've given every bit of strength I have to this climb. My soul has been so emptied of arrogance it booms like a big pot drum. Surely by now the Flame Bird knows I'm worthy?

In the north, a thunderous roar rises and works its way south through the glacial fissures. It's deafening.

I grip the handholds hard as the roar builds and the cliff shudders so violently it's impossible to search for footholds.

There's a faint snap when the ledge beneath my left hand cracks off. As my body swings outward, my right hand smoothly slides from the handhold. I'm so tired I don't even panic as I go over backward.

Is this real? Am I falling?

I'm lying on my back, staring at a vast canopy of swirling snow. Somewhere out there mastodons trumpet, and I hear the far-off growling of giant lions. It's pleasant to listen to their melodies while cold air rushes around me.

As I pass the last place I saw him, I try to see the other boy clinging to the cliff . . . but he's not there. Did he fall, too?

Maybe none of this is real? Maybe I'm deep asleep in the camp and dreaming. That's why my fingers continue to curl over ledges that vanished moments ago, and my feet brace hard against darkness that feels like the cliff. My mind doggedly insists I'm not falling. It's the world that's moving. Not me. Has to be a dream . . .

Then a powerful gust flips me onto my belly, and my arms spread like a condor soaring. The ground is rising toward me, just like in our Beginning Time stories of First Woman. After the Jemen created her, she fell through a hole in the sky. Ancient wolves saw her falling and began digging holes to pile up snow to make a soft place for her to land.

I'm weightless, flying . . .

What a view! When the snow gusts, I see wavering glimpses of the shore below. Arms of zyme crawl over the snow like the distended veins of a dark green monster. Is that the zyme hissing, or wind whipping past my ears? I twist in midair, trying to see home—the sea cave where Sky Ice Village nestles—but I can't. They must all be asleep anyway, wrapped in warm bison hides with streamers of snow falling through the smoke holes and melting upon their peaceful faces. Is Little Fawn worried about me? I'm worried about her and my other little sisters. Will they be all right without me to guard them?

Chunks of ice the size of my family's lodge tumble no more than an arm's-length to my right, torn from the cliff by the ice quake. They're so close I can smell the distinctive scent of the Ice Giants, old and musty, like mammoth carcasses that have been frozen in darkness for a thousand summers.

I am falling. I'm sure of it now.

Inhaling a burst-your-lungs breath, I splay my fingers and try to drag air.

Inexplicably, I flip to my back again and find myself eye to eye with huge boulders somersaulting right above me. They resemble the black boulders that create the parents' shelter, and it occurs to me that Mother and Father may be falling, too. Perhaps the entire cliff shattered in the quake?

"Father?" I scream. "Mother? *Mother!*"

The instants pass like centuries. I practice the things Father told me to do if I fell: bring my knees up, curl into a ball so that

I roll when I land, forget about the brokenness inside me. Keep rolling. Keep breathing.

Across the canvas of my soul, I imagine plunging into the deep snow, rolling across the shore until I stop, then rising and dusting snow from my pants. Father and Mother will land softly beside me, and they'll run toward me, smiling. Father will tell me how proud he is that I almost made it to the top. *It will be enough, Kujur,* he'll say, *you've proven you are a man of great bravery and strength.* Laughing, we will walk home together and I will be able to live like a respected man among the Sealion People.

My chest aches with hope.

Why hasn't my spirit helper come?

What did I do wrong?

. . . Something's happening below me.

Can't get air now. Light's fading.

The snowy ground darkens as though a gigantic shadow flaps through the storm.

Then a voice cries out, and my name soars upward on a gust of icy wind. It's a long drawn-out wail that rises and falls like an eagle's shriek.

29

---❅---

RABBITEAR

R abbitEar, wake up! Did you hear that?"

I lunge up out of my hides and stare wide-eyed at Quiller where she's rushing to shove her feet into her boots.

"What?" I ask in confusion. It must still be night. Snow drifts down through the smoke hole. "How bad is the storm?"

"Bad. There's six hand-lengths of snow on the flats and giant drifts piled everywhere."

Shoving out of my sleeping hide, I crawl over to the fire to sit beside her. Her bushy red hair tangles around her freckled face. "Why aren't you sleeping?"

"I heard Jawbone scream. Didn't you hear him?"

"No. I heard nothing. You were probably dreaming. You're just worried and imag—"

"It was his voice, RabbitEar! I know my own son's voice."

Our gazes lock and hold. My heartbeat speeds up until I feel my cold face flush. "He wouldn't try to climb the cliff when it's dark, Quiller. He's smarter than that."

"Is he?" Dread creases her face. "Something's wrong. I feel it."

Trying to force the sleep from my mind, I rub my eyes. "Maybe you heard the wind? We've had some fierce gusts tonight."

"Wasn't the wind." She swings her cape over her shoulders.

"Wait, all right? Just wait a moment." I'm trying to wake up enough that I can think straight. "Let's say it was Jawbone. Maybe he had a nightmare and cried out, but we told him to stay put if a storm rolled in. He would not have disobeyed us. He must be sleeping warm in one of the children's caves."

Quiller reaches for a wooden cup and dips it into the teabag hanging from the tripod. As she hands it to me, she says, "Drink this and get dressed. We're going after him. When he gets scared, he does crazy things."

"Yes, he does, but he—"

"And maybe he had a spell. Did you think of that?"

Sipping the wildflower tea, I swallow and let it warm my throat. "What do you want to do? Try to climb down in the blizzard?"

Her brows draw together as she grimaces at the fire. "I have to make sure he's all right."

Wind whips snow through the crevice. I watch it spin in the firelight, then settle on Quiller's shoulders in a powdery white haze. "I assume you mean, if it's safe to climb down."

"I'm climbing down, RabbitEar."

"Even if it's still snowing and wind is blasting the cliff?"

The lines at the corners of her eyes deepen. "Yes."

"Just . . ." I hold out a hand to tell her to give me some time to get used to the idea. "Tell me what you heard."

Roughly, she throws a chunk of dung on the fire and cinders pop across the floor. "He screamed '*Mother*.'"

"That's it? That's all you heard?"

"That was enough!"

I can tell that she's been in a state of panic since the scream woke her from a sound sleep. No matter what I say, I'm not going to change her mind. Not only that, what if she did hear our son scream? The possibility terrifies me.

I squint down at my reflection in the tea cup. My bearded

face is puffy with sleep, but my eyes are hard and green. I feel more awake this instant than I ever have.

"All right, but we need to plan this out."

"I have. While I'm climbing down the quest trail, you'll hike to the shore and search for Jawbone down there. He might have gotten scared and decided to climb back down. If he's not there, you can climb up from the bottom and meet me in the second camp. That way, we'll know for sure."

I don't answer while I ponder her plan. "I don't like that plan. Not only is there a monster storm out there, hungry predators are going to be slipping through the snow using it as cover to sneak up on prey. Let's think of something where we stay together. We need to be able to guard each other's back."

As though she sees something moving out there, Quiller fixedly peers at the snow falling beyond the shelter. She can't seem to convince herself to look away, and I wonder if she's conjuring a vision of Jawbone trotting through the storm, smiling, ducking into the shelter, and leaping into her arms. Jawbone would be proud of himself for making it to the top, eager to tell tales of his harrowing adventures.

The images are so clear, even I expect to see our son duck into the shelter. My hand starts to shake. I have to set my cup aside and clench my fist to stop it.

Quiller turns and searches my face. "Get dressed."

"Yes, all right." I set my half-finished cup of tea down and reach for my boots.

30

JAWBONE

My name wavers on gusts of wind.

Growing louder and louder, as though it seeps down through the dark mound of snow that covers my body. Someone saw me fall.

Is it Mother? Surely Mother and Father heard me cry out? They must have rushed to the edge and seen the cliff let go of me.

Right above my face, I hear clawing. Frantic digging. Soft pings and chirps.

I blink my eyes open. The blackness is going gray, then lighter gray, and finally I see moonlight shining off huge talons, turning my icy tomb into a sea of silver flashes. If there's moonlight, the storm has broken. How long ago did I hit bottom? How long have I been buried in this drift?

Am I alive?

Can't feel my heart beating, but I'm so focused on the strange face emerging through the blanket of snow I don't care. Silver eyes and sharp teeth glint.

It's the Flame Bird . . .

She's so beautiful. Her scales have a rainbow shine. Gripping my arm with her talons, she drags me out of the drift. My eyes seem frozen wide open. I can't blink. Pale lances of moonlight slant through the drifting clouds.

The Flame Bird drags me against her and covers me with her wing, sharing her warmth. Her scales are downy soft. I thought they'd be spikey, like the tips of bone slivers.

I want to thank her, but there's no air in my lungs.

Flashes of light wink behind my eyes. I'm confused at first, then I realize they're words. If I can just string them together, I'll understand what she's saying.

Stay brave now, Kujur. Don't close your eyes. The doorway approaches. See it out there rolling across the face of the Ice Giants?

Can't answer. My voice is dead.

Probably I am dead, and she's showing me the way to the afterlife where my ancestors wait to greet me. Oddly, that does not frighten me. Instead, I'm wildly glad. I will see my old family. I have missed them so much.

Just dream awake until it arrives, then you must not lose sight of me. I'll try not to get too far ahead of you, but you can't lag behind. Do you understand? I'm going to take you home, but you must keep up. I don't know how long I have.

She gestures northward with her long snout, and I see something moving. What is that? It rolls like a monstrous black tidal wave, blotting out the campfires of the dead as it comes on.

With her shining talons, the Flame Bird pulls me to my feet, and holds me up as the towering darkness looms above us.

Nothing to fear, Kujur. It's always been there, hiding in the crevices inside you, waiting for you to see it. Just let the door open inward. The other boy will find you.

Panic surges through me. "No! He's dead! I—I can't let him find me!"

He walks in a landscape of terror that he can't escape. You must help him.

When the Flame Bird gazes down, the tiny scales that cover her head glimmer.

Look up now. See the doorway turning in the sky above us?

Before I can answer, the blackness swallows me and rolls me over and over, until I tumble out across a vast desert of pure endless night. There's nothing here, just an empty wasteland so black it shines. And eerily silent, as though all echoes are stillborn.

This must be somewhere along the path to the campfires of the dead. It's the only thing that makes sense. The cliff let go of me and I fell. Boulders and chunks of ice landed on top of me and crushed me to pulp. I'm just as dead as the other boy. But where's the Road of Light I'm supposed to follow? There's no light at all and . . .

Silver eyes wink in the black wasteland ahead.

Can't stop, Kujur. We will fall in love with the darkness. Come.

I trot out across the blackness where her eyes are the only lights.

31

RABBITEAR

While I shrug into my coat, Quiller slides through the gap in the parents' shelter and disappears into the gale. It takes another thirty heartbeats before I've pulled on my mittens and I'm ready to follow her into the storm.

Wind Mother rages across the Ice Giants, piling enormous drifts of snow against anything that dares to defy her fury. Boulders, trees, crevasses, all have vanished into a featureless expanse of white. Worse, there's no light, not even a hint of zyme glow, and the temperature has plunged. As I stagger through the drifts, breaking trail, I can feel the water freezing in my eyes.

"Quiller?" I put a hand up to shout, "Where are you? I can't see you."

"Over here! Stretched out on the edge of the cliff."

When I make out a human-sized mound beneath the snow, I get down on my hands and knees and crawl toward her. Before I can drop to my belly beside her, Wind Mother almost shoves me over the edge. Quiller grabs my sleeve and drags me close. "Did you see something down there?"

She's shivering, her teeth chattering. "No. I haven't even g-glimpsed him climbing the trail. Either he fell, or he's holed up in the second or third children's c-camp."

"Then let's go back to the parents' shelter! This is killing cold! We'll not survive out here for more than a hand of time."

"No. No, I have to find him. He could be—"

"Look at me!" I shout in her face. "If he fell, he's dead, and there's no point in rushing down to the shore. If he's in one of the children's camps he's safe, and if he tried to climb the cliff in the storm, there's no way we can get to him! It's too dangerous."

I grip a handful of her sleeve and drag her backward toward the shelter. She fights me for a few moments, then I hear her muffle a sob. Finally, she says, "You're right."

We both slide away from the edge on our bellies before we dare to rise to our hands and knees so we can crawl. The trail I broke through the drifts moments ago is almost gone, filled in, but the shelter's black boulders, warmed by our fire, waver in and out of the ground blizzard. I lead the way back and wiggle through the gap into the firelight.

Quiller shoulders through behind me and crawls to the fire, where she drops like a rock and gives me a heartbreaking look. "When the storm—"

"Yes, we'll leave immediately." Frowning at her ice-crusted hair, I say, "Let me get you a hot cup of tea."

Shivering, she stammers, "Thought I might . . . see him."

"In this ferocious blizzard? You have to be smarter than this!"

Retrieving a cup from where it rests near the tripod, I dip it into the tea bag, and then lean around the fire to set the cup by Quiller's hand. "I only filled it half full. Didn't want you to slosh the tea onto the floor before you got it to your mouth."

Carefully, she grips the cup in both hands. As she sips, she blinks ice-encrusted eyelashes at me. "Wind Mother is tr-trying to stop us. Why?"

"Probably because Jawbone is wrapped in a warm buffalo hide sitting before a fire, and she's trying to save our lives."

Quiller clamps her jaws for a time to force her teeth to stop chattering. "Even if we can't climb d-down," she stutters, "we can still hike to the s-shore."

"Once the storm eases up. Even then, if the wind is still gusting, it's going to be tough cutting a trail through the drifts. Some of them are taller than I am. And that's up here on the top, where the wind sweeps the ice constantly. What about at the bottom? The drifts piled against the base of the cliff are going to be one hundred hand-lengths tall and just as wide. Breaking trail will take at least a day, maybe two, and if we lose sight of each other in the ground blizzard, it's over."

Quiller shivers hard before she answers, "We'll rope our-selves t-together."

"We're not going to find Jawbone down there anyway. He's safe and warm and—"

"Then we'll climb up and s-search the camps."

I almost ask her what happens if Jawbone isn't there either, but I stop myself. I'm not sure what that would mean. It might mean Jawbone managed to climb up the trail and was waiting for us in the parents' shelter. Or it might mean something I don't want to consider, not yet, for there's always the chance he got confused in the storm and started inching his way across a ledge far from the quest trail.

Quiller takes a deep breath and her whole body shudders. "He can't have fallen far from the vertical line of the handholds, RabbitEar. If the snow is deep enough, he may be alive, but we have to hurry or—"

"Stop saying he fell." I give her a penetrating look. "We don't know that."

"You didn't hear him scream. I did. It was . . . terrible."

I reach around the fire to smooth a hand over her hair. "You thought you heard him scream, but you were sound asleep. You could have been dreaming, or it could have been the wind or the howling of a lone wolf in the distance."

Clutching her cup in both hands, she whispers, "Not g-going to argue, but I've been over and over it. I know what I heard."

"Fine, but I'm not ready to accept that yet."

As she sips her tea, her eyes glaze over, as though she's already digging through drifts for our son's dead body.

"Talk to me, Quiller."

She tries to hide them, but she's still suffering uncontrollable bouts of shivering. She was out there for less than fifty heartbeats and it completely drained the heat from her flesh. I'm certain she won't be warm any time soon. Just as certain that in less than one hand of time, my wife will be on her feet and heading out the door into the ground blizzard, off to shovel through drifts at the bottom of the cliff.

"RabbitEar," she says in a pained voice, "Jawbone shouted 'Father,' then he shouted, 'Mother.' Twice. But he called out for you first."

I pause as my heart thunders. "Why did you tell me that?"

"He n-needs you."

The fire is burning down. The light that plays upon her anguished face has changed from amber to a reddish hue. I need to add more bison dung, but I'm concentrating on her expression. She truly believes she heard our son call out for us.

Quiller says, "While I warm up, c-can you get us packed?"

"Yes." I answer reluctantly. "But we're not leaving until the storm breaks. While we're waiting, we'll eat and get as warm as we can."

Quiller's head jerks in a nod, but I can tell she thinks I'm wasting precious time.

32

KUJUR

The rich aroma of roasting meat wakes me, but I'm so tired I just roll to my side and tug the curly buffalo hide more tightly around me. The fur has been turned in for warmth, creating a soft cushion for my aching body. If only I could sleep here for a moon, I'm sure I would heal.

Still half asleep, I think I'm in Sky Ice Village, but I don't feel my family moving around me, and Mother and Father always rise before I do. Every morning since they adopted me, I have wakened to the soft sounds of their voices, and it's made me happy. Not only that, the pungency of zyme does not suffuse the air.

Instead, dust fills my nostrils.

Where am I?

Pushing down the hide, I see the Flame Bird nestled in a hole she's dug in the ground five paces away from the campfire. She's clearly been taking a dust bath, for dirt coats her scales.

"I didn't know that creatures without fur or feathers took dust baths."

The Flame Bird scratches up more dirt and flops onto her side to roll her right wing in it, then she switches, flops to her other side and rustles around, throwing a haze of firelit dust into the air.

I blink at the rocky cliff that seems to lean over our camp.

There's no snow or ice, just massive ridges of blood-red sandstone that slither serpent-like across the desert. Searching the campfires of the dead, I try to find some pattern that seems familiar. The Wolf Pup constellation should be right there, and Bear Hunter should be over there, but they're not. I don't recognize anything. Bewildered, I scan the entire sky from horizon to horizon.

Slowly, the truth dawns on me.

"Am I dead?"

Rose-red light rims the Flame Bird's nostrils as she flares them to smell me.

Hard to say. Life and death blur in both directions.

"If I'm dead, where are my ancestors? My ancestors are supposed to greet me."

The Flame Bird rises, shakes off the dirt, and walks through the dust cloud to stand on the opposite side of the fire from me. With her long, toothy muzzle she points to the stick of roasted meat leaning over the flames keeping warm.

"Thank you." I grab the stick and take a cautious bite of the hot meat. "This is good. I haven't eaten in . . . well, I don't know how long, but it seems like forever. What is this meat? I've never eaten it before."

Desert cottontails died out before the zyme was born.

While I chew the tender meat, I notice for the first time that the Flame Bird is so thin her ribs catch the firelight. They resemble bright bars down the length of her scaled chest. Is she sick?

"Are you hungry?" I hold out the stick. "Do you want part of this?"

The Flame Bird extends her neck, rips off a hunk of the meat, and gobbles it down.

I alternate with her. First I take a bite, then she takes a bite. Chewing slowly, I let the strength of the desert cottontail seep into my body. After I've eaten enough, I hand the rest of the meat to her and she snatches the stick from my hand with her talons, tears the last chunk off, and swallows it whole, bones and all.

"This place smells strange," I whisper as I sniff at the fragrances drifting on the night breeze—damp earth and some sort of blossoms I don't recognize. On occasion, I hear owls hoot, but their calls are very different from the owls I know. It's as though we have journeyed across the shining blackness and stepped into a bright new world.

"Why is it so warm here? I didn't know there was a warm place left in the world."

Sometimes souls get lost. Random coordinates draw you to look over the edge of the precipice.

Frowning, I ask, "You mean I'm lost?"

I'm lost.

She heaves a sigh and slowly blinks at the ground. I think maybe she's sad or lonely.

"So . . . we're lost?"

The Flame Bird suddenly tilts her head and listens to the night. She stands so still her silver eyelids glow as though aflame. It takes a long while before she whispers: *Hear them?*

I listen. "What?"

Voices so sublime they make moths weep because the creators made eyes instead of ears on their wings.

I listen harder. Finally, the warm breeze carries the lilting melody to me through the darkness. The notes are deep and resonant, like millions of buffalo singing in unison as they run across endless meadows. Even the campfires of the dead seem to stand motionless in the sky lest they disturb the song with their sparkling.

"Feels like they're runnin' in my chest," I whisper.

Don't let them get too far ahead.

The Flame Bird rises, and a wave of reflected brilliance moves over her body. She starts marching southward—at least I think it's southward.

"Is this the way to the Land of the Dead?" I leap up and rush to follow in her steps.

The buffalo call us home.

"Is it far?"

Home is always far away and a long time ago. But you must not let your heart be dried out by the vast empty places you must search. Do you understand?

I think about it. "If you're with me, I'll be all right."

Gazing around at the towering red cliffs, I notice the swath of big bird tracks in the dirt before me. "That's a lot of tracks. How often do you take this trail?"

Never. I exist, Kujur, but I'm not real. In summer, others follow the flash of fireflies. In winter, they follow the breath of the buffalo.

I rub my dust-clogged runny nose. "If you're not real, why do I see you?"

There are little shadows that run across the grass and lose themselves in the sunset. I'm right there. Between the shadow and the sunset. That's where you see me.

The Flame Bird picks up her pace and lifts into the air to fly above the trail. It's stunning to see her huge body flapping over my head.

I have to run hard to keep up.

33

LYNX

Wandering aimlessly around Quancee's cave, I arrange and rearrange the ancient books on the shelves in the rear. The Rewilding Reports are especially heavy and very fragile.

I don't know what else to do.

Quancee is still gone. The crystal panes that cover the ceiling and walls have a faint glow, but they are slowly, inexorably dimming. Where is she? I haven't felt her presence at all, and she hasn't called to me.

Running a hand through my long black hair, I walk over and gently touch the pane that has blinked three red, three green, and three red lights for as long as I have known Quancee. It's gone completely dark, like a black wound in her midsection. She's no longer crying out for help. What does that mean?

"Are you all right?" I softly ask. "Where are you?"

The silence has a ring of eternity to it.

"You didn't leave without me, did you?"

Letting my hand fall to my side, I sit down cross-legged beside the cup of water I filled long ago, but haven't taken a single sip of. I brace my back against Quancee. She's usually warm. Not today. This morning she's cold.

It's a curious sensation, sitting here beside her without the nuances of thoughts and dreams—subtle as fragrances on the wind—that have always pierced my heart with beauty. The cave feels devastatingly empty. I haven't had the strength to build a fire, so the only light is her faint glow.

Leaning my head back, I blink up at the patchwork of panes I glued back in place. They create an irregular mosaic of black squares. A few drips of pine pitch run down the panes like dark tears. I didn't notice them until now.

"Do those hurt?" I whisper. "Do they restrict the energy flow?"

Quancee never told me so, but she wouldn't have. She doesn't criticize. Even when Sticks got so frustrated that he started throwing things at her, she just retreated into the qubits until I managed to talk him down. Toward the end, his tantrums became constant and unbearable. It was as though he wanted to destroy her very existence. And mine, too.

Tenderly, I pet the panes beside me.

"Did you walk into the wasteland where the others wait for you?"

I expected her to be here. She's always been beside me, guarding me, loving me, as unobtrusive as my own shadow, even when I was a child, though I didn't know it at the time. Would things have been different if I had known it? I've often wondered. Arakie did, as well. I recall one long winter night after a brutal mathematics session, when Arakie looked at me and softly inquired, "Wonder what happened in a future where I said yes." I asked what he meant, and he gave me one of his enigmatic smiles. "When you'd seen barely four summers, Quancee asked if she could bond with you. I said no, that you were too young to understand. I suspect I made a poor decision that day."

A future where he said yes . . .

Who would I be now? What would have happened to the Sealion People if Quancee had been teaching me my whole life? Would they be thriving and happy, rather than doomed to extinction?

"Can you hear me?"

The cave magnifies my voice, making it sound as hollow as a cast-off old flute.

A short distance away is a small pile of pane fragments too shattered to be glued back together. I pick up one, a tiny triangular shard, and frown at it as though I've never seen it before. Laying it down, I pick up another and turn it in my hand, examining the spiderweb-like cracks. Shimmers used to play through the depths of these fragments, turning them into translucent gemstones. No longer. I feel like I'm holding the brittle bone of some long-dead magical creature.

Drawing it back, I clutch it over my heart.

"I'm right here, Quancee. I'll be here until you come back, no matter how long it takes you to find your way home."

For a moment, dark swirls of galaxies appear in my mind, whisperings of fragmentary visions, but they vanish almost as quickly, and I wonder if Quancee is living in a future where Arakie said yes. A place where I'm smart enough, knowledgeable enough, and strong enough to actually protect her.

Gently, I replace the shard in the pile of pane fragments, and turn to . . .

Outside the chamber, fabric rustles. It has the distinctive whine of trayalon.

"Oh, no," I whisper. "They're already here. They've come for me and Quancee."

Trayalon scritches on stone as the person outside walks closer.

"Who are you?" I shout.

More rustling.

Then a deep voice answers, "May I enter?"

Leaping to my feet, I watch Thanissara step into the doorway.

The elder Dog Soldier's bushy white hair frames his dark face like a wreath of clouds.

"What do you want?"

Slowly, so as not to alarm me, he pushes his silver cape back over his shoulders, revealing the green-painted shirt decorated with red designs. I'm not sure what the designs mean. "Forgive me. I didn't wish to disturb you. You sounded forlorn."

"You . . . you stood out there listening to me? What did you hear me say?"

His gaze moves over Quancee. "Nothing you should be ashamed of."

As the old Dog Soldier ducks through the doorway and into Quancee's chamber, he grimaces at the strange crystal walls. He's much taller than I am, so I must look up at him. The lump of rust he wears has left an orange arc across the front of his cape.

Gesturing to the softly glowing panes, he says, "Is that it?"

I extend a hand to Quancee. "This is Quancee, but she's not here right now."

He gives me a curious glance, as though my words were nonsense. Gazing upward at the panes over his head, then to the single black pane in the center, he asks, "What fuels it?"

I'm backing away from him when I answer, "Light. Time. Uh. Time crystals and entanglement. Bits of light hooked together."

"Bits of light." He shows no emotion. Just returns his eyes to Quancee. "Strange. I feel no evil coming from it. Nor good, for that matter."

Thanissara walks forward, but warily stops when I move to place my body between him and Quancee.

His dark eyes tighten. "I will not hurt it. I give you my oath. I'm just curious about it."

I glance at my spear, which I foolishly left propped near the doorway. I figured I'd hear the Rust People coming and grab it on my way out of this chamber to face them in the caverns beyond. "Elder, what are you doing here?"

"I needed to see it."

I look over his shoulder, expecting the rest of the war party to appear at any instant. "Are your warriors outside?"

"There are no warriors, though the other five elder Dog Soldiers stand in the first cave reading the stories painted on the walls." He squares his shoulders. "I came to meet you alone. I didn't want to risk anyone but myself. After the stories Sticks tells, I thought you'd kill me with a word long before I could enter this chamber."

"The stories Sticks tells are nonsense. I have no powers."

A smile touches his lips. "No waving your hand and having condors fall dead from the sky, eh?"

"Not likely."

"That probably also means you can't breathe upon dead heroes and bring them to life."

"Sorry, no."

"Oh, that's all right," he sighs. "No need to apologize. I'm well aware that Sticks is an inventive liar. I served as his teacher for a decade before he came to you." Extending a hand, he asks, "May I walk closer to it?"

Instinctively, I thrust out a fist to stop him. "You're too close right now."

Thanissara nods respectfully and backs up a step. "I didn't know. I meant no offense."

It's such an accommodating gesture, I frown at him. "Elder, what do you want?"

"I was hoping you could tell me about it. About . . . her. Sticks says you believe her soul is female."

I stare at him in confusion. "Quancee is female, yes, but that's a surprising question given that you've been listening to Jorgensen tell you she's nothing but a bunch of mechanical parts."

Thanissara looks toward the rear of the cave, where the Rewilding Reports fill the top shelf. His expression slackens with awe. "My people think he is the last of the Jemen to walk the earth. They believe he is a god."

"And you, elder? What do you think?"

His gaze has fixed on one particular volume, but I can't tell which one. "I think he's strangely lacking in godlike qualities."

In the pause, I hear the faint rhythms of the paleo-ocean washing the shore outside. This old Dog Soldier is a surprise. Because of the low domes of their skulls and their big ears, Sealion people have always considered Dog Soldiers to be half-human beasts. But Arakie told me that Dog Soldiers are the oldest human species on earth. Long before either Sealion People or Rust People evolved, Thanissara's Dmanisi species of *Homo erectus* was surviving saber-toothed cats, Etruscan wolves, and hyenas the size of lions, as they trekked across half the world in search of better lives.

Using his chin, Thanissara gestures to the Rewilding Reports. "Would you mind if I look at your books?"

I have to think about that before I answer. Rust People believe Dog Soldiers can read, but when I first met him, Sticks could not. He told me that no Dog Soldier could actually read. I've always wondered if he was telling the truth.

"Can you read, elder? Sticks says you can't."

"Sticks is a novice. He's never been initiated into the secrets of Dog Soldier society." He looks at me as though waiting for an answer to his question.

"I would not mind if you look at my books."

Thanissara veers wide around Quancee, scrutinizing her glued panes, as he makes his way to the Rewilding Reports. His hand hovers for a moment before he thoughtfully trails his fingers down the ancient spines. "You taught Sticks to read."

"I did."

"I suppose you regret that now."

"No, elder. I wish he'd read more. Quancee and I wanted him to return to the Rust People villages and teach others what he'd learned here."

"That's interesting."

"Why?"

Thanissara has his back to me and his silver cape has a soft gleam. "He told us . . . myself and the other five Dog Soldiers . . . that you ordered him not to reveal anything he'd learned here. He said it was secret knowledge, and that sharing it would violate the trust of the ancient gods and bring their wrath down upon us."

"Ridiculous."

My angry tone makes him give me an askance look, then he turns back to the Reports. "Interesting. I've always suspected Jorgensen was behind that order. Jorgensen wants to keep us ignorant, though I'm unsure why."

"He likes people to think he's a god."

"He certainly does." The old Dog Soldier reaches up and runs his fingers over the vials on the shelf. "What are these clear tubes?"

"Uh . . . powdered medicinal plants."

"I see." He moves down the shelf, pulls out Volume Delta, and opens it.

"Careful!" I throw out my hands in warning. "They're extremely fragile."

"Yes, I see that." Thanissara frowns at the words, glances at me, then closes the book and carefully replaces it upon the shelf. "Is Quancee mentioned in the Rewilding Reports?"

I'm not sure what to make of him. He's made no threatening moves toward either me or Quancee. Neither has he explained why he's really here.

"She's mentioned often. But not even her Jemen creators

really understood her. My teacher, Dr. John Arakie, told me that Volume Omega was entirely devoted to the question of what Quancee is."

"Yes," he says thoughtfully. "Volume Omega is mentioned in several old story fragments. It was entitled, 'The Origin of Quantum Consciousness,' wasn't it?"

Now I'm truly intrigued. "Do you understand what that means? Quantum consciousness?"

"Does anyone?" He smiles. "Where is Volume Omega? I don't see it here."

My eyes narrow. He may have simply deduced Volume Omega was not here from what I said, or perhaps he really can read the spines.

"It's not here."

He frowns as though he senses I am not telling him the whole truth. "Have you seen it elsewhere? In another cavern, perhaps?"

When I don't answer, Thanissara nods to himself, and turns to Quancee again. "You know, I assume, that Dog Soldiers are storykeepers? We spend our lives finding and memorizing story fragments, trying to piece together the story of how our world came to be."

"Sticks told me."

He steps closer to Quancee and lifts a hand, but lets it hover above the panes. "May I touch her?"

I've apparently been holding my breath without realizing it. My lungs hurt. I have to suck in air before I can answer, "Please be gentle. She's far older than the Rewilding Reports, more than one thousand one hundred summers old."

Lightly, he places just the tips of his fingers on the closest pane, and with great reverence strokes her face. "I would give my very life to know her story."

An ironic smile turns my lips. "Well, sadly, your people are going to kill me soon, and Jorgensen is going to tear Quancee apart, so neither of us will be able to tell you her story."

Thanissara's white brows angle down over his wide nose. "Would she tell me her story?"

"Of course, elder. Quancee is a teacher. That is her purpose in life. And mine, as well."

He continues stroking Quancee, and I wonder if he hopes to bring her back or to wake her. "That's not what Jorgensen says. He says her purpose is to deceive and destroy. He says she was created as a weapon."

"That is not true, elder. The Jemen used Quancee as a weapon, but it was never her purpose."

Pulling his hand away, Thanissara closes his fingers, as though to hold onto the feel of Quancee. "She has a cool, waxy texture. Almost like dead flesh."

The words are lance thrusts straight to my heart. "Usually, she's warm and silken, not cold and waxy."

Swallowing hard, I turn and walk to the dark tears of pine pitch. Was Jorgensen right? Did I hurt her when I mended her panes?

Thanissara watches me, clearly trying to fathom my relationship with Quancee. "Is that what you meant? When I first entered, you said Quancee was not here. I didn't understand."

I consider telling him that he doesn't have the background to understand quantum wave theory, but that would make me no better than Jorgensen. Not only that, I know very little about Dog Soldier society. He may have the background. If he knows the title of Volume Omega, perhaps the Dog Soldiers know the contents, or at least some of the basic questions posed. If so, he may know more than I do.

"Elder, I have heard that Dog Soldiers send their souls flying to other realms. Is that true?"

"It is." He nods.

"Into the past and future?"

"Yes, indeed."

"Quancee also sends her soul flying."

Apparently fascinated, he stares hard into my eyes. "Where does she go on these journeys?"

"To a place where she is both alive and dead," I say, expecting that to end the discussion.

"Ah. The wasteland." Thanissara stands so still that Quancee's wan gleam paints his cape with an edge of white fire. "That makes sense."

"Does it?" I'm actually frozen in place. He knows about the wasteland.

"Oh, yes. When Sticks returned saying that Premier Elektra was the Old Woman of the Mountain, it contradicted all of our stories: Elektra was a young woman, not an old woman. Elektra was human, not made of crystal tears. Elektra was buried in darkness, not suspended in a glittering timeless world where no shadows fall."

The phrase startles me. "You . . . You have a story about the place where nothing casts a shadow?"

"You have heard of it?"

"I have."

"Well, it's a fragment from a story we call 'The Last Days,' a story Dog Soldiers have spent hundreds of summers piecing together. Some of the fragments don't quite fit. The most curious fragment speaks of the capture of the Old Woman of the Mountain. It says the doctor who captured her had to travel far, far away, to an ocean of light where no shadows fall and death does not exist."

His deep voice is spellbinding. I long to hear him recite the entire tale.

Thanissara's gaze roams the chamber as though understanding Quancee for the first time. "Blessed gods, I'm standing in the sacred tomb of the Old Woman of the Mountain, aren't I?"

The stunned expression on his dark face makes me back up a step. "Maybe. Arakie thought our stories about the Old Woman of the Mountain might be about Quancee, but he wasn't sure, and neither am I."

Against the dying glow, the Dog Soldier appears to be suspended, floating above the floor, his silver cape like a haze of moonlight. An almost breathless mixture of desperation and hope strains his elderly face.

"Blessed Teacher, may I sit down and ask you more questions about her?"

I lick my lips nervously. "For a little while."

Thanissara walks over to sit cross-legged in front of the dead fire and gracefully folds his hands in his lap, as though he's waiting for me to join him. When I don't, his hope fades. He gestures to the other side of the fire where my water cup rests beside the hearthstones. "Please, sit with me."

"Elder, I don't have much time—"

"Lynx, stories also exist in a realm where they are both alive and dead. Only our breath gives them life. Please, let her story live. I came here to listen."

He gestures to the other side of the fire again.

Girding myself, I walk over and sit down. "How can I help?"

His astonished eyes return to Quancee. "First, tell me what she is?"

"Well, I'll try, but that's a more difficult question than you think. You see, Quancee both is and is not." I drag over my cup and dip my fingers in the water. As I lift them and let the drops fall back into the liquid, I hold it out for him to observe. "Do you see the waves?"

He leans over the cup, looks inside, then lifts his gaze to me. "What I see is an illusion. Shadows walking on the wall of Plato's cave. What do you see?"

Awestruck, I draw my cup back and begin to reevaluate everything I think I know about Dog Soldiers. I suddenly realize I am not the teacher here. "I don't know who Plato is."

"But Sticks said you studied with a Jemen teacher, Dr. John Arakie."

"I did."

"And he did not tell you about Plato? How can you ever hope to understand Quancee if you don't know Plato?"

I give him a helpless shrug. "I . . . I don't know."

"Ah." He nods pleasantly. "Well, then, let us share stories. I'll explain Plato's allegory of the cave, and you can tell me about the ocean beneath the waves."

34

KUJUR

My legs feel rubbery as I walk through the dark desert in the Flame Bird's tracks. She's tired, too. She started to stagger a while ago, but just on occasion. Mostly, she resolutely marches in a straight line, heading for the odd rim of light on the southern horizon. She hasn't stopped to rest for even a few moments. It's as though she's afraid to pause for fear that she won't make it to our destination.

Breathing hard, I frown at the rim of light. It's like a hoarfrost glitter of purple ice crystals blowing across a vast plain. But this place is so warm, it can't be ice.

"What is that?" I call.

Threshold.

The Flame Bird stumbles sideways, rights herself, and heaves a shuddering breath.

"You're very tired. Why don't we rest?"

She turns to look at me, and my soul is overwhelmed with visions frightening and wonderful: turquoise lakes covered with crystal spiders that have lived on sunlit reflections since before the Beginning Time, twin mountains of gold so bright every tree and rock casts double shadows, and dancing fox skins that yip. Flame Bird memories . . . miracles she has seen in her long life.

When she blinks, water shimmers in her silver eyes, and I'm suddenly afraid. Do Flame Birds weep?

"You're completely exhausted! You need to sleep. Lie down! It will be all right for a little while."

Can't. No more . . . coordinates.

She starts forward, but one knee gives out, and she falls. Weakly, she shoves up again, and stands with her legs trembling, gazing longingly at the brilliant rim on the horizon.

Running forward, I hug her leg. "What's wrong? Can I help you?"

Those who never live at the right time can never die at the right time. That's all this is.

The Flame Bird rests her snout on the top of my head, and her breath smells like wormwood in the air.

"Are you dyin'?" Panic fills me. "You can't die! What will happen to me?"

Affectionately, she nuzzles my hair with her snout, then steps away and plods onward toward the rim of light that grows more luminous with each step.

Trotting along behind, I look up and see the campfires of the dead melting down from the cobalt sky, thousands of them, raining upon us like bright tears.

"Do you see that?"

Land of the Dead falling.

"But why?"

The Flame Bird halts and cranes her neck to watch the heavenly conflagration. She's breathing very hard, panting as though she can't get enough air.

Shadows need light. Must find the place where no shadows fall.

She forces her shaking legs onward.

It isn't until I place my feet in her tracks that I see the glittering trail of scales she's leaving behind. Is this normal? Is she shedding?

I race to catch up.

Like silver petals, her falling scales light my path.

35

LYNX

I have my eyes closed as I massage my aching temples. It's been a long five hands of time. We've gone back and forth with questions, suppositions, and answers that are, more or less, merely deeper questions. The elder Dog Soldier is by no means half-human, nor is he ignorant. In fact, the nuances of his understanding of consciousness seem to far exceed mine.

"I don't think I'm able to answer that question, elder. No one really knows where personality comes from. Is it simple illusion spun by the observer, as you ask? Probably."

I hear Thanissara stand up, and I open my eyes. His face, flickering with firelight, seems particularly dark in contrast to his silver cape. He's frowning, but his gaze is far away, seeing into some distance inside him that I cannot fathom.

After a lengthy interval, he looks down at me where I sit cross-legged before the low flames. "For many summers, I have known that there was no objective world out there, Lynx. My only question was about myself. Am I the observer spinning this illusion, as many philosophers have hypothesized in the past? Or am I merely part of another observer's created world? Which would mean my consciousness is contingent. Like the flame, without some basic fuel, I could not burn."

"My Jemen teacher, Arakie, told me the only thing I could be certain of was that there is one observer: me."

"Ah!" Thanissara says and waggles a finger in my direction. "I disagree."

Pulling up my knees, I lock my arms around them. He's started to pace back and forth. "Why?"

"Because the waves upon the water do not exist only when we look at them. Just as Quancee can be in two places at once, or suspended between places, this . . . superposition . . . implies that the waves follow two paths at once. That means there are at least two objects. Perhaps two observers. The wave and me. I myself may produce the results of my measurement, but I must be measuring something."

"I don't think so, elder. If there is no objective reality, then your 'something' is mere illusion."

"Yes, but that doesn't mean it doesn't exist." He blinks, and his eyes narrow. "In fact, I suspect the only reason I exist is that the wave is observing me. The wave knows not just if I am looking at it, but if I'm planning to look. The wave experiences all of time at once. It can create me only because it knows I *will* see."

My head feels cottony, like it's stuffed with bison wool. I massage my aching temples again. "There are times," I say in frustration, "that I fear Jorgensen is right. I'm not smart enough to understand these things."

"Nonsense. My point," Thanissara says with glittering eyes, "is Quancee."

I have a powerful headache building, so I open one eye and squint up at him. "Yes?"

The Dog Soldier gazes down at me for so long his halo of white hair resembles a bonfire of cobwebs. He folds his arms, and his silver cape flashes. "Can human consciousness act as a quantum wave?"

"As I understand it, yes, in certain circumstances."

"Then we are not that different from Quancee, are we?"

"No." I shake my head. "On that score, we are the same. But I think we are different in other—"

"I do not."

Thanissara walks back to stand in front of the Rewilding Reports. He stares at the ancient spines for a long time. "We have a library, you know. Dog Soldiers, I mean."

"I didn't," I say in surprise. "Sticks never mentioned your library."

"Yes," he answers in a soft contemplative voice. "Seventeen precious books. We guard them with our lives."

Curiosity fills me. Since the moment I learned to read, my need for books has been insatiable. "I would like to see your library sometime, if it's allowed."

"No. Only initiates can look upon the sacred artifacts. Besides, they are not kept in one place. Each initiate has a special talent. Two are healers, one builds lodges, two have dedicated themselves to feeding the hungry. Each is given volumes relevant to his talents to read and memorize, and each is required to hide and protect those volumes. That way, if we are attacked, we hope a few of the books will escape destruction."

I prod the fire with a branch and sink back to rest my shoulders against Quancee. It comforts me to touch her. "And what is your talent, elder?"

"Me?" Thanissara touches his chest with three fingers and smiles. "I speak with the dead."

"You mean that you send your soul flying to the Land of the Dead to speak with the ancestors?"

"Sometimes. More often I find the lost souls wandering along the Road of Light and sit down to ask them questions about their lives." His gaze moves to Quancee. "When the time comes, I hope I will find her. Perhaps she will allow me to ask her questions about myself and why I exist."

Thanissara raises a hand and traces the edges of the glued

pane with his finger, following the pitch as it zigzags across Quancee's faintly luminous face.

"Lynx, you mustn't be sad that she's dying."

"She's my whole world, elder." I pull over the water cup and watch the waves glitter as they collide. As they decohere. "I can't help it."

Thanissara gracefully walks to stand and peer down at me. "You have told me that decoherence is like a bubble bursting."

"Yes."

"When it bursts where does it go?"

"I . . . what?"

"I'm trying to tell you that Quancee knows you're looking."

I shake my head in confusion, wondering why he said that. "But if she dies—"

"Death, my young friend, is in the eye of the observer."

A smile flicks at the corner of his lips, then he steps into the corridor outside and is gone, his steps as silent as a hunting lion's.

36

QUILLER

Wind Mother dies down at sunset, leaving dusk to fall like gray smoke across the snowdrifts that sculpt the shoreline. Everywhere I look, the ocean is a blanket of white; but out across the distances, beams of zyme light shoot upward into the dove-colored sky. It's a rare sight. A forest of green lances standing on end.

RabbitEar cuts trail ahead of me. His muscular shoulders swing back and forth as his legs hew a dark swath through the white. The mammoth-bone point of his spear, which he's using to test the snow depth, glints as he moves.

"Slow down, RabbitEar," I call. "I'm falling behind."

He slows, but continues resolutely forward.

Freezing, my eyes water constantly. I have to flex my numb fingers to ease the ache. The quest cliff looms no more than one hundred paces away. A ghostly powder of zyme glow covers the smooth vertical face. It's clear now that snow filled in the handholds and footholds, turning the trail invisible. Even if Jawbone had wanted to, he would have never been able to climb up to us.

I cup a hand to my mouth and shout, "Jawbone? Jawbone, do you hear me?"

Desperately, I stare upward, praying to see our son step to

the edge of one of the ice caves and wave to us. The caves are dark. There's no firelight reflecting from the ceilings.

"RabbitEar, do you see him?"

"No." Propping his spear, he leans on it to steady his tired legs, and scans each crack that might be large enough to shelter a climber. "Maybe he was caught in the storm, couldn't see the handholds, and took a different path to get to the top."

"You mean he may have tried to work outward along one of the horizontal fissures? Gods, I hope not. His arm muscles aren't strong enough to support his weight."

RabbitEar shouts, "Jawbone! Answer me! Son, are you up there?"

When no answer comes, I rub my eyes. I'm half snowblind, just as RabbitEar is. "I told you I heard him scream."

When my husband turns to look at me, he's white-lipped and silent, unable to say the words neither of us can bear to hear. His hand moves instinctively toward me, reaching out, and I slog through the snow and into his arms.

As he pulls me against him, he says, "If he's here, we'll find him."

He can no longer tell me I'm wrong, that our son is fine and just holed up in one of the children's camps in front of a warm fire, and it breaks my heart.

RabbitEar hugs me so tight, it's hard to breathe, but I say, "We should never have forced him to climb this cliff. Not this time of summer when storms are the most unpredictable and fierce. The instant he begged us to take him home, we should have done it!"

"Don't . . . Don't do that, Quiller. We can't be absolutely sure he fell until we've searched the camps. He could be lying by his dead fire, senseless from cold."

I push away and stare at him. "You believe that?"

"I have to."

RabbitEar turns and wades through the snow to look up at the cliff, the place where the trail should be, then he stares at the tortured drifts piled against the base. My husband is trying to calculate where our son would have landed if he'd fallen from different points on the trail or tried to work his way along one of the fissures.

"We know he made it to the first camp," I say, slogging forward to stand beside him. "And we saw him climbing toward the second. My guess is that he made it to the second camp. So if he fell, it would have been while climbing up from the second camp to the third." I extend my arm and draw a line across the appropriate snowdrifts. "Which means he should be somewhere in there."

RabbitEar gives me a faint nod. His gaze has fastened on a different location, on the worst drifts. The zyme light is so faint, they resemble huge, rounded gray humps, seventy handlengths high. We both know what's beneath them. "If he fell straight down from anywhere along the trail between the first and second camp, he would have landed in the same place as Little Gull."

My gaze ascends the cliff as I imagine my son's small body tumbling through the air and crashing into the massive black boulders at the bottom. I feel it, too, that haunted certainty that our son's dead body is right there in front of us, lying broken and bloody beneath the snow.

RabbitEar says, "Let's dig a snow shelter in one of the drifts, and we'll get started at daybreak."

"No. I know there's not much light left . . ." My words trail away, for I know it's a foolish thing to ask. Darkness is falling fast and we're both exhausted and bitterly cold.

RabbitEar sighs. "I'm not going to talk you out of it, am I?"

I shake my head. "I have to start digging."

"All right, but we still have to find shelter." He looks around for any sort of quick shelter that doesn't require scooping out the drift, shaping and compacting the interior into a bell-like shape, and fashioning an elevated sleeping platform inside that's higher than the entrance to create a heat trap. A big crevice might work. "I'll make a bargain with you. If you find us some sort of quick shelter, I'll start digging. Acceptable? I can clear more snow than you can before it's too cold to search."

"Yes. Good. Thank you."

He trudges toward the buried boulders, while I head northward.

I know this stretch of shoreline as well as my own village, but everything looks different in a sea of windswept snowdrifts. All the usual landmarks are gone, swallowed up as though they never existed. Nonetheless, somewhere ahead, sandstone ledges create overhanging shelves. I must find them.

As I hike, the hiss of zyme grows louder, and I hear faint trickles of glacial meltwater flowing beneath the snow. I can imagine green arms methodically creeping up the trickles. Soon, no ocean will be visible along the shoreline. The zyme will have reached the cliffs and begun to climb them like perverse vines. By midsummer, these cliffs will be solid green walls.

When the drifts to my left slope downward, I stop. Using my sleeve to break the ice crust from my eyelashes, I have to blink several times to clear my vision before I can distinguish the fine details that might tell me what lies beneath. In several places, zyme light throws shadows, meaning the drifts are undercut.

Wading through deep snow, I make my way around to the front, and kneel down to start excavating beneath the ledge. The sun-warmed sandstone must have held its heat after it was buried, for there's a dry cavity inside. How deep is it?

"Quiller?" RabbitEar calls. "Where are you? I can't see you."

"Over here!" I wave a hand. "I found the ledges. I'm going to see if we can sleep comfortably beneath one of these overhangs."

"Don't get out of my sight!"

I wave back, and he bends down again. In the green gleam, I see a haze of glittering snow fly as he tosses it out of his way, searching for our son.

The campfires of the dead burn brilliantly tonight, creating points of light across the sky. I can't help but wonder if Jawbone is sitting around one of those campfires with my dead mother and father. I know they would have run to meet him when he stepped from the Road of Light into the villages of the dead.

Suddenly, it's as though it's me stepping off the Road of Light and watching Jawbone running toward me with his small arms open. He's laughing, excited to see me . . .

The vision is so clear I have to shake myself, as though from a dream, before I can turn back to my task.

Sliding beneath the ledge on my belly, I clutch my spear and drag it along beside me as I wriggle forward, stopping often to feel out the shape of the dark hollow. When I hit the back wall, I lay my spear aside and use both hands to measure the space. The cavity is about two body-lengths deep, but it's very shallow back here. I may be able to roll to my side, but Rabbit-Ear will have to sleep on his back. His shoulders are too wide. Nonetheless, we'll be able to rest comfortably stretched out side by . . .

"*Quiller!*" RabbitEar shouts, and my heart stops.

Terrified of what he's found, I'm shaking when I scurry from beneath the ledge and get to my feet to search for him. "Did you find Jawbone?"

RabbitEar must be crouching down, or hidden in the hole he dug in the snow bank, for I don't see him.

Instinctively, I start running toward the last place I saw him, then I see a dark shape lunging toward me through the zyme light.

"Get back!" He's bashing his way through the snowdrifts, waving frantically with his spear. "Get back under the ledge!"

I'm confused for an instant, then I see the pride of giant lions trotting absolutely silent through the snow behind him. They have their massive heads up. Their eyes flash.

"Blessed gods!"

I scramble back beneath the ledge and slither to the very rear with my heart slamming against my chest. In less than ten heartbeats, RabbitEar's body blocks the light and his cape scrapes across the sandstone as he crawls toward me on his belly.

"How many?" I ask.

"Can't tell. Ten, maybe."

Ten lions.

Both of us go quiet, concentrating on sounds. I hear nothing except the distant washing of waves and the rumbling of the Ice Giants. That's what makes lions terrifying. You can't hear them until they're right there staring into your eyes in the darkness. By then, it's too late.

Panting . . .

I grip my spear tighter, but RabbitEar is the one in front. He'll have to fight them back. There's nothing I can do.

Their feral smell seeps beneath the ledge—a mixture of lion musk and blood-scented breath from their latest kills.

RabbitEar whispers, "They've eaten recently."

I nod and try to identify the scent before I whisper back, "Smells like bison blood."

"Probably been up high hunting newborn calves."

We both heave relieved breaths. Means they're not starving. If they were, it would be virtually impossible to keep them out.

Low growls vibrate the darkness, but most are simply panting from their run.

My ears track their movements as they circle our shelter, seeking the way inside.

RabbitEar shouts when a huge paw swipes beneath the ledge.

Instinctively, he lunges forward, spears the paw, and leaps back.

A cacophony of growls and roars erupt and echo across the beach outside.

"There's at least two trying to squirm under the ledge!" RabbitEar says as he shoves me hard against the rear wall.

"They can't get inside," I cry. "Their heads are too big to fit beneath the ledge!"

"But they can reach in for us!"

Paws thud on the roof right over my face, then sandstone screeches as claws slash at the rock like knives. A cacophony of growls erupts. The pride starts loping around the shelter in frustration.

Then I hear paws digging snow.

"They're trying to dig us out, Quiller!"

37

LYNX

Gripping my spear in one hand and a birchbark torch in the other, I duck out of Quancee's chamber and head for the paleo-ocean. The vast expanse of water is mirrorlike, with skeins of blue bioluminescent algae trailing across the surface for as far as I can see. As I walk, my footsteps fill with water and leave a shining blue path behind me.

Quancee's glow is still fading, and I can't bear to stay in there and watch her die.

Planting my torch in the sand, I slump beside it with a deep sigh and rest my spear across my lap, while I wait for our enemies to arrive.

It comforts me to sit here, for I remember so many times when I sat here with Arakie and listened to him tell me magnificent and terrible stories of the long-lost Jemen. Gods, I wish he were here right now. Even if his advanced age wouldn't allow him to fight at my side, his sense of humor would lighten the tension that twists and turns in my belly.

I must come up with a plan to defend us, but I can't seem to think. I'll probably wait in the door to Quancee's chamber and fight them off for as long as I can, but I have never been a warrior. My paltry skills will hold them off for a few moments, perhaps, but not much longer than that. I can already envision how it will be: Two or three Rust warriors will break down the door. When I cast my spear at the first warrior to enter, the next warrior's spear will pierce my chest.

Absently, I pick up a pebble and hurl it out across the ocean. Where the pebble skips, phosphorescent blue dots appear. As I pick up a larger pebble, a thought occurs to me.

Rocks scatter the shore. Can I use them to build a fortification in front of our chamber to hold off the warriors for a short time?

My torch sputters, and the gleam dances over the vast tracery of gigantic black beams that dangle from the roof, and reflects on the fallen beams that thrust up from the water. They remind me of giant gambling sticks tossed out in an ancient game.

"Quancee, where are you?"

Leaning my head far back, I try to imagine how the beams were connected to form lodges. Arakie said that many summers before the Battle of the Stronghold, thousands of Jemen sealed themselves in these caverns, both for protection from the advancing glaciers, and from the war raging outside. Hundreds went mad in the final days and killed one another trying to find a way out.

"Quancee?"

My voice echoes around the beams and comes back three or four times, growing weaker each time.

I expel a breath.

Thanissara left four hands of time ago. I have no idea what he told Ganmor when he returned to the Rust People villages. Even if he now has some sort of sympathy for me and Quancee, it might not matter. The Rust People may choose to believe Sticks and Jorgensen over Thanissara. I assume Thanissara has the support of the other five Dog Soldiers, but I have no way of knowing how much sway they have among the council of elders.

Casting a glance back over my shoulder, I study the square opening that leads back to Quancee's chamber. It has a barely visible glow.

She's still alive.

Gripping my spear, I replay my conversation with Thanissara and wonder what he meant at the end. *Quancee knows you're looking.*

It will take me time to understand the things he told me, and I'm sure it will take Thanissara a while to process what I told him and to explain it to the other Dog Soldiers. Will they come to the right decision?

More importantly, what will Jorgensen do if it looks like the council is turning against him?

My blood goes cold.

Feeling helpless, I lay back on the sand and stare up at the torchlight fluttering over the black beams like translucent orange wings.

"Where are you?" I call out to the empty cavern.

38

KUJUR

The Flame Bird staggers to a stop at the edge of the shimmering violet haze, and her feet seem to go out from under her. When she topples onto her side and her talons claw the ground as she tries to rise back up, I run forward with tears welling in my eyes.

"Flame Bird?" I fall to my knees at her side. "Tell me how I can help you."

She struggles to rise again, but it's a futile effort. Her huge head thumps the dirt.

"There must somethin' I can do!"

The buffalo will wait, but not too long. Go. Go now.

Her breath is hot, fevered, and she's lost so many scales on our journey that her hide has dark splotches amid the silver.

"I'm not goin' until you're strong enough to come with me," I say.

Lying down beside her, I pet the scales beneath her luminous eyes. My closeness seems to comfort her, for the Flame Bird leans her heavy head against mine, as though we are two old friends together for the last time.

"You're goin' to be all right. I'll make a fire to keep you warm while you sleep."

Her nostrils flare as she sniffs the fragrant desert wind, then her enormous shining eyelids flutter closed.

These final moments are quiet—the wind sighing through the sage, a single owl hooting, and the sounds of my sobs muffled against my sleeve.

"I'll be right here," I promise. "You rest now."

For another half hand of time, I stroke the scales that run down her beautiful throat. She's a huge, hulking creature, but gentle and otherworldly. I knew the moment I saw her that she was an ancient being. Like me and dire wolves, I suspect she was re-created by the Jemen, but I'm sure her kind flew the skies millions of summers before our most ancient ancestors were born.

"I'm here," I say to let her know she's not dying alone.

Suddenly, beneath my hand, her muscles contract, then a shudder works through her. When it fades, her body relaxes and her breathing slows until I can barely feel her chest move.

"Don't go. Please don't go!"

Something amazing and precious is about to pass out of the world forever, and I am the only witness. How can that be? I pet her muzzle beneath her pointed teeth.

She doesn't move.

"I'm building a fire right now." Rising, I run out toward the violet haze to gather dead sticks from beneath the sagebrush.

As I move along, I study the haze. Like a wall, it seems to rise from the earth and shoot straight upward into the sky. I bend down to pick up another stick, and smell the haze. It has the brittle mustiness of the deepest crevasses in the Ice Giant Mountains, but somewhere out there, buffalo sing in deep rumbling voices. Calling and calling . . .

I long to step through the haze and find them, but I won't leave the Flame Bird when she needs me the most.

Turning, I tiptoe back and lean my sticks together like lodge poles, then I pull my firesticks from my belt pouch.

After I have a good fire going, I silently stretch out with my back pressed against the Flame Bird's. Her chest faintly rises and falls. I hold my breath while I wait for it to rise again. The black pupils of her silver eyes have narrowed to slits.

She's so still.

I wait and wait, but her chest never rises again.

Burying my face against the Flame Bird's scaled throat, I cry. Then . . .

In the firelit darkness, music glitters. Buffalo songs. I feel their rumbling voices slip around behind my clenched teeth and, weightless as spider-silk ribbons, twine their way toward the hide that sways in the back of my head.

As though born of the music, a shadow springs to life and runs toward me. Quick and light. Then a gray-mantled child steps from behind my eyes and into this world. It wavers and disappears like a trick of moonglow in the forest.

I sit up with my heart pounding. "Who are you? What— what's happenin'?"

He's out there, standing just beyond the firelight, but he's not quite solid, more like see-through ice, filled with pale rec- ollections of light that gleamed long, long ago in a faraway place I cannot even imagine.

"Come on, Kujur! We must hurry."

My breath catches.

One thousand summers from now in the villages of the dead, I'll know that voice. I scream, "No! Leave me alone!"

The other boy steps forward and extends his hands to me. "I didn't mean to run! I couldn't help it! Stop blaming me!"

There's something familiar about his voice. I stare at him, breathing like I've run for days straight. "What? You ran?"

"Mother told me to! I know I should have picked up my spear and killed the lion that took Father, but I—I was so scared

I couldn't think. I couldn't . . ." Sobbing, he covers his face with his hands. "Don't you remember?"

"No, what are you . . ."

Like a flame in a dark lodge, understanding flickers through my terror. Slowly, it drains away until all that's left is a hollow throbbing in my heart. I recognize those sobs, for they are mine. I heard them three summers ago on the night the lions killed my whole family.

"You . . ." I shake my head, trying to get my thoughts to fall into some sort of order. How is it possible that I did not know him? Couldn't I face him?

He mews, "I didn't mean to run."

He looks so small and thin standing there. I swallow hard. "But . . . if you hadn't run, who would have saved Little Fawn, Loon, and Chickadee? Who would have kept them safe until Quiller found you hiding in that boat?"

The other boy lifts his head and stares at me with tears running down his cheeks. "There was no one but me. Everyone else was dead."

"That's right. If you hadn't run and protected those three little girls, you'd all be dead. There wouldn't be anyone left of the White Foam clan."

He wipes his nose on his sleeve. In a pathetic voice, he asks, "We are all that's left?"

"Yes." I frown at him. I don't understand why he has not been able to move on from that night. It's like he's stuck, living it over and over. "But because of you, we lived, and we are happy and loved. We were adopted by Sealion People. No one could have taken better care of us than Quiller and Rabbit-Ear have."

The other boy sniffs and smiles at me. When he edges closer, I do not run.

Quietly, he says, "Kujur, we should go. The buffalo are running away. We must catch them."

I take a deep breath and hold it in my lungs, allowing the truth to filter through me. I finally understand why the Flame Bird died to bring me here.

"I'm ready. I'll follow you."

39

LYNX

My hand is resting against Quancee when her gleam dwindles, flickers, and fades to darkness.

"Don't do this," I plead. "Quancee, no. No!"

As numbness spreads through me, my gaze drifts around the chamber. For the first time in over one thousand summers, this room is lit only by pale firelight.

My fingers press harder against Quancee, as though my touch alone is enough to call her back from the dead. Instead, I hear Arakie's elderly voice seep up from my memories: *Love is atonement. Get used to it.*

I've been preparing myself for this moment for three summers, and now I discover I am not prepared at all. She's always been a tower of strength and magic. Three summers ago, Arakie told me she was dying, but it didn't seem possible.

As the pane beneath my fingertips turns to ice, I see thousands of spiderweb-like cracks in her panes that I've never noticed before. They were hidden beneath her glow. Was she so old and broken that she simply could not go on?

Turning away from her is the hardest thing I have ever done.

I resolutely walk to the pile of rocks I collected along the shore of the paleo-ocean. Each stone is colorful and glacially smoothed to perfection. I select a large gray rock about the size of my head, lift it, and place it on the huge pile I've already built in front of the closed door to Quancee's chamber, then I fall back a step to survey my work.

The barricade will hold them off for a little while, maybe one or two hands of time, if I'm lucky. Eventually they'll batter it down and force their way inside. What are their orders when they come in? To destroy Quancee? To kill me?

My spear leans against the wall to my right. I'll fight for as long as I can, but I suspect I'll only get in two or three good spear thrusts before they drag me down and kill me. Not that it matters. Centuries from now, my death will be nothing more than a small detail in a larger story about the defeat of a luminous evil being. I imagine the story will begin with the Battle of the Stronghold when Quancee shut down. No one will ever understand why she stopped fighting; they will only remember that her betrayal allowed the enemies of the glorious Jemen to overrun these caverns. The story will be repeated around the winter fires of the Rust People, for by then Sealion People and Dog Soldiers will be long gone. No one will remember the truth.

Bending down, I pick up another rock, carefully place it on top. This is a useless last effort. I know that. But I can't let go of the hope that, out there somewhere, Quancee's wave function still exists, and if I can protect her body here, one day she will come back and this room will flicker and blaze to life again.

The tangy fragrance of pine-needle tea rises from the boiling bag hanging from the tripod by the fire. My half-full cup rests near the hearthstones. I walk back and sit down beside it.

Before I reach for the cup, I run my dirty hands through my hair. My cold fingers feel good against my aching skull. I've never felt this empty in my life.

What will I do now? Where will I go?

Bowing my head, I close my eyes and feel my way around the edges of her loss. Like a blind man, I seem obsessed with judging the size and shape of the abyss, as though knowing such things will help me understand the darkness.

"Oh, Quancee." I lean back to rest my shoulders against her panes. "Did you find your way across the wasteland to the place where no shadows fall?"

Firelight dances across the ceiling, flows into the widest crystal cracks and flares in the clefts like tiny campfires of the dead. My sense of time has vanished. I gathered and hauled rocks for what seemed an eternity. Is it dawn yet? Midday? It must be close to . . .

Voices rise outside.

Cocking my head, I strain to recognize the speakers. I don't hear Sticks or Thanissara. Certainly not Jorgensen. I'm sure he will not be here until the danger has passed, then he will simply walk in and pick through the pieces of Quancee that he wants.

I hear several different men now. Their footsteps are heavy, pounding down the corridor beyond the blocked door. I suppose they've sent their bravest warriors to face me. After all, I'm the man who can kill with the wave of his hand and bring the dead back to life.

"They're coming," I say as I reach up to stroke Quancee.

"*Come out, Blessed Teacher!*" a man shouts. "*Don't make me kill you.*"

Someone pounds on the door. It echoes around the small chamber.

I reach for my tea cup.

There's plenty of time to finish it while they throw themselves at the barricade.

40

QUILLER

Lying on my side with my back pressed tight against the stone wall, I feel RabbitEar move. When he edges forward, I blink at the brilliant zyme light wavering over the roof above me like green flames. The predawn air is filled with the soft roar of ocean waves, the birdlike chirping of Ice Giants, and the feral musky urine of lions.

"Careful," I say. "They could be bedded down waiting for us."

"I'll let you know soon enough."

RabbitEar cautiously slides forward on his belly. I stay put, afraid that he's going to come rushing back at any moment.

When he reaches the opening, he sticks his head out to listen. Lions post sentinels to keep watch while the pride sleeps. If the sentinels spot him, we'll hear soft growls, then the pride rising to its feet and stretching awake in the freezing wind.

RabbitEar slides out with his spear gripped in his fist and silently gets to his feet. All I see now are his lower legs silhouetted against fluorescent zyme hillocks that rise and fall on endless waves.

He walks out of my sight. I remain motionless, just listening, waiting for him to tell me if it's safe to come out.

It takes another twenty heartbeats before he calls, "They're gone, Quiller."

"Thank the gods."

Grabbing my spear, I work my way forward on my belly, eager to escape this cramped shelter. At the mouth, I see the deep grooves in the sandstone. They dug hard, even after they hit solid rock.

After I stand up, I sniff the pungent wind. "They must have spent half the night urinating around our shelter."

"Marking their territory, telling the dire wolves and short-faced bears to stay away from their trapped prey."

"Which means they'll be back later to see if we're still hiding beneath the ledge. We'd best find better shelter before that happens."

"Agreed."

Two of the brightest campfires of the dead glitter on the western horizon. RabbitEar glances at them, then turns to face the quest wall that rises into the sky like a luminous jade-hued monster. The handholds and footholds are still filled and smoothed over with windblown snow, but the cracks that hold the children's camps are black ovals.

My gaze clings to them. There's no sign of life, not even the soft red glow of a fire burned down to coals. RabbitEar has his head tilted far back, as though he's scanning the rim, praying to see a little boy standing up there waving to him.

Mounting agony encompasses my body. I clench my fist around my spear. "I think you were digging in the wrong place last night."

"Tell me where to dig, and I'll do it."

My gaze locates the place where the trail must run between the second and third camps, then I calculate the drop point. My chin gradually lowers until I'm staring at the massive drift at the base of the cliff where our son's body would have landed. The sea wind has sculpted and molded the drifts into flowing curves twenty times the height of a man.

"There." I draw a line with my finger. "Somewhere in there."

RabbitEar heaves an agonized breath. "All right. Could you make breakfast while I get started?"

"Yes."

He trots toward the cliff.

In the meantime, I force my legs to take me to the ocean's edge, where dead clumps of zyme and sticks of driftwood lie upon the wave-scoured sand. I collect firewood until my arm is full. Searching the shore for a place sheltered from the prevailing wind, I spy a curious wind-hollowed drift near where RabbitEar digs snow.

"Take me home, Mother. Please, take me home."

Despair beyond anything I've ever known fills my chest.

Many summers from now, when I'm spearing fish, or netting snowshoe hares, I'll find myself looking down into Jawbone's terrified blue eyes, begging me to help him, and I'll remember that I killed my son. No one else. I could have reached down, taken his hand, and walked him back home.

Guilt is a finely honed knife. It carves and shapes the soul. I have the feeling mine is just beginning to feel the blade.

I force my legs to walk toward the wind-hollowed drift; it has a curious circular shape, open to the north, looking up the shoreline. Kneeling in the drift's shadow, I dump my armload of driftwood and arrange the larger sticks, then I pile small twigs inside atop the clump of dead zyme, and open my belt pouch to draw out my fire-sticks.

Three paces away, RabbitEar scoops snow with his hands and throws it aside. The windborne white haze that surrounds him makes him resemble a ghostly apparition engaged in some strange burial ritual.

While I spin my hardwood dowel in the punky stick, I listen to the sounds my husband makes. RabbitEar digs snow as fast as he can. He must be feeling the same half-fright, half-desperation that I am, wondering if it would be wiser to run home, assemble the entire village, and return with more hands to search for Jawbone. In the end, it would take less time. But the truth is, wisdom plays no part now. Neither of us is going to leave here until we know for sure what happened to our son.

When red coals glow in the punky stick, I tuck it inside the driftwood tent and tap them out over the dead zyme and twigs, then carefully blow until the zyme catches and tiny flames lick up through the tinder. The firelight is weak and frail, but I can see the circular drift better now. It's so oddly shaped, I wonder if days ago the lions buried a carcass here. Is that why the pride returned last night—to dig it up and carry it off to eat? Absently, I examine the floor searching for claw marks, but don't see any.

I add more twigs to the fire. The larger sticks catch and began to burn in earnest. Chunks of ice litter the ground, as though they fell from a great height and shattered on this spot. As soon as the fire really gets going, I'll pull my boiling bag from my pack and toss a couple of the chunks inside to melt for tundra wildflower tea.

Blessed spirits, it's cold this morning. Rubbing my freezing arms, I notice a dark discoloration to my right. It's a faint shadow in the snowdrift. The shadow cuts a straight vertical line about eight hands wide down through the drift. Bending my head back, I try to chart its course. It's as if something, maybe a boulder, fell from the rim and knocked a hole through the drift all the way to the ground.

My gaze traces the shadow down to where the drift meets the sand, and I frown at the tan object hidden in the firelit snow. Could simply be a dead animal the lions buried . . .

"RabbitEar! Gods, no! RabbitEar!"

Scrambling to my hands and knees, I lunge forward and

thrust my hand into the drift. As I close my fingers around the object, I realize it's a small arm.

"NO!" I shout.

"What is it?" RabbitEar screams as he rushes toward me.

It takes all of my strength to tug my son out of the drift and drag him onto my lap. By that time, I'm breathing hard, staring wide-eyed down at his bluish face wavering in the firelight. His eyes are half closed, his blond hair frozen solid.

RabbitEar's boots pound across the shore.

Then there's a dreadful moment of silence.

"NoNoNoNo!" He sobs the words as he drops to his knees beside me, pulls his son from my arms and lays him on the ground. "Did you check to see if he's breathing?"

"No. I—I . . ."

RabbitEar places his ear against Jawbone's chest. "He's not breathing."

"Heart—heartbeat?"

With his ear still to Jawbone's chest, he grabs our son's wrist and waits with desperation in his eyes.

At the same time, I reach down to place my fingers against the big artery in Jawbone's throat. "I don't feel—"

"It could just be really faint. Maybe we should . . ."

My ears don't hear him anymore. There is only the thunder in my chest. Slumping back against the drift, I concentrate on the sound of air stuttering in and out of my lungs.

"Let's go!" I order and gather our son into my arms.

"Go?" he asks in confusion. "Where?"

As I stagger to my feet, I gently shift Jawbone to carry his stiff body over my left shoulder. "We have to get him home right now."

"H-home?" RabbitEar's eyes are eerie reflections of zyme light bouncing off the cliff. "Right now? Why?"

"So Elder Hoodwink can bring his soul back to his body."

"Back? But Quiller, he's—"

"No!" I shake my head angrily. "That's not true! You don't know that! This could just be one of his spells. He always looks dead when he has a spell."

RabbitEar shakes his head like a fawn struck in the head by a rock. "His soul is already on the way to the Land of the Dead. All we can do—"

In a booming voice, I shout, "This is just a spell! That's why he fell, and that's why he's not awake now. We must get him home so Hoodwink can call his soul back to his body."

RabbitEar weakly rises and stares at me, bewildered. I know he loved Jawbone. I've never seen a man love a child so deeply, so I'm stunned when he says, "This is madness. You're a warrior. You've seen death many times over. How can you not see it now?"

"He's alive, RabbitEar! I know he is!"

"No, Quiller," he says softly. "We must carry him home and build a burial scaffold."

"Don't you dare tell me my son is dead! He . . . he's not dead." I clutch Jawbone's body in trembling arms, and see a familiar blend of desperation and sympathy in my husband's eyes.

"I know this is hard, Quiller. It's killing me, too, but we must—"

"Stop it! He's a special child, touched by spirit power. You know it as well as I do. He—he's gone, but he's coming back to us."

He stares at me dumbly, unable to find more words.

"He's coming back!" I repeat and wait for him to nod or agree, to give me hope.

Finally, he says, "Yes, Jawbone is touched by spirit power.

Let's get him home to Hoodwink. We can take turns carrying him. Why don't you let me start?"

He reaches out and I reluctantly transfer my son's body into his muscular arms.

Then I turn and take off at a dead run for the trail that leads back to Sky Ice Village.

41

KUJUR

Forested mountains rise around me, their peaks hidden by moon-varnished clouds.

Blessed Spirits, it's beautiful here, but I'm tired. Really tired. Sweat mats my blond hair to my face and trickles down below my armpits. My hide shirt is drenched. I've been running behind the other boy for hands of time with no idea of where we're going or when we will arrive.

Twigs crack in the pines ahead of me, and I see the long-horned buffalo bull again, loping through the forest shadows. When he steps out into a patch of moon-glow, I stare at him. The bull met me the instant I stepped through the glittering wall, and has never left my side. He just trots a short distance away, always within sight, like a guardian.

I wasn't born buffalo clan, but I know this bull has special power. White hairs fringe his black nose, which means he's old, far older than the number of long winter nights he's stood keeping watch over his herd. I'm sure he was standing guard the night the world was born.

The bull silently edges onto the trail and breaks into a trot. I follow him up over a rise, and when I plunge down the other side, for the first time since I left the Flame Bird, I see dawn swell above the dark mountains.

The bull suddenly roars like a lion and charges down the trail with his tail flying.

In the distance, I see the other boy running headlong after a buffalo herd that thunders on pounding hooves toward a brightening valley below.

Behind them, the spirit bull lopes in a cloud of dust.

Gasping, I stumble to a stop to watch the herd curl like a breaking wave over a hilltop, then disappear with dawn light flashing from their horns.

My heart actually aches at the serene vista.

The sky is shading pink, revealing a blue river that winds through endless rolling green hills. The buffalo charge down to the river and spread out along its banks to drink from the clear water, but the other boy keeps running. I see him flying down the trail toward a copse of pines with his short legs pumping and his arms open as though he sees someone he loves running to greet him.

All I see is a peaceful mountain valley.

I fill my lungs with the pine-scented air and ponder this strange feeling in my chest. I've never felt this way before. There's no shame here. No fear. I have lived with both for so long, I'm not sure who I am without them. I miss Quiller, RabbitEar, and my sisters, but somehow that's all behind me now. The farther I run through this magnificent world, the more my memories of them fade. And losing them doesn't hurt now. Somehow, it's right and exactly as it should be.

When the youngest orange calves finish drinking, they dash out into the meadows and run headlong through the tall grass, bleating in sheer joy, while they kick their heels up and bound around like bouncing hide balls.

I smile, and my gaze roams the high, forested peaks, silhouetted against the dawn. There's something strangely familiar about all this, as if I remember this valley, the playing buffalo, the sunlight being born into a warm world. I wonder if this place has always existed inside me, perhaps behind the swaying buffalo hide where the other boy lived? Is that why he kept calling me? He wanted me to come here?

A breeze rustles the pine boughs and the scents of fresh grass and wet earth rise. Taking a deep breath, I hold it in my lungs for as long as I can.

The herd is beginning to move away from the river. The lead cow starts out at a slow trot, then the rest of the herd falls in line behind her, moving toward the trail to pursue the other boy, who's running very hard now. They thunder away with their tails flying and hooves kicking up dust.

As though wondering where I am, the big bull charges back up the trail and stands four paces away with one hoof lifted. Father Sun has just crested the horizon and yellow flashes fall through the pines and flit across his back like secretive butterflies hiding in his fur.

Lifting his huge head, he rumbles to me.

"I'm comin'," I answer.

The bull whirls and charges away to catch up with the herd.

Breaking into a tired sprint, I pound down the trail behind him.

I don't know where the buffalo lead me.

All I know is I'm going home.

42

QUILLER

As the zyme glow fades, Father Sun rises over the jagged blue peaks of the Ice Giants, and a wave of yellow lights the world. Grains of sand glitter like points of flame on the beach.

RabbitEar sprints down to the beach trail three paces ahead of me, dodging the slithers of zyme.

Jawbone's head lolls in front of me. His mouth dangles open. A few clumps of ice continue to shine in his blond hair, but most of his head and clothing have melted out. He's dripping wet. Trickles of water run down his cheeks. If I didn't know better, I'd think they were streams of tears.

After running for hands of time staring into my son's glazed eyes, I should know he's dead. But I refuse to believe it.

Despair and rage are eating my soul. What will I do if my son is dead? This is different than watching friends or family die in battle. It's different than watching them die of sickness or old age. Those deaths are comprehensible. Jawbone's death will come with an unfathomable burden of guilt.

I'm trying hard to hold back my sobs, but white clouds of breath puff from my mouth in time with my steps.

RabbitEar slows down to a labored trot as we round a curve in the shoreline and Sky Ice Village comes into view, nestled in the firelit sea cave perched above the water line. Black dots of people move around outside, going about their daily duties, completely unaware that the world has changed forever.

RabbitEar stumbles, lunges forward, and almost drops Jawbone.

I call, "RabbitEar, stop! It's my turn. Let me carry him for a while."

"No, you're just as exhausted—"

"He's my son, too. Give him to me!" I run forward with my arms thrust out.

RabbitEar turns with tears in his eyes and I wonder how long he's been crying. He's been doggedly staying ahead of me, probably trying to keep me from seeing. "Be gentle, Quiller."

"Yes, of course."

When I extend my hands farther, he clutches Jawbone against his chest, then tenderly lifts our limp son into my arms.

Smoothing a hand over Jawbone's icy cheek, I stare down into his face. One eye is half-open, the other almost closed. The stiffness has gone out of his body. When I heft him to carry him over my shoulder, his arms and legs flop around as though boneless.

"Let's go," I say and fall into a steady distance-eating lope.

RabbitEar silently trots beside me.

As I splash through a stream of meltwater, darkness suddenly covers me like a condor's shadow, but immensely more huge. The shadow hovers above me for a long while, then ripples across the sand and vanishes over the cliff top.

Craning my neck, I search the sky. "What was that?"

RabbitEar follows my gaze.

Clouds drift through the sunlight with their bellies glowing golden, but there's nothing else up there, not even a single bird.

RabbitEar says, "Must have been a trick of cloud shadows."

43

LYNX

Stone axes slam against the door and shudder through the fragile ancient panes that surround me.

I sink back against Quancee with my spear across my lap. They've been at this for seven hands of time. Long enough that my fire has burned down to a bed of coals, leaving the chamber cold and bathed in wavering red light. I should add more wood, I suppose, but at this point it seems a waste.

There's a pause, then the cacophony begins again as my attackers switch off. As best I can tell, there are two warriors outside who take turns. One man is larger, more muscular, for when he swings the ax it feels like the world is coming apart.

I nuzzle my shoulders against Quancee. "I'm here. I'm not leaving you."

Doesn't matter that her wave function has ceased to occupy this realm, I suspect she can still hear me, though I can't explain the mechanics of that possibility. It may be a form of entanglement that can't be explained—a sort of quantum superposition of thought that is neither in this realm nor that realm.

Three more great booms shudder the air, and a haze of dust seeps into the chamber and glitters in the red gleam.

I clutch my spear in both hands, preparing to thrust it into the first body that bursts through. Already, a thread of clean blue light, streaming from the paleo-ocean, outlines the top and left side of the door. Won't be long now.

"Gods, what is this material?" the big man demands to know. "It looks like wood, but every time my ax dents it, the door repairs itself!"

"Let me strike at the hinges with my granite hammer. They're just leather, aren't they?" the second man suggests. "If we shatter them, we can lift the door off."

"Go on, then, but they are not leather," the first man says, and I hear his steps move back.

Hammerfalls ring out. The hinges groan off and on for a finger of time, then fall silent. The odor of stale sweat filters around the door.

"Why didn't the Sticks warn us about this door? He studied in this very chamber with Lynx, didn't he?"

"So he claims," the big man answers.

"You don't believe it?"

"Sure, I guess. Even if Sticks didn't know about the door, Jorgensen must have. He's a god. They know everythin'."

Through a heavy exhalation, the second man says, "Not this one. Did you hear that heated conversation he had with the Blessed Thanissara?"

"'Course I did. Who didn't? They were growlin' at each other like foamin'-mouth dogs. Not that I understood any of it."

Feet shuffle on dirt. "I know what you mean. That was a weird question Thanissara asked."

"Which one?"

"When he asked Jorgensen if humans could act as waves."

"Waves? Like the ocean?"

"Don't ask me. I was asking you."

Sheepishly, the second man says, "I was standing guard at the edge of the trees. I didn't hear the part about the wave. What did Jorgensen answer?"

"He said it was possible, and Thanissara shouted, 'Then Quancee is not so different from us, is she?'"

Rising to my feet, I tiptoe to the door to listen more closely to their conversation. If Thanissara asked that question, he must have been seeking confirmation from Jorgensen that what I'd told him was correct. Or perhaps he wanted the other five Dog Soldiers or the council to hear it from the Blessed Jorgensen himself?

Hope actually makes me lightheaded. Did they understand?

Boots scrape dirt again, as though the second man shifts his feet uneasily. "Sounds like they're saying humans are oceans, doesn't it?"

Irritated, the first man replies, "Don't ask me stupid questions. I don't have time for your nonsense."

Both men retreat a few steps and began to quietly converse in frustrated tones.

At last, the first man trudges back. He has distinctive heavy steps. "For the sake of the gods," he shouts, "if you are alive in there, surrender and I will spare your life."

I don't respond. No sense in clarifying the issue.

The second man asks, "What are we going to do now?"

"Maybe we can pry the door open? You know those black beams in the water outside? There has to be somethin' we can use as a lever."

A hesitation. "You want me to wade out into that water searchin' for a lever? What if somethin' lives in that water?"

"Great gods, you're stupid and a coward!" the big man shouts. "I'll do it myself."

Heavy steps stride away.

Gingerly, I climb up on one of the rocks and peer around the edge of the door at the corridor outside. Pale blue light penetrates the dust kicked up by their efforts. The second man, tall and muscular, has his mouth quirked, watching the empty place where his friend disappeared. Displaying relative calm, he brushes away a clump of dirt on his silver shirt, and leans back against the wall to await the big man's return.

Then, as though he knows I'm watching him, he offhandedly calls, "Be best to quit, Lynx. War Leader Menash keeps his promises. Quit and you'll walk out of here."

Unwisely, I reply, "And then what?"

The tall man straightens up and walks toward the door. His gaze moves around the edges, as though searching for a dark spot that blocks the reddish gleam and will tell him where I'm standing. "There's an entire war party out at the mouth of the cave. You can't get away. Less you really can fly, like the Blessed Sticks claims, what's the use in holdin' out?"

"Did the Dog Soldiers accompany the war party?"

"What do you care? They can't save you. The village council has made its decision. They want that evil beast in there torn apart."

Climbing down, I gently touch Quancee. Her crystal panes, glued here and there with pine pitch, have absorbed the reddish gleam of the coals, and each crack casts a shadow. She appears to be cobwebbed with a gauzy black shroud.

"Don't listen to them. I know who you are."

My heart beats in my ears like a pot drum, and I wonder if she can sense my pain. Arakie once told me that strong emotions altered the behavior of quantum systems—changed the quantum probabilities—and he knew it because they affected the outcomes of his measurements.

Resting my forehead against Quancee, I focus my emotions, doing everything I can to alter the quantum probabilities.

"I'm looking, Quancee. If you're out there, I want you to know that I'm looking."

44

QUILLER

Quiller, hand him to me. You're very tired, and it's my turn to carry him again."

I lift Jawbone into RabbitEar's arms. I have slowed to a stumbling walk as we near the trail that slants down toward Sky Ice Village. "Be careful. Don't run so fast that you hurt him. He's completely limp."

"I'll be gentle," he says in understanding. "Come when you can."

While I watch him sprint away with Jawbone bouncing over his shoulder, I remain in the trail like a carved wooden statue. Unfeeling. Just watching him put distance between us.

Everything seems to be moving more and more slowly. The clouds have frozen in place over my head. The zyme barely rises and falls on the distant waves. Even the Ice Giants have gone quiet, as though out of respect for my loss.

My gaze instinctively seeks out the high point in the distance where two warriors stand guard night and day, and I try to recognize the closest man just from the way he braces his feet and carries his spear. Mink, maybe.

Filling my lungs, I breathe out slowly.

If I don't go down to the village, I'll never have to hear Hoodwink's verdict. I can remain suspended in this numb state of uncertainty forever. Why do I so long for that? Is not knowing better? Once RabbitEar and I accept the truth, we can begin building the burial scaffold while the village women wash our son's body and dress him in his best clothing. Then we can carry him up to the high point where the scaffold stands. It will be covered with soft buffalo hides and decorated with brightly painted ribbons that flutter in the sea breezes. Together, Rabbit-Ear and I will lay our son to rest where he can look up at the campfires of the dead. The entire village will gather around him to sing his soul to the villages of the ancestors.

Jawbone will never again be cold or hungry. And he'll be greatly loved. My son will be all right.

Then why can't I let him go?

Mink shouts to me and abandons his guard post. I watch him charging across the tundra toward me with his long cape flapping behind him.

Suddenly, the clouds begin to move again, drifting eastward, pushed by the sea wind, and the Ice Giants awaken. When they stretch, the ground beneath my feet quakes. Waves crash across the shore below . . .

If only I could believe in an afterlife. Unfortunately, I'm a warrior. I've witnessed far too much death and destruction, and I know the next moon will bring the death of my soul, for I will be condemned to watch my husband sitting beneath the scaffold, watching his son's body decay while he tears himself apart with guilt.

A commotion breaks out in Sky Ice Village when RabbitEar pounds down the cliff trail and into the village plaza. People drop whatever they're doing and race toward him. My guilt is magnified a thousand-fold when my three little girls duck beneath the flap of Gray Dove's lodge and run toward their father.

Little Fawn screams, *"Jawbone!"* and it shivers the blood in my veins.

How could I have allowed RabbitEar to face this alone?

I gird myself and run hard, forcing all emotion from my thoughts. I must be able to think straight when I get there. Someone has to answer all the questions. Someone has to make the decisions.

Mink meets me halfway there, shouting, "Quiller? What happened?"

I stop and manage to say, "Jawbone fell off the quest cliff."

Mink's dark eyes go wide. "Is he alive? I saw RabbitEar carrying—"

"Of course he's alive," I say a little too stridently.

Mink grabs my shoulder, forcing me to stare into his eyes. Long black hair blows around his face. Mink is a father of two sons. "Does RabbitEar think he's alive?"

Wearily shaking my head, I look away from him. "No, I . . . I don't think so, but . . . Mink, I have to get down there to help RabbitEar. I shouldn't have let him enter the village alone. My girls need me."

"I'll go with you." He releases my shoulder.

When I break into a run, Mink is right there beside me, shoulder to shoulder, just in case I need him.

By the time we're halfway down the trail, people are streaming out of lodges, running for RabbitEar, who has rested Jawbone on one of the buffalo hides around the central bonfire. Lying on his back with his legs akimbo, my son looks pale and broken. His lips are blue.

What is it inside me that insists he's still alive? He can't look like that and be alive. But something inside me insists that I saved him once, three summers ago when his village was destroyed by lions, and I can save him again. I must save him.

"Father?" Little Fawn tugs on RabbitEar's sleeve. "What happened to Jawbone?"

RabbitEar crushes his daughter to his chest with one arm and opens the other arm so that Loon and Chickadee can run to him. As he kisses their blond heads, he says something soft that I cannot hear.

At the far end of the village, Elder Hoodwink ducks from his lodge, clutching the knob of his walking stick. He scans the gathering, then lifts his gaze to watch me and Mink trotting down the trail into the plaza.

Within heartbeats, RabbitEar is surrounded by people calling questions. He ignores them all and shouts, "Elder Hoodwink? Please, hurry? Jawbone fell!"

Hoodwink hobbles forward as fast as he can, shoulders through the murmuring assembly. When he kneels beside RabbitEar to bend over Jawbone, gray hair swings around his face. "Please, give me some room."

My daughters cry out, "Mother!" in unison and run to grab me around the legs and waist.

"Mother?" Little Fawn cries. "Is Jawbone going to be all right?"

"Why won't Jawbone wake up?" Loon asks.

The youngest, Chickadee, just gazes up with tears streaming down her face.

I pet their hair. "He fell off the quest wall into a deep snowdrift. Hush now, Elder Hoodwink must be able to hear your father."

Hoodwink lays his walking stick aside and quietly runs his hands over Jawbone's skull, arms, and legs, then lifts the boy's drenched shirt to probe the ribcage. A mystified expression comes over his elderly face. He grabs Jawbone's wrist and simultaneously bends down to place his ear against our son's lips. After a few moments of listening, Hoodwink straightens and sits back.

Before he can pronounce our son dead, I shout, "His soul is loose, but I feel it nearby. Can you bring it back?"

All the kindness in the world fills Hoodwink's eyes. "If it's close, I'll find it," he says and turns to RabbitEar. "Why don't you strip him out of these wet clothes and swaddle him in a fire-warmed hide while I fetch my healer's bag."

"Yes, elder."

Mink crouches beside RabbitEar. "I'll help you."

"Thank you, Mink."

RabbitEar and Mink work on different arms, tugging Jawbone's shirt over his head. As they work, the tiny, gray soapstone sculpture of a buffalo falls out and bounces across the floor. RabbitEar picks it up, and a sob catches in his throat.

"Quiller, could you come with me, please?" Hoodwink grabs his walking stick and grunts as he shoves to his feet. "It would help if you could carry my heavy bag."

"Of course, elder."

Elder Stone Bowl and Elder Crystal Leaf trail behind us, but the rest of the village crowds around Jawbone where he blindly stares at the cave ceiling with half-open eyes.

When we've walked twenty paces away, Hoodwink quietly asks, "Can you tell me how long your son's soul has been gone?"

"I pulled him from the drift before dawn this morning, elder. I don't know exactly when he fell, but the blizzard had been raging for long enough that huge drifts had built up at the base of the cliff. I could see the tunnel his falling body made as it knocked a hole in the snow."

As though confused, Hoodwink frowns. "But the blizzard didn't get bad until well after nightfall."

"Yes, I know. For some reason, and I can't imagine why, he must have tried to climb the quest trail in the middle of the night."

Propping his walking stick, Hoodwink halts and motions for Elder Stone Bowl and Elder Crystal Leaf to join our small circle. They hurry forward, and Hoodwink whispers, "Can you guess how high Jawbone was when he fell?"

"Maybe five hundred hand-lengths above the shore?"

Stone Bowl and Crystal Leaf stiffen. Tears fill Stone Bowl's eyes.

Hoodwink glances at them, then lightly shakes his head. "It makes no sense. The boy appears dead, but—"

"He's not dead!" I stubbornly say.

"He may not be." Elder Crystal Leaf folds her stick-like arms over her chest. "Little Gull fell from a much lower height and his skull was shattered. Why isn't Jawbone's?"

"Yes. It's very curious," Hoodwink agrees.

"Does the boy have any broken bones?" Stone Bowl asks.

"No." I shake my head. "Not that I could find. I think the big snowdrift cushioned his fall."

Crystal Leaf softly says, "Perhaps. Doesn't seem possible, but . . ."

Stone Bowl says, "Even if the drift cushioned his bones, the boy could still have a split liver or pulverized lungs. He may have bled to death inside and would show no signs, except bloodless flesh."

"His flesh is blue." Hoodwink clutches his walking stick. "But he was lying in a drift for many hands of time."

I shift to brace my knees. Though I've thought about all of these things, hearing them from the mouths of respected elders makes them somehow more real.

By the fire, I see RabbitEar disintegrate. He's always been a tower of strength, but now he seems to be shaking apart. When he gathers the girls into his arms, a sob escapes his lips.

I square my shoulders. I have to be able to bear this. One of us has to bear this.

Hoodwink must have noticed my gaze, for he places a hand on my forearm and gives it a comforting squeeze. "Thank you, Quiller, for speaking with us. Please go back to be with your husband. He needs you more than I do. Crystal Leaf and Stone Bowl will help me carry my things."

45

THANISSARA

Soft green twilight seeps through the air.

I halt at the mouth of the cave and wait for the five elder Dog Soldiers to gather around me. Only the young Sticks does not stand with us. It's a strange feeling, for our sacred stories tell us that Dog Soldiers have stood together for over one thousand summers. This split has been coming for a long time—since Vice Admiral Jorgensen's mysterious appearance.

On the other hand, Sticks is young and spiritually inexperienced. If he did see Jorgensen change from a wolf into a man, it was a grand moment of religious ecstasy. He witnessed a god come to life before his eyes. At that instant everything else became paltry in comparison. Including Dog Soldiers.

I gaze down the slope to where Sticks gazes worshipfully at the last Jemen to walk the earth. Jorgensen leans against the stone wall with his arms crossed and a smile on his lips. His hair has gone entirely white and wrinkles cover his lean face. It's a shocking change.

Elder Homara quietly walks to stand close beside me. "Immortality is fickle, isn't it?"

"How so?" I glance at him. He's tied his long gray hair behind his head, but strands flutter over his dark face.

"It seems his life is tied to the device's life. As it dies, he dies. I find that interesting."

Smoothing a hand over my chin, I reply, "As I do, but what does it mean?"

"Unknown. If they are indeed tied together, you'd think he'd be doing everything he could to keep the device alive."

"Yet," Elder Pyara whispers as he moves closer to us, "her death apparently gives him hope."

We three stare at one another. Pyara's broad nose spreads across the middle of his face, and long, black-streaked gray locks hang over his cheeks.

I say, "The only logical conclusion is that by tearing Quancee apart he hopes to build a life raft."

"I'm not sure I understand," Pyara replies.

"I'm not sure I do either."

The ocean shimmers with green fire as the zyme brightens, and the drifting clouds go from the lavender of dusk to the luminous green of night. The sound of waves carries to me on the cold breeze.

I study the lines of Rust People carrying torches up the trails through the forest. Everyone wants to be here when the legendary holy man of the Sealion People faces death. Already strange tales travel the villages. Many expect Lynx to clap his hands, transform into a ball of light, and soar to the campfires of the dead like one of the Meteor People.

"If you are right about the life raft"—Homara's head dips in a subtle nod—"should we stop it?"

"Can we stop it?" Pyara asks.

My gaze moves from one Dog Soldier to another, assessing their opinions from their nods or uncertain shrugs.

"I have spoken with Elder Ganmor about what to do with the Blessed Lynx if he survives the battle, but I did not wish to discuss Jorgensen with him."

As darkness intensifies, light filters up from the vast paleo-ocean inside the caverns and turns the opening into a flickering blue square. Hundreds of people have climbed the slope and array themselves in a semicircle. A few have already built campfires to wait through the night if necessary. Here and there, children laugh, and their breath condenses into small glistening clouds and glides across the zyme-lit face of the mountain.

When a ragged roar erupts from the caverns, accompanied by the angry shouts of warriors, the mountainside goes quiet, then people surge forward with torches.

"It's over." Homara exhales the words. "We must decide."

"Yes," I answer.

Jorgensen straightens up where he stands beside Sticks. As he flips up his lion-hide hood to fend off the cold wind, he shifts to stare directly at me. Inside, where his face should be, I only see glowing blue eyes floating in darkness. I pull myself up to my full height and narrow my eyes to gaze back.

For a timeless moment, I cannot move. The feeling of threat is overwhelming.

Homara whispers, "Don't look away."

"Not about to."

Jorgensen says something to Sticks, and hobbles forward so stiffly he resembles an ancient wraith in dark rags. He waits a few paces from the entry.

Another hoarse roar echoes up the throat of the caverns as two warriors drag Lynx through the blue glow and into the gleam of countless torches. Blood streaks his chest, arms, and legs from a number of spear wounds. Despite his injuries, his face is a mask of defiance as he struggles against his muscular captors.

"Homara," I say, "please find Elder Ganmor and inform him the Blessed Teacher is badly wounded and no longer a threat. As we discussed, he should simply be escorted to Sky Ice Village, where his own people can care for him."

"What if the rest of council intervenes and demands death?"

"We'll face that if the time comes."

"Yes, Thanissara." Homara bows and sprints down the slope through the crowd.

Down along the seashore, seven buffalo walk into view, four cows and three calves. As though they've absorbed the zyme light, their woolly coats glitter and their horns shine as though made from polished jade. Some of our oldest story fragments say that long-horned buffalo are the guardians of the dead. Sometimes, especially after a battle or a long illness, the souls of the dead become confused. They wander around lost and weeping, unable to find the Road of Light that leads to the afterworld. When the buffalo see them, they thunder down, surround the soul, and herd it into the sky where the soul can at last clearly see the villages of the ancestors. I wonder if they've come for the Blessed Teacher Lynx.

"Release me, you fools!" Lynx rages. "Let me go!"

Two more warriors stagger out of the cavern behind him, clutching belly wounds.

"He must have fought like an enraged short-faced bear," Pyara says.

"I only hope the struggle didn't destroy the crystal chamber."

In a powerful voice, Lynx shouts, "You're killing our future! Can't you see that? Jorgensen is not a god! He's a liar. If you allow him to tear Quancee apart, we're all dead!"

"Do you believe him?" Pyara leans sideways to ask.

Across the slope, heads shift to peer at Jorgensen. The last Jemen looks faintly amused, which sends an eddy of whispers through the crowd. Jorgensen and Sticks boldly walk into the cavern and disappear into the flickering blue depths.

"I do." I motion to the four Dog Soldiers behind me, and we climb as one to meet the warriors before they can drag Lynx in front of the crowd that eagerly awaits the miracle that will accompany his death.

"War Leader Menash, please release the prisoner and back away."

Menash frowns in confusion. "But Blessed Thanissara, my orders from the council—"

"Elder Ganmor is on his way here. You'll receive new orders when he arrives. I'll take responsibility for releasing the prisoner."

"Yes, Blessed Thanissara." Menash bows respectfully and turns to his warriors. "Release the prisoner and step away."

The warriors blink, grumble in low voices, but obey.

When they release Lynx's arms, he staggers and almost topples before he manages to steady his shaking knees. Clutching the wound in his side, which is pouring blood down his right leg, he gives me a pleading look. "You must hurry. Hurry."

The words are like stones placed upon the grave of the dead. Each has a final thump to it.

Softly, I answer, "There is neither life nor death, slayer nor slain. Isn't that what Quancee taught you?"

The lines at the corners of his dark eyes tighten. "Yes."

Motioning to War Leader Menash, I say, "Order your warriors to escort the Blessed Teacher to a fire where he can stay warm and guard him until Elder Ganmor arrives."

"Of course, Blessed Thanissara." Menash bows again, then gestures to two warriors. "Escort him to a fire. Give him a hide to keep him warm."

Menash remains standing beside the entry while his warriors grip Lynx's arms and support him down the mountain to the closest fire. Lynx keeps turning around to stare pleadingly at me.

All along his path, people gather to whisper in awed voices as he passes. A few disbelievers pelt him with rocks or chunks of ice.

The Dog Soldiers close the circle around me and, one by one, I give each a questioning look. None speaks while he mulls the issue.

Then Pyara says, "I do not believe we have a choice."

Nods go around the circle.

My head dips in the barely discernible nod that seals the decision. "Then let us proceed."

I gesture to Menash. "War Leader, please escort us."

"Of course, elder. Where are we going?"

"I will lead the way," I answer.

Following in Jorgensen's tracks, I resolutely march deeper into the glowing blue caverns with the other Dog Soldiers in single file behind me. Menash brings up the rear, but he doesn't look happy about it.

46

QUILLER

Firelight flutters across the ceiling of the sea cave.

RabbitEar and I sit on either side of our son's body waiting for the final verdict from our sacred elders. One hand of time ago, they gathered on the far side of the village to talk in low voices. I'm certain they are delaying to give me and RabbitEar more time to accept the truth before they must tell us what we already know.

Running my hand over Jawbone's bloodless face, I say, "RabbitEar, he's very cold. Can you fetch him a hide from our lodge?"

"Yes, of course."

He walks away with our three girls trailing like ducks behind him. I'm relieved to have a few moments alone with Jawbone. He looks so peaceful now. His mouth curls into a faint smile and both of his eyes are closed. He could simply be asleep and dreaming. I want to believe this.

RabbitEar ducks from the lodge carrying a caribou hide with our girls trotting behind him. The children have gone as silent as rabbits hiding in the brush from a hunting wolf. They long ago stopped crying. Now, they just follow us wherever we go in the village.

"This will keep him warm, Quiller." RabbitEar kneels and drapes the hide over Jawbone.

Little Fawn hovers behind RabbitEar's shoulder. After a few

heartbeats, she whispers in his ear, "Are you cold, too, Father? May I fetch your heavy coat?"

"No, but thank you," he answers. He sits back down in front of Jawbone, pulls the caribou hide up beneath the boy's blood-less chin, then gently tucks the edges around Jawbone's arms and legs.

"We're right here, son," I whisper. "We've been here all along."

The elders' circle breaks up, and Hoodwink resolutely hob-bles back toward the fire.

RabbitEar watches him like a warrior who knows he's about to be ordered to throw down his weapons. His fists clench.

Hoodwink gives us a tight smile as he lowers himself to sit beside me and slips an arm around my shoulders. In a soft voice, Hoodwink says, "Your son is running the Road of Light to the campfires of the dead. You should not be sad, he—"

"No!" I say. "His soul is here in the village! I feel it here right beside me!" I drag Jawbone's limp body into my arms to protect him from the villains who want to take him away.

Hoodwink peers into RabbitEar's eyes, imploring him to do something.

RabbitEar reaches out to touch my hand. "Quiller, it's time to prepare our son for the burial scaffold."

"You're not putting Jawbone on a burial scaffold! I'll kill you if you try to do that!"

The hatred in my voice stuns even me. I sink back on my heels, and watch the soft firelight fall across RabbitEar's sad face while I gaze into his eyes, eyes I know so well—and so lit-tle. We grew up together, but we've only been married for three summers. At this moment, I don't know him. He's shared my bed, saved my life a dozen times on war walks, and helped me raise four children, but right now he looks at me with the eyes of a baffled stranger.

Petting Little Fawn's hair, RabbitEar rises and walks across the cave to crouch in a spot overlooking Mother Ocean. The waves of zyme are an endless blanket of light green and dark green, adorned with moonlight.

Relatives and friends gather around RabbitEar, trying to talk to him, to ease his grief, but he breaks into sobs and shouts, "Get away from me!"

Rocking my son in my arms, I say, "It's all right, Jawbone. Everything's going to be all right."

But my gaze glides to Hoodwink. Most of the village is looking at him, waiting for what they know comes next. After a decent interval, the sacred elder stands and raises his hands to get everyone's attention, then his melodic voice lifts in the death song. Villagers join in, announcing to the ancestors that an honored child of the Sealion People is on his way to share their campfires.

Only Mink does not sing. He watches me.

Finally, he crouches at my side. "Tell me what to do."

"I—I don't know. I can't think."

Mink sits with me in silence for a time, listening to the singing as he stares out at the ocean. "You've never flinched at death, Quiller. You face everything head on. RabbitEar isn't as strong as you are. He needs you more than you know."

"I can't even help myself, Mink."

"You don't have to do this alone. The entire village is here to help. I'm here to help you."

Mink casts a glance over his shoulder. "Several of the women have already begun quietly gathering the things they'll need to wash and dress your son. You won't have to do that."

Like water draining from a cracked bowl, all of my strength seeps away. I bend down and kiss Jawbone's cold forehead, then I bury my face in his hair and just breathe in my son's scent.

"Mother?" Little Fawn strokes my hair. "Jawbone wouldn't want us to be sad."

For the first time, sobs silently shake my chest. I can't speak.

Mink holds out his arms. "Let me take him? I'll be gentle."

Before I realize it, I've made my decision. I lift my son into my friend's arms, then stagger to my feet.

"I . . ." I'm suddenly at a loss for words. After a deep breath, I continue, "I'll find a place on the rim above the village to build the burial scaffold. I don't think RabbitEar could bear it. Not only that, he needs to rest."

"With your permission, I'd like to carry your son into your lodge and place him beside the fire where the women can care for him."

"Yes, he—he's been cold a long time. Do you think you can convince RabbitEar to stay with him? He's completely exhausted. Maybe he'll get some sleep."

Mink nods. "I can."

I gaze into my old friend's dark eyes. "After that, will you help me build the scaffold?"

"Of course. Let me take care of Jawbone and speak with RabbitEar, then I'll meet you on the rim. Is there anything special I should bring?"

I think back to the day we were throwing rocks into the silver tube after visiting the cavern of blue faces. "Our son would want soft buffalo hides to rest upon, and colorful ribbons fluttering from the mammoth-rib posts. Red and blue. Hoodwink keeps a basket of ribbons in his lodge."

"I'll see to it." Mink rises with Jawbone clutched in his arms and walks away.

The strange otherworldly roars of the Ice Giants seem tortured tonight, as though they, too, grieve the loss of this Sealion child. My gaze scans the children sitting with their parents around the village. We have so few children left. I frown when I see Loon and Chickadee sitting alone in front of our lodge, waiting for their brother.

Little Fawn lovingly pats my back. Long blond hair drapes down the front of her hide cape, and her eyes are as blue as pieces of sky fallen to earth.

"Are you all right?" I ask.

"I'm all right," she answers bravely. "But Mother, I told Loon and Chickadee to sit down and wait. I told them you'd come and explain what happened. They need to hear someone tell them the story in detail, so they can understand."

"Gods," I say and rub a hand over my face. Of course they are waiting for me. "I—I'm sorry. I should have already done that. Forgive me?"

"Father needed you. We could wait."

Dragging myself to my feet, I take Little Fawn's hand and gather every shred of strength I have left. My little girls watched their old families torn apart by lions, just as Jawbone did. They don't need coddling; they need the truth.

As we walk, I say, "Your brother loved you very much, do you know that?"

"Yes," she answers in a trembling voice. "I loved him, too."

I squeeze her hand. "I know you did."

All day long I've been searching behind my eyes for the cave covered by the buffalo hide. The place where no one is looking. The place where I am innocent.

I can't find it.

47

KUJUR

Stopping on a rise to catch my breath, I gaze across the forest that fills the valley bottom. Pines and trees with spreading branches cast shade over the river. Charging down the trail in a cloud of dust, the buffalo head straight for the rolling hills in the distance, joyously rumbling, bucking, and kicking up their heels. Far ahead now, the buffalo flow up a hill and disappear down the other side.

Only the big bull remains, placidly grazing in the tall grass to my right.

Where is the other boy? After he crested the rise where I now stand, he vanished. I have not seen him since.

Using my sleeve, I wipe sweat from my face. I don't know why—there's nothing here to fear—but I'm suddenly afraid. The other boy is gone. The buffalo herd is gone.

As I force my feet to continue down the trail, my only companion is the big bull. He stays with me, striding at my side toward the pines that line the river. My heart almost stops when I see tiny threads of gray rising above the trees.

"Is that smoke?"

As we get closer, I glimpse lodges hidden in the shadows. They are not the dome-shaped lodges of Sealion People, but the trayalon tents of Rust People, like the lodges I grew up with.

Familiar sounds drift to me: voices, laughter, dogs barking playfully.

Warm wind blows down from the surrounding mountains, flapping my sleeves around my arms. As I slow to a walk, the mixed scents of wet earth and wood smoke rise.

A tall man in a silver cape steps out of the trees carrying a bowl. When he dumps it on the ground, a gray haze of ash blows through the air. He starts to return to the village, but stops, lifts a hand to shield his eyes, and studies the trail where I stand beside the buffalo bull.

Suddenly, the man cries out, drops the bowl, and puts a hand to his chest, as though in pain. In an instant, he leaps forward and pounds up the trail toward me, his silver cape billowing behind him.

"He's here!" he shouts.

Other people duck from lodges and stand watching, talking excitedly. Suddenly, a woman shoves through the crowd and flies up the trail behind the man.

Tears slowly fill my eyes.

Why has it taken me so long to recognize my old mother and father? It's been three summers since I've seen them, but they look exactly as they did before the lions came. Father is in the lead, his arms outstretched, running toward me as hard as he can.

"Father! Mother!"

I race down the hill and throw myself into Father's arms. Mother is right behind him, crying, "My son! My son!"

Off to the right, almost invisible in the pine shadows, I see the big buffalo bull expel a deep contented breath. He watches me for a time, then leisurely lopes for the distant horizon to find the rest of his herd.

48

THANISSARA

As we walk along the shore of the paleo-ocean, our footprints fill with water and turn luminous and blue. It's one of the curious wonders of these caverns that never ceases to astound me.

Elder Pyara points to the massive beams that hang from the ceiling and jut up from the water. They are so black that light seems to slide off them. "The Hive. Don't you agree?"

"That was my assessment, as well," I reply.

The other Dog Soldiers mutter and nod. We're all thinking about the story fragment that says in the final days the Jemen turned themselves into insects and lived in hives to hide from their enemies. Though some Dog Soldiers in the past proposed it was literally true, we have always suspected the fragment was to be taken symbolically. The Jemen lived *like* insects. But none of us could ever have imagined the magnitude of this hive. The gleam of the blue algae only carries so high. What we see is the bottom tips of beams that vanish into darkness high overhead, and extend across the ocean for perhaps two days' walk into the distance.

"What other marvels do these caverns hold?" Menash whispers.

"Once we have settled this matter, perhaps we can all begin searching them. But first things first."

"Yes, Thanissara."

The caverns quake as the Ice Giants let out a deep-throated roar, followed by several grating shrieks.

We continue onward, marching in silence around the curving shore until we hear the faint voices of Sticks and Jorgensen.

I say, "The square tunnel that leads to Quancee's chamber is narrow. We will have to enter in single file."

"And it's strewn with rocks and debris," War Leader Menash says. "Lynx tried to barricade the door. It was a fierce fight."

"Very well," Pyara says. "Shall I lead?"

"If you wish to, yes," I answer.

"Apologies, elders," Menash says, "but I think I should take the lead. Not that I believe Sticks or Jorgensen would attack you—"

"But there's no sense in taking risks," I say. "Thank you, War Leader. You're right. We'll follow you."

Menash walks toward the voices, stops at the mouth of the tunnel to listen, and then ducks low to enter. I trail behind him. The other Dog Soldiers follow me. Someone must have stoked the fire in the chamber, for firelight wavers over the tunnel's walls and I see faint inscriptions that I did not see last time I came here. It's a flowing script that rises high and loops. Unfortunately, I do not understand the language of the writers.

Whispers drift down the tunnel, then fade.

My breathing sounds loud in the silence. I move up close to Menash and call out, "Sticks? Jorgensen? We are coming in."

Menash pushes forward, steps around the door that rests on its side to the right, and sidesteps several rocks, before he enters the firelit chamber. "Put down your spear, Blessed Sticks. No one is going to harm you. The elder Dog Soldiers only wish to talk."

When I enter behind Menash, I see the large stones that

litter the chamber. In many places, blood streaks the crystal panels. A fierce fight, indeed.

"Do you feel it?" Pyara asks as he moves up behind me and a shiver goes through him. "There's a strange feeling here."

"Yes. I noticed it the first time I entered this chamber, but it's more powerful now . . . as though something old and wise watches us from a vast distance."

Sticks stands guard with his spear in front of Jorgensen, who has his arm thrust into a gap in the rectangular panels. Jorgensen appears to be feeling around for something. Many broken panels lie scattered across the floor, as though torn out in a hurry and tossed away like refuse.

I say, "War Leader Menash asked you to put down your spear, Sticks."

"Stay back! The Blessed Jorgensen needs more time!" Sticks cries and defiantly keeps his spear aimed at my chest.

"What is he searching for?"

The other Dog Soldiers crowd into the chamber, glance at Sticks, and stare around as though awestruck.

"This is Quancee?" Pyara asks. "These crystal panels on the walls, roof, and ceiling are the evil device?"

Sticks replies, "Yes, of course, and you must stay back while we kill it!"

Menash fingers his spear. "Kill it? Looks dead to me. During the fight, I never saw it move or make a sound."

"Doesn't matter. I studied here in this chamber, and not even I can be sure it's dead. Besides, the Blessed Jorgensen assures me the device is still alive."

Sticks foolishly aims his spear at Menash, and the War Leader's eyes narrow. Quick as lightning, Menash bats the spear from Sticks' hands and picks it up. "Don't mean any disrespect, Blessed Sticks, just don't like people pointin' spears at me."

"You've seen the device, now leave," Sticks orders.

I'm watching Jorgensen. "Vice Admiral, what are you searching for?"

Jorgensen's face contorts as he shoves his arm deeper. "It's right here behind the cryoperm shield, but . . ." He ferociously tugs on something behind the panel. "Why won't it just—"

"Perhaps some part of Quancee is alive and she does not wish you to remove her heart."

"It has a heart?" Menash gives me a curious look, then fixes his gaze on Jorgensen, awaiting his answer.

Jorgensen's deep wrinkles slacken as he pulls his arm from the hole. "Quancee has no ability to—"

"During the Battle of the Stronghold, you didn't think she had the ability to shut parts of herself down either, did you? She surprised her creators then, why not now at the last?"

"Do you have any idea what you're saying?" Jorgensen draws in a halting breath. "Or are you just repeating something Lynx told you?"

"Dog Soldiers have stories about the Old Woman of the Mountain and the ancient battle for her heart." Absently, I gesture to the hole in the panels. "Until this instant, I did not know exactly where to find it."

Jorgensen hobbles forward like a man with a bad case of joint-stiffening disease. His labored breathing sounds loud in the small chamber. "I need that quantum processor. Menash, I order you to reach in there and pull it out. I'm . . . I'm too weak to do it."

Menash turns to me. "Elder?"

"No." I shake my head.

"You morons! You have no understanding—"

"Why do you need her heart?"

Jorgensen wheezes, coughs, and staggers sideways to brace

his shoulder against Quancee, obviously having trouble staying on his feet. "Lynx told you to do this, didn't he?"

I walk over to join the other Dog Soldiers who stand around the fire. "He told me you would be looking for her heart, and I would have a choice to make."

Jorgensen looks furious. Sweat beads his brow. "Where is Lynx? I must speak with him immediately."

"I will find him and bring him here, Blessed Jorgensen," Sticks says as he hurries for the doorway.

"No," I say to Menash, and the War Leader instantly steps to block Sticks' path.

"Why not?" Sticks whirls around to face me with his jaw clenched. "Am I a prisoner?"

"Not at all," I say with a sigh. "It's just pointless. By now, the Blessed Teacher is on a litter and being carried home to his people in Sky Ice Village."

"Fools!" Jorgensen shouts, then falls into a coughing fit that doubles him over.

I study the last of the Jemen, wondering what the world will be like without his kind. Dog Soldiers will be extinct soon, as well, and so will Sealion People. What will the world be like without any of us? There are many story fragments that say we were all extinct once before, along with mammoths, mastodons, and giant lions, and Mother Earth was lonely and desolate without her ancient companions. This time, there will be no one to breathe upon the bones of our ancestors and re-create us. Perhaps that is the true way of existence—the dead should stay dead—but I pray Rust People can find a way to survive the expanding Ice Giants.

I turn to Menash. "War Leader, please escort Sticks outside while we speak with the Blessed Jorgensen. We'll be out as soon as this is over."

Menash glances at Jorgensen, and gives me a doubtful look. "Are you sure you want to be alone—"

"Yes. Thank you. If any part of Quancee is alive, I'm sure she will keep us safe."

Menash gives me a worried look, glances at the curious crystal chamber, and uses his spear to gesture to Sticks. "Don't try to run, Sticks. Understand?"

"This is ridiculous," Sticks says through gritted teeth, throws up his hands, and strides for the door.

When they are gone, Jorgensen's legs wobble. Slowly, he slides down the panels to sit among the broken crystals flashing with firelight, and puts a hand to his chest. "You're working with Lynx? That's a . . . a surprise." He exhales and fluid bubbles at his lips. "You have no idea what . . . what you . . ."

I fold my hands before me. The chamber suddenly fills with the scent of fear sweat, and the hate in Jorgensen's eyes fades to blind terror as he looks around.

Tilting my head to the side, I see no shred of the godlike figure who has paraded through our villages with such arrogance over the past three summers. The figure before me is just a skinny, white-haired old man with a strangely shaped skull.

I nod to the other Dog Soldiers, and they quietly walk over and form a semicircle around Jorgensen. When I join them, I kneel and stare into Jorgensen's strange blue eyes. His deep wrinkles cast a web of shadows over his face.

Softly, I ask, "Do you know the Dog Soldiers' prophecy about the last Jemen?"

He laughs. "Idiotic—"

"Our prophecy tells us of a time," I say as I pull the book from my cape pocket, "when the last Dog Soldier will give the last Earthbound Jemen our most sacred book. We have protected that book for him for over one thousand summers. For you, I suppose. It is said that when we give the book to the last

Jemen, he will breathe upon it and the book will come to life and sail far away beyond the Road of Light until it finds the Sky Jemen and brings them home. Then the Ice Giants will melt and the world will warm and become the paradise it once was."

Jorgensen desperately gasps for air. "Get it through . . . your skulls. Nobody's coming. Ever."

The last of the Jemen coughs so hard and long, he loses his balance and topples onto his side, where he sprawls across the floor. He struggles to rise, but his shaking arms won't support him. He rolls back against the firelit crystal panels.

Pressing my lips to the sacred book, I hand it to Jorgensen. "This is yours now."

When he makes no move to reach for the book, I gently place it on the floor in front of his mouth where he can't help but breathe upon the ancient pages, yellowed with age.

"Let us begin," I instruct and rise to my feet.

Pyara lifts his voice in the sacred chant that our order has memorized for centuries, but never once spoken aloud. As each of us joins him, our deep voices reverberate from Quancee's crystalline body until the entire chamber rings.

Hallowed be the names of the Blessed Jemen who created the universe: Hammeroff and Heel-Catcher, Penrose and Posner, Heisenberg and He-Laughs, Fisher and the White Stone . . .

The resonance in the small chamber is so unearthly, it's stunning.

Jorgensen vents an ugly laugh and whispers, "Cl-clowns."

As we continue our chant, his gasping grows more hoarse and desperate, until he sprawls across the floor with his mouth gaping. I watch the light go out of his strange blue eyes.

"Pyara? Please make certain?"

Pyara crouches and places two fingers on the big artery in Jorgensen's throat, waits, then gives me a nod. "Yes. Gone."

"Very well."

Stepping around the Jemen's body, I walk to the hole in the crystal panels and gently stroke Quancee's face. "If you can hear me, I assume you know who I am, and that I mean you no harm."

I neither hear nor feel an answer, and so fear tingles my spine as I slip my arm into the hole and pat around until I find what feels like a shield. Reaching behind it, I find a round object about the size of my fist; it's intensely cold. When I grasp it, the object seems to slide into my hand of its own volition . . . as though giving itself to me.

I pull it out and hold it in my open palm to examine it.

"Is that her heart?" Pyara asks in awe as he moves closer to me. "It resembles a silver eyeball with a black stripe running across it."

"It must be." The heart is so cold the warm air around it condenses and forms wisps of cloud. "It's freezing. I can't hold it for long."

"What do we do now?" Pyara asks.

Tucking the egg in my cape pocket, I look at the other Dog Soldiers. "Let's gather these rocks and wall up this chamber forever. That way, if she wishes to return, her crystal body will be unharmed and waiting for her."

49

QUILLER

Sister Sky dances spectacularly tonight. As her skirt whirls, pale green curtains of light ripple and flash across the heavens.

Mink holds the last mammoth rib in position while I use sinew to tie it to the bed of the scaffold. We've both been quiet as we work, occasionally glancing up at Sister Sky. I have only been into the high Ice Giant Mountains twice, but I was amazed at the different sky colors. Along the shore, the zyme light mutes the colors, but if you climb high enough, Sister Sky's ripples are teal, turquoise, and lavender. Not only that, the Road of Light is so clear you can almost reach out and touch it. This evening, the Road is barely visible as a pale streak cutting through the campfires of the dead.

My voice is hollow when I ask, "Do you think my son is already there?"

Mink follows my gaze. "If he is, he's no longer cold or hungry. The ancestors are holding him in their arms. He's happy, Quiller."

I bend down to pick up the long red and blue ribbons of painted mastodon hide, and my throat constricts. It takes me a few moments to swallow my grief before I can say, "How was RabbitEar when you accompanied him to our lodge?"

I hand half the ribbons, each as long as I am tall, to Mink.

He takes them, pulls out a red ribbon, and carefully ties it to the northwest corner of the scaffold. "After I placed Jawbone in bed, he curled his body around his son. RabbitEar was asleep in heartbeats. The women with the burial preparations sat down outside to wait."

Tears blur my eyes. I wipe them on my hide sleeve and walk to the northeast pole to tie a blue ribbon. "Thank you."

Mink follows me and ties a red ribbon beside it. We are both silent, lost in our own thoughts. I'm remembering the sweet high-pitched laugher of my son the first time he cast his boy's spear and hit a target painted on a rock.

From Mink's expression, I suspect he's remembering other scaffolds, other deaths. There have been so many. Each loss weighs on my chest like a granite boulder, making it hard to think. When we walk to the last pole, I find my knees are shaking, and I have to grab for the scaffold to steady myself.

"Why don't you sit down for a time?" Mink softly asks. "I'll finish tying the ribbons."

I place my remaining ribbons in his hand, say, "Just for a moment."

Sitting down, I try to clear my jumbled thoughts.

The slopes of the Ice Giants are alight with Sister Sky's dance. It's an unearthly sight, for thousands of reflections leap and shoot through the air above the glaciers like flickers of fox-fire. In the low growls that shudder the mountains, I hear Ice Giants whimpering and gnashing their teeth as though in despair.

"Did my girls follow RabbitEar into the lodge?"

Mink carefully ties another ribbon to the scaffold—a blue ribbon that whips and snaps when a gust sweeps the shore. "Yes. Loon and Chickadee went to sleep. Little Fawn sat beside her brother and stroked his hair while she whispered to him. I couldn't hear what she was saying."

I'm suddenly totally exhausted. "She'll be all right. She's a strong girl, and she knows her sisters and father need her."

"And her mother, too, I think," Mink adds with a sad smile.

When lions roar, I scramble to my feet and reach for my spear where it leans against the scaffold. "Sounds like the pride has come down from the high country to hunt the tundra."

"Yes." Mink walks a short distance away to scan the darkness. "They sound close. Do you see them out there?"

In the wavering gleam, everything appears to be moving. But there are dark shapes on the trail to the north. I point at them with my spear. "What's that?"

As they get closer, they crystallize into trotting humans. Their silver capes shimmer with zyme glow.

"Four Rust People. Looks like they're carrying a litter."

"Think they're coming here, to Sky Ice Village, or just passing by?" I ask.

"We'll know soon enough."

Mink walks back and retrieves his spear from where it rests on the ground.

We stand side by side with our spears held across our chests as the party winds along the rim trail. When they spy us, the lead warrior, calls, "Don't cast! We are on a peace mission. Just bearing the body of the Blessed Teacher Lynx back to his family."

Barely audible, I hear myself say, ". . . body?"

Mink exchanges a glance with me and we break into a run, charging for the procession. Mink calls, "I am his brother. Is he injured?"

"Of course," the lead warrior calls.

Mink and I halt on either side of the litter, gazing down upon a man we both love. Spear wounds slice Lynx's clothing and leak blood down onto the litter. A lot of blood.

Mink shouts, "What happened?"

The man gives him an irritated shrug. "Your brother tried to protect the evil device and War Leader Menash stopped him. Be glad he's alive. If it had not been for Elder Thanissara, your brother's bones would be cracking between the jaws of dogs right now."

Lynx seems to rouse. He weakly lifts his head and blinks at me and Mink, then his gaze goes to the burial scaffold. "One of the . . . elders?" he asks.

"No." I exhale the words. "My thirteen-summers-old son."

Agony tenses his face. "Oh . . ."

As Lynx closes his eyes and sinks back to the litter, Mink walks forward and grasps hold of one of the litter poles. "Release the litter to us. We will carry him to our healers so they can bandage his wounds. You and your warriors may return home."

"Gladly."

The warriors step back and allow us to grasp the litter poles. Mink takes the top and I take the bottom. Neither of us speaks while we watch the Rust People trot away into the darkness.

I carry the litter past the burial scaffold toward the cliff trail to Sky Ice Village. As we walk, trying not to jostle Lynx, Mink looks down at his brother.

In a sympathetic voice, he asks, "Is Quancee dead?"

"She's gone, Mink. That's all I know."

50

LYNX

I've been lying beside the central fire for most of the night listening to the weeping that fills Sky Ice Village. Elder Hoodwink bandaged my spear wounds, but they seem small measure compared to the death of a child.

It's about two hands of time before dawn. A few people wander about the village, mostly elders. Mink sits beside me, feeding driftwood to the central fire to keep me warm, but his gaze constantly slides to Quiller where she sits on the lip of the sea cave. Once or twice, Mink went to speak with her, but no one else wants to be shouted at. I haven't seen RabbitEar or her daughters at all. Though earlier in the evening, village women came and went from their lodge, carrying bowls of water and clean clothing. No one has told me, but I assume they've bathed and dressed the body of the dead boy.

I did not know Jawbone well, but the sounds of grief that have issued from the lodges throughout the night tell me he was greatly loved.

As always before dawn, the pungency of the zyme is powerful. In the distance, it rides the waves like a rumpled green blanket. The only happy sound tonight is the cooing and laughter of Mink's newest child that drifts from his lodge. I can imagine Gray Dove holding the baby to her breast, smiling down at him as she feeds him.

The world goes on . . .

We have all watched companions, lovers, spouses, and children vanish from the world. The fortunate ones simply drifted away in their beds like leaves torn from trees. Most did not die in peace. Those are the hardest vigils.

I wonder if Quancee died in peace. Was there still a shred of consciousness in her body when Jorgensen tore her apart? Did she wonder where I was? Why I was not there to protect her? Did she weep in loneliness?

Tears lodge in my throat.

My life will forever be inextricably, deeply, and eternally bound to the moment of her death. I am convinced that I was only really alive when she was looking at me, and now I am just one of the odd shadows moving across the wall of Plato's cave—a dim and amorphous shape. Not real.

Quancee said death was a tiny stepping stone in a vast universe of time coordinates, and that the coordinates least observed, least distinguished, were the best coordinates, because wave functions move on. Splashes and disturbances make the flow rocky and painful. It's easier, she said, if a wave can merely flow unnoticed through the vast sea.

But I am too stupid to grasp what that means. All I know is that she is gone from my heart, and all that remains is a gaping chasm where she once loved me.

"Are you awake?" Mink whispers.

"Yes."

"You must be hurting. Let me dip you another cup of willow-bark tea."

"Thank you, brother."

Mink picks up a wooden cup, dips it into the bag hanging from the tripod, and carries it around the fire to set it beside me. In the firelight, his heavy brow ridge casts a shadow over his sunken eyes. I'm sure mine does as well. We look so much alike.

As Mink crouches, he casts a glance at Quiller. Bushy red hair blows around her freckled face, which has a green tint from the zyme.

"I'm glad you're here, Lynx. She's going to need a friend."

"She has RabbitEar."

"RabbitEar is as broken as she is. You've been her best friend since you were children. She trusts you. Guilt is her greatest enemy now."

"Because she took her son to climb the quest wall?"

Mink's black brows pull together over his wide nose. "Yes. The elders told her it was necessary to heal the boy, but she didn't want to do it. Quiller thought it was too dangerous this time of season, and it turned out she was right."

Quiller straightens slightly at the sound of our voices, as though she heard her name and knows we're talking about her. With great difficulty, she rises on shaking legs, stiffens her spine, and gazes out at the luminous ocean. Finally, she strides to the fire.

Mink stands up, says, "Are you hungry? Gray Dove is making fish stew for breakfast. When it's cooked I'll bring you a bowl. You'll feel better if you eat."

"Thank you, Mink. I am hungry."

Quiller sits down beside me and watches Mink walk to his lodge.

Neither of us says anything for a time. We just sit in companionable silence. She is the bravest person I have ever known, but she's trying to still her quaking hands by clasping them together in her lap.

"Are you all right, Lynx?" she inquires.

"I will be. Hoodwink says the punctures in my arms and legs will heal. He's only worried about the one in my side. It missed the liver and the guts, but it's still deep, and he's worried about . . . evil spirits nesting in the wound."

I always have to stop myself from saying things that will make no sense to them. Words like "bacteria" would be a barrier to understanding, not an aid, and I am acutely aware that I must not allow myself to get so far from my people's perception of the world that I start to view them as intellectual insects, as Jorgensen does.

"I'm more concerned about you, Quiller. Are you all right?"

"No."

She heaves a tired breath and cocks her head as though listening to the distant deep-throated roars of the Ice Giants. Reflections dance across the highest peaks, green as grass and luminescent as polished jade.

I don't say anything for a time, just lick my own internal wounds. Lonely, frightened, and more helpless in the face of life than I have ever been, it's hard to imagine how I can help her.

But I softly say, "It's all so complicated, isn't it?"

"What is?"

"Loss. The person I knew as Lynx died yesterday. The person I knew as Quancee died, too. The world I loved died. I'm grieving so many deaths it's impossible to breathe. I was wondering if you feel the same way."

Slowly, she turns to stare at me. "None of that was your fault, Lynx, but this is my fault. I killed my son. Now I have to learn to live with it."

Reaching out, I pull one of her hands from her lap and hold tight to it. "No one has told me how it happened."

She shakes her head, and I think she means she can't, then she says, "I told you my son was sick, having sp-spells. The elders said he had to go on a spirit quest, because only a spirit helper could heal him."

"And because you loved him you took him to the quest wall."

"Yes." She whispers the word as though afraid to say it aloud.

"Standing at the bottom of the trail, my son begged me to take him home and I . . ."

She can't go on and looks away.

"Quiller, you tried to heal your sick son. What happened is no one's fault. You mustn't blame yourself or RabbitEar."

Quiller gazes at the fire. "I don't blame RabbitEar. If I had taken my son's hand and led him home, RabbitEar would have just sighed and followed us back to Sky Ice Village. That's what I should have done."

"Maybe. I don't know."

Her brow furrows. "How can you say that?"

"Something Quancee told me, I . . ." I stop, afraid that I'm about to make myself even more alien to my people than I already am.

Quiller exhales a deep breath that frosts in the cold air. "What did she tell you?"

"I'm not sure I can explain . . ." I helplessly shake my head, but I continue, "Quancee would tell you that you did take his hand. You led him home a hundred times in a hundred different places, and in those places he may still be alive. What you must ask is why, in this place, did he die? There is always a reason."

"A reason? For the death of an innocent child? There's no reason for any of this."

"I know it feels that way."

The lines at the corners of her eyes deepen. Sharply, she says, "Explain better. What do you mean he may still be alive?"

"I mean . . ." I shift to ease the pain of the spear wound in my side, which has started to throb. "There are other worlds. They are all around us, and we are embedded in them, moving through them, part of them."

"Blessed gods," Quiller hisses through gritted teeth. When she hangs her head, red hair falls around her face. "You've become so odd."

"I try not to be."

She lifts her head. "Why do you think Quancee died?"

A swallow goes down my throat. "I don't know. There is an answer. I just . . . I don't know what it is."

"And it's killing you inside, isn't it?"

"Yes."

The tear that falls from her eye onto my hand is warm. "I will bury my son this morning, Lynx. This is the only world I care about."

Pulling her hand from mine, she rises and returns to sit upon the lip of the cave and stare out at the brightening sea.

I am alone and I have failed, not just failed to save Quancee. I've failed to help my best friend and my people. I've lived as a hermit in a cave with a magical creature they will never understand. My greatest failure is me. Though I tried, I never learned enough. I never understood enough.

The flames burn higher and heat bathes my cold face. My bones feel hollow, as though I'm fading away and there's too little left to tie me here. Perhaps my quantum wave is moving on . . .

Sinking back against my hides, I watch the firelight fluttering over the cave ceiling, and wonder why I'm such a fool. How could I have expected my words to comfort Quiller? They do not comfort me. Eventually, I believe, they will ease my pain, but at this moment all I know is that Quancee is not here in this world; she is just as dead as Jawbone is for Quiller, and there's no understanding any of it.

51

MINK

O f course I'll stay, elder."

"Thank you, War Leader." Hoodwink turns to give Lynx a worried appraisal where he lies beneath a mound of hides beside the central fire. "I know you wish to attend the burial, but your brother's fever is bad this morning. He's confused and raving. Someone must remain to care for him in case he tries to rise. Can't afford to have those wounds break open again."

"I understand."

Hoodwink pats my shoulder. "I will explain to Quiller that you will not be able to help carry the burial litter today."

"Thank you."

Hoodwink props his walking stick and gingerly hobbles to where Quiller has crouched on the lip of the cave all night. When Hoodwink sits down beside her and slips an arm around her back, she gives him a vaguely disapproving look.

The cave is a flurry of activity. Five children quietly slip through the village with dogs trotting at their heels. My wife and two boys stand over the small fire outside our lodge. The cradleboard that carries our newest child leans against the cave wall a pace away. I can hear the baby gurgling as it watches Gray Dove stir the big bag of glypt stew that swings from the tripod. When the burial is over, everyone will return here to feast and tell stories about Jawbone.

"Mink?"

"I'm right here, brother." I crouch at Lynx's side.

He gazes up at me with dazed eyes. "Where's Siskin? Tell her to come back, please."

I pull the hides up beneath his chin and smile down at him. Siskin, his wife, died three summers ago. "I don't know where she went," I answer. "I'll have someone find her."

The words seem to ease him. Lynx swallows, and his head falls to the side to face the fire. He blinks lazily at the flames.

I feel his fiery forehead. "You're very hot. Let me dip you another cup of willow-bark tea."

As I reach for his cup and sink it into the tea bag, Lynx grimaces as though an unpleasant thought just occurred to him.

"She . . . Siskin is dead, isn't she?"

"Yes, brother. She was killed by lions three summers ago."

"But she was just here."

I pull the cup out dripping. "That's good. Did she tell you that you're fevered and need to drink this cup of tea?"

"I miss her. It's been . . . a long time."

I slip an arm beneath his back and gently lift him while I push the cup against his lips. "Drink this."

Lynx—obedient as one of my young sons—gulps noisily. Then, turning his head away, he says, "Bitter."

"Very, but it will help your fever." I tilt the cup again, and he draws a deep breath and drinks more. When he chokes and coughs, I pull it away. "Sorry, not trying to drown you."

"Thank you. For helping me."

"I'm your brother. I don't have a choice."

Lynx gives me a dazed smile. "Nonetheless."

As I rest the cup beside the hearthstones, his eyes follow me, a vague stirring of concern in them.

"Quiller . . . She buries her son today, doesn't she?"

"Yes, she does."

A slow knife of grief cuts its way through my body, penetrating clean through even my death-hardened warrior's soul. I'm not as tough as I think I am, though I work hard to give a good imitation of it.

"When?"

"Soon, I think. Don't worry, I'm staying with you. You're fever-stupid. I don't want you to rise and think you can walk on air out beyond the cliff edge."

His gaze wanders to the ocean. "Arakie told me . . ." He seems to lose his thread of thought. "He—he told me the Jemen thought zyme would be their salvation. It would feed people, be fuel, and cool the world."

"Didn't work out so well, did it?" I say with a hint of sarcasm. Zyme is an empty-hearted monster; it kills everything that gets within its reach. But there are ancient stories about the Jemen and the zyme. Our elders tell them around the winter fires . . .

"Mink? Quancee is dead, too, isn't she?" He shifts uncomfortably as though easing the ache in his side. "I can't . . . feel her presence."

"You told me yesterday that she was gone."

Tears well in his eyes. "Neither slayer nor slain. Just a tiny step to another coordinate. Why can't I believe that?"

"I don't know, brother. I don't understand a word you're saying."

Lynx closes his eyes, and I ease his body back to the hides where he can rest. His long sweat-soaked black hair sticks to his flushed cheeks. "Try to sleep, all right?"

Incoherently, he murmurs, ". . . cold lap . . . alien stones . . . afraid. Afraid."

"Don't be. I'm right here. I'm not leaving you."

When I see RabbitEar duck out of his lodge carrying a blanket-wrapped bundle in his arms, my heart turns to stone in my chest. Their three daughters follow behind him, along with Quiller's black dog Crow. Crow keeps smelling the bundle and using her teeth to tug at the hides that wrap the dead boy as though intent upon unwrapping him. RabbitEar bats the dog's nose away and tenderly lays the body on the litter I built last night, then he staggers back a step and searches for his wife.

Quiller rises, helps Elder Hoodwink to his feet, and stares at RabbitEar with blank, unfeeling eyes. She's walled off the pain so she can do what must be done. As she stoically walks past me, I stand up and say, "Just a little while longer. It'll be over soon."

"I know." She nods back—one warrior to another—and walks to pick up the top litter poles. RabbitEar lifts the back, and together they solemnly carry their precious son up the cliff trail. The elders follow, then the rest of the village falls into line behind them. The sacred songs ring out as they climb toward the burial scaffold.

I wait until they move beyond my sight before I exhale the breath I've been holding. I've been trying not to imagine what I would do if it was one of my sons on that litter, but it's hard to keep the images out of my head. I keep seeing my eldest's son's face beneath the hides, his skin white and bloodless, his lips blue. Turns my blood to ice.

"Brother?" Lynx whispers. "They're coming."

"They just left. It'll be at least one hand of time before they return. Sleep while they're gone. The village will be loud with weeping and songs when they return."

"No, not . . ." he says in a hushed voice. "Listen."

I cock my head. "All I hear is a couple of bison bulls roaring and the rumbles of the Ice Giants, but . . ."

My voice trails away when I see five men, all Dog Soldiers,

marching down the trail. Their silver capes sway around their tall willowy bodies. The old man in the lead has very dark skin and a bushy shock of white hair. "Blessed gods, is that the legendary Thanissara?"

Lynx suddenly blinks as though coming back to himself. He twists his head to look. "Yes."

"How did you know they were coming?"

He weakly shakes his head.

I squint at the lead Dog Soldier. "I've never seen Thanissara up close. He carries himself with an odd dignity, doesn't he?"

"I need to s-speak . . . with him."

"Truly? After your words about being afraid of alien stones, I'm not sure you can speak with anyone and make sense."

Lynx weakly tries to shove up on one elbow. "Can you help me sit up?"

"I don't think that's a good idea, but what if I rearrange the hides behind you to prop you up a bit?"

Lynx nods, and while I keep one eye on the Dog Soldiers, I move around to lift his shoulders so I can pile the hides up behind him. They've just entered the sea cave and are surveying the seven mammoth-hide lodges and numerous fires. After whispering to one another, four of the Dog Soldiers turn their backs to me and look up the trail, as though guarding the path. Only Thanissara walks forward.

I stand and bow respectfully to him. "Elder. Welcome. Please allow me to thank you for saving my brother's life. How may I help you?"

"I must speak with the Blessed Teacher, if he is well enough."

It's always strange hearing my younger brother referred to in this manner, but I extend a hand to Lynx. "Go ahead, but he is fevered from the wounds your warriors gave him. I'm not sure he can carry on a—"

"Hopefully, I can help with that." Thanissara shoves aside

his long cape and unlaces his belt pouch to pull out four clear tubes filled with colorful powders. I've seen them many times on the rear shelf in Quancee's chamber. As he kneels beside Lynx, he says, "I thought you might need these medicinal plants." He places them on the ground at Lynx's side.

Lynx manages a feeble smile. "Yes. They will help."

I shift to brace my feet. "Elder, your people almost killed my brother. It was very risky coming here. Weren't you afraid—"

"It was worth it," he says curtly. "I had to see Lynx."

Lynx blinks as though trying to focus his eyes. "What happened? At the end? Please, tell me."

Thanissara reaches back into his belt pouch and draws out a silver eyeball-shaped object. "I found this. Though our order would like to protect it, I believe she would wish you to have it."

He hands the object to Lynx and as my brother turns it in his hand, I see the thin black stripe that cuts across one side like a thin pupil. "What is it?" Lynx asks. "It's very cold."

"Ah," Thanissara says with a nod. "You've never seen it before. That makes sense. I would not have known what it was if I hadn't seen Jorgensen reaching for it through the crystal pane he'd broken out."

"Jorgensen?" Lynx asks with a tremor in his voice. "Is he—"

"Dead."

In astonishment, I glance between Lynx and Thanissara. "Did you kill him? You killed the last of the Jemen?"

"We did not, War Leader. He died from extreme old age. The last thing he wanted"—he points to the silver object—"was Quancee's heart."

Lynx suddenly seems to comprehend what he's holding in his hand. As tears fill his eyes, he clutches it against his chest. "Thank you, elder. I will guard it with my life."

Thanissara rises to his feet. "I know you will. If you ever need my assistance—"

"Yes. I—I do, elder." Lynx lifts his fever-brilliant gaze to the old Dog Soldier. "When I am better . . . there's something I would like to show you."

"Very well." The Dog Soldier graciously inclines his white head. "I'll be waiting for you. Come find me when you are able."

Thanissara bows to me again, a deep respectful bow, turns and walks away. When he nears the other Dog Soldiers, a pathway opens between them, allowing him to walk through, then they fall into line and march up the trail out of my sight.

I frown down at Lynx, who is holding the object like a rare gem. "What is that thing? He called it a heart."

"Purpose," he replies, barely audible. "I was so lost without her. I didn't realize that it doesn't matter if she is gone. I am still her caretaker."

Lynx squeezes his eyes closed and holds the silver eyeball to his lips. His words are nonsense to me:

"Are you looking, Quancee? I am looking. I will always be looking."

52

THANISSARA

Two moons later . . .

We have been hiking through the Ice Giant Mountains for four days. With Lynx's healing spear wounds, he cannot walk very fast, and at night he groans from pain, which means none of us has gotten much sleep.

I rub my tired eyes and take a moment to look out across the vista. To the north and east, the glacial slopes shine wetly. In the heat of summer, they always shimmer with meltwater, but today is especially glorious. The ice gleams like polished azure, broken here and there by islands of pines, and black crevasses that seemingly drop away into the endless rumbling depths of the underworld.

Pyara and Homara hike behind me, but my gaze seeks out Lynx, who is cautiously propping his walking stick in the washed gravel of the trail before he dares to take another step. He moves like an old man, and I know this journey causes him great pain in more ways than one.

Pyara hikes up beside me, breathing hard, and says, "He's having a difficult day."

"Yes. I suspect by now he wishes he'd waited another moon to bring us here."

"He's still told you nothing about our destination?"

"No. Just that it's a crevasse and an answer to a question I once asked him."

I wait for Homara to catch up, then I begin methodically leading the way up the icy slopes to the place where, three summers ago, Lynx says he climbed out of the monstrous crevasse that almost claimed his life.

"Careful here," I tell my companions. "The trail has been melting out. It's running water."

As I walk, I study the rivulets that trickle down the trail. My hide boots are soaked, my feet ice cold.

When we crest the hill, I see Lynx standing before a dark triangular maw. The entry to the crevasse? If so, it's almost hidden among a cluster of head-high black boulders.

"Is that it?" I call.

"Yes." Lynx nods. "It's a miracle we found it so easily today."

"It isn't always this easy?"

"No." Lynx leans heavily on his walking stick, and I note that his legs are shaking. "The entry constantly melts closed, then opens in a new location. I've been coming here for three summers and rarely found it in the same place. Today's entry is a good distance from where I originally escaped the crevasse."

When I reach the entry, I glance at Lynx and then down into the darkness. Moans and shrieks echo from the maw, rising from deep inside the earth, as though the Ice Giants are warning us to turn back.

"Do you need to rest for a time before we explore the crevasse?" I ask. "You're exhausted and in pain, Lynx. I can see that."

"No, elder. If we're going to make it back to our camp before the lions and wolves hunt in the darkness, we should light our torches and hurry." He gestures to the other Dog Soldiers.

Elder Pyara draws a stone bowl of hot coals from his belt pouch, while Homara pulls two torches from the quiver over his left shoulder.

Lynx doesn't wait for the light. Ducking low, he walks inside and disappears into the darkness. I follow him.

The first thing I notice is the mossy scent of water. I stop and wait for torchlight to waver over the cavern walls. As Pyara and Homara enter, they suck in deep breaths.

A vast underworld ocean spreads to our right. It's so black the torch's gleam seems to skim off the surface.

Lynx calls, "It isn't far."

I see him up ahead, moving at the edge of the light. As we follow, our breathing is magnified a hundred-fold, until the cavern hisses like a gigantic serpent.

Walking deeper takes an act of courage, for the cave opens up to a huge cavern that arches at least three hundred hands over our heads. Smaller caves and tunnels jut off in every direction. The torches flare as we move past each entry and continue down into the groaning darkness.

Pyara and Homara mutter amongst themselves, stopping often to examine some curious tunnel, but I march onward without delay. I don't wish to lose sight of Lynx.

My feet crunch gravel as I curve around the edge of the water and glimpse a monstrous ice wall ahead. Lynx leans one shoulder against the wall as though propping himself up to wait for me. His long black hair trembles where it hangs down the front of his cape, and I wonder how much longer he can stay on his feet.

I turn and call, "Please bring up the torches."

Pyara and Homara quickly trot forward.

I head toward Lynx in a bubble of torchlight that seems alive, flying over the walls and ceiling.

When I stand beside Lynx and gaze at the torchlit ice wall, I cannot speak.

"Blessed gods," Pyara blurts and stops dead in his tracks. "What is this place?"

"It . . . it's unbelievable," Homara whispers as he comes to stand at my side to peer at the fantastic shapes buried in the ice. The flickering light catches in the angles of the frozen pyramids and rectangles that topple over each other as they recede far back into the glacier.

"There are stories . . ." I say in awe, "of ancient Jemen cities buried in the belly of the Ice Giants, but I never thought I'd see one."

"We need to walk a few more paces down into the caverns." Lynx shoves away from the wall with a grimace and slowly makes his way down the trail.

"Thanissara?" Pyara says. "Would you mind if we remained here to study the ruins?"

"Not at all. I'd like to study them more myself. Please hand me one of the torches."

Pyara extends a torch, and I lift it high to light the way ahead. Lynx is waiting for me. "Please, continue on."

We follow the curving ice wall to a new part of the frozen city, where Lynx halts.

"This is what I wanted to show you." He extends a hand to the ice. "You'll have to get close to see it."

"What is it?" I lean forward with my nose almost touching the wall and squint into the torchlit depths of the ice where line after line of shelves extend for as far back as I can see. "Are those . . . books?" I ask in an astonished whisper. "The colorful spines of books?"

"Yes." Lynx grasps my hand that holds the torch and moves it slightly to the left. "Can you read the spine of the book that is shelved seventh from the right on the closest shelf?"

The torch's gleam flashes around the ice like lightning, bouncing from the spines so that the titles waver, appearing to rush close to me before they dance back. I squint hard, and when I finally make out most of the letters, my whole body tingles.

I straighten and stand with my mouth open for a long moment before I can ask, "Volume Omega?"

"Yes. You said you would give your very life to know Quancee's story. It's right there, elder. Twelve hand-lengths away."

My gaze searches the towering ice wall. "But how can we get to it without destabilizing the entire cavern and bringing it down on top of us?"

Lynx leans more heavily on his walking stick. After a lengthy pause, he says, "Quancee taught me that you should never reach for truth unless you know full well it may bring your entire world down on top of you. I suspect Volume Omega will destroy everything you believe."

I stare at the title on the spine of the book—*The Origins of Quantum Consciousness*—and desperate longing fills me. "Are you asking me if I think her story is worth it?"

The Blessed Teacher blinks at the torchlight fluttering over the cavern. "It may be worth it for you."

He turns and walks back toward the entrance.

"It isn't worth it for you?" I call.

He pauses briefly, softly replies, "No, elder," and continues to walk away.

I trot after him, but Homara grabs my sleeve. "Please, speak with us about the frozen city. We must discuss what it means for our stories. Do you think this is the city referenced in our fragment about Seacouver?"

"It may be. Let's discuss it around the campfire tonight. I must speak with the Blessed Teacher now."

"Of course, forgive me."

I hurry after Lynx.

When I finally duck outside into the brilliant sunlight, I see Lynx sitting with his back leaned against one of the black boulders with his legs outstretched and his eyes closed. He looks utterly exhausted. Concerned, I ask, "Are you well?"

He opens his eyes and watches me trot down the trail to stand over him. "I hurt, elder. In more ways than I can count."

"Can I help?"

"The pain is my burden to carry."

As I breathe in the glacial fragrances, I see his hand drift to his belt bag. I do not know what rests inside. It seems to take an act of will for him to reach for the laces and pull the bag open.

"Ah," I murmur when I see the glimmering silver orb inside. "I wondered if you kept her with you at all times, as I would."

He speaks quietly, but not to me. "When I was lost, you found me here. Remember?"

Quancee's heart is silent, flickering in the sunlit reflections. But Lynx cocks his head, as though straining to hear her answer.

"Is it still cold?"

"No. She's warm. I keep her warm."

Gently, I say, "Lynx, I hope you understand that you are no longer alone in your search to understand her. Even if we never manage to extract Volume Omega from the ice, over the long summers ahead, we will speak of Quancee around a thousand campfires. Perhaps you can find some peace in those discussions."

"I will be very happy to talk about her with you, elder. But not if you've read Volume Omega. In that case, you will never see me again."

Taken aback, I stare at him. "But why? I don't understand. Don't you care how the Jemen created her? How her consciousness emerged? How she—"

"No." The word is spoken with a brutal finality. "They never understood her. They thought she was a tool. A weapon. And it broke her heart." Tenderly, he draws the silver orb from the bag and holds it to his chest. "I will find no truths in Volume Omega, just misunderstandings, and I cannot bear to read them or hear them repeated by those who know less about her than I do."

The anger in his voice is tempered with tears.

"I see. I think."

I slump down beside him and frown out across the slopes of the Ice Giants. As the sunlight shines upon the dark boulders, they gather the heat and warm the air around us. I unlace my cape and let it fall open to the cool breeze while I try to fathom what it must have been like for him to live with a creature that could hold the winds of time in her hands and journey to places that have not yet existed. All I know are bits and pieces of old stories that speak of the dangerous powers of the Old Woman of the Mountain.

"What did you mean when you said she found you here?"

He seems to be deciding whether or not to answer. "I was trapped in this crevasse, alone in the darkness, freezing to death, when I heard my dead wife Siskin calling to me. She appeared and led me outside. She saved me."

"Your dead wife?"

Lynx props a fist upon the ground, as if trying to control the agony of the memory. "I didn't realize until much later that it was Quancee taking the form of my wife to help me. Recently I've been seeing Siskin everywhere, just glimpses. She appears and disappears. It's as if she's searching . . ." His jaw trembles before he clenches his teeth.

Slowly, I begin to understand the depths of his loneliness. "You hope she will find you here, as she once did."

"It's possible, isn't it?"

Reaching out, I rest a companionable hand on his fist. His fingers are cold. "Of course it is."

I bow my head and heave a sigh when I realize the implications of what he's saying. Blessed Spirits, why do the gods dangle eternal truths before my eyes and then snap their fingers and make them vanish before I can grasp them? But there are truths that humans are too feeble to grasp, and even the faintest understanding will be misconstrued and used for evil purposes . . . as the Jemen did with their understanding of Quancee.

I open my mouth, then close it. I have to take a deep breath and hold it to fortify myself for what I am about to say.

"As of this moment, I declare this to be holy ground, just like her cave. No one but you will ever enter this place, Lynx, at least not so long as Dog Soldiers exist."

Lynx stares at me for a long while. "And Volume Omega?"

Some of the most difficult words I have ever spoken come out of my mouth. "Neither I, nor any of the Dog Soldiers, will ever try to reach the books stored here. Volume Omega will remain a sacred mystery."

Lynx scrutinizes my expression, judging the truth of it. "Will you keep my stories about her? Quancee and I would appreciate that very much."

My throat goes tight, for deep inside me I see all the firelit faces of the Dog Soldiers who have traveled to the campfires of the dead. Their wide eyes watch me, bearing witness. "I give you my solemn oath that we will faithfully keep any story you tell us."

Lynx places her heart back in the bag and pulls the laces snug.

As cloud shadows meander across the ice around us, the world goes from light to shadow and back again, but all I see is the Blessed Teacher, who has braced his walking stick and is struggling to rise.

I grab his arm to steady him while he gets stiffly to his feet. "Let me help you down the mountain."

"I'd be grateful."

Behind us, I hear Homara and Pyara step out of the cavern.

Their words are soft with awe as they discuss the magnificent wonders they have seen.

I don't think Lynx hears them. He seems to be lost in the echoes of voices long gone. Finally, he inhales a deep breath and lets it out slowly.

As he props his walking stick and heads down the mountain trail, he begins, "She danced with crystal spiders that only existed for an instant in time and sailed upon the light of suns that died billions of summers ago . . ."